ALSO BY HANNAH TUNNICLIFFE

*The Color of Tea*

# SEASON *of* SALT *and* HONEY

A NOVEL

# HANNAH TUNNICLIFFE

Touchstone

New York  London  Toronto  Sydney  New Delhi

Touchstone
An Imprint of Simon & Schuster, Inc.
1230 Avenue of the Americas
New York, NY 10020

*Opposite Contraries: The Unknown Journals of Emily Carr and Other Writings*, written by Emily Carr and edited by Susan Crean (Douglas and McIntyre: 2003). Reprinted with permission from the publisher.

First Touchstone trade paperback edition September 2015

For information about special discounts for bulk purchases, please contact Simon & Schuster Special Sales at 1-866-506-1949 or business@simonandschuster.com.

The Simon & Schuster Speakers Bureau can bring authors to your live event. For more information or to book an event, contact the Simon & Schuster Speakers Bureau at 1-866-248-3049 or visit our website at www.simonspeakers.com.

Manufactured in the United States of America

10   9   8   7   6   5   4   3   2   1

Library of Congress Cataloging-in-Publication Data

Tunnicliffe, Hannah, 1979–
    Season of salt and honey : a novel / Hannah Tunnicliffe.—First Touchstone trade paperback edition.
        pages ; cm
1. Life change events—Fiction. 2. Grief—Fiction. 3. Domestic fiction. I. Title.
PR9199.4.T836S43 2015
813'.6—dc23

                                                2015024603

ISBN 978-1-4516-8284-7
ISBN 978-1-4516-8285-4 (ebook)

For Sian

What do these forests make you feel? Their weight and density, their crowded orderliness . . . How absolutely full of truth they are, how full of reality. The juice and essence of life are in them; they teem with life, growth, and expansion. . . . As the breezes blow among them, they quiver, yet how still they stand developing with the universe. . . . They stand developing, springing from tiny seeds, pushing close to Mother Earth. Fluffy baby things first, sheltering beneath their parents, mounting higher, spreading brave branches, pushing with mighty strength not to be denied skywards. Tossing in the breezes, glowing in the sunshine, bathing in the showers, bending below the snow piled on their branches, drinking the dew, rejoicing in creation, bracing each other, sheltering the birds and beasts, the myriad insects.

Emily Carr, *Opposite Contraries: The Unknown Journals of Emily Carr and Other Writings* (edited by Susan Crean)

# SEASON *of* SALT *and* HONEY

# Chapter One

· · · ·

Aunty Connie's cucumber sandwiches, stripped free of plastic wrap, are lined up on a rectangular plate on Mrs. Gardner's table, pointed tips dried and turning stale, like rows of teeth. Four rows, the jaw of a great white shark. I stare at them too long and feel my father's gaze turn towards me. I force myself to blink. He watches me from across that room filled with people wearing black and charcoal. It isn't the weather for these colors; it's unseasonably hot and the musty smell of clothes pulled from the backs of drawers mingles pungently with spring sweat.

I glance over at Mrs. Gardner by the door; take in the fine, smoke-gray cashmere sweater and the black pants with a neat line pressed down the center of each leg. She is speaking to a woman, the fingers of one hand placed lightly against her pearls, her expression as though she painted it on with her makeup: cordial, pleasant, cheeks and eyes and a little smile arranged in the correct way, showing perfectly tethered and restrained grief.

A group is in the yard dressed in long shorts fraying at the hems, their salt-cracked heels in rubber sandals, cigarettes between fingers. They're huddled together, looking down at their drinks, which are in red plastic cups because Mrs. Gardner can't abide to see them drink out of cans. Among them, a young woman, her long hair under a hat, who glances at me, then away again, her eyes red from crying.

The air inside the room feels thick. I look back at the sandwiches that Zia Connie never makes for family, only for these kinds of events. For *merigans,* though she wouldn't use that expression in this company. I imagine the cucumber slipping against my teeth, the thick butter coating the roof of my mouth, the cloying stick of bread in my throat. These are the same sandwiches Zia Connie served at Teresina's husband's funeral. The difference is, he was seventy-five. Alex is only thirty-one. Was thirty-one. Must remember to say "was." Papa makes his way across the room to me; I see him out of the corner of my eye. My mouth begins to water in that way that lets you know vomit is about to follow.

I start to move. "Excuse me . . . sorry."

My stomach lurches. I move faster. My feet take me to the door, high heels beating out a fast and desperate little rhythm down the front steps. Spring air, new-green and fresh, fills my lungs.

"Frankie?"

That's Papa. I want to turn and step into his arms, but by now there will be people turning to watch, looking out the windows. Mrs. Fratelli, my boss at the council, my aunties, Alex's work colleagues, guys he played hockey with and their wives. My cousins, Vinnie, Giulia, and Cristina—Cristina with the new baby on her hip. My uncles Mario and Roberto, both holding plates piled with food. Some of Mama's family, distant relations whose names I can't remember and whose eyes keep seeking me out. Gardners. Caputos. More Caputos than Gardners, but watching all the same, plates full and faces solemn.

"That poor girl," they'll be saying. "First her mother, now this." They will be shaking their heads, privately thanking God it isn't their sister or daughter or niece. Thanking God it isn't them.

I wobble too fast across the hot lawn as though I am drunk. Air tastes good out here, better than inside, so I gulp it down and keep walking. *Escape.*

"Frankie?" Papa again, by the door.

"I'm okay." My voice is crooked. It's clear to both of us that I am not okay.

I don't turn to see his face because I know it will be pale and old. The way he looks when he disagrees with Uncle Mario, or that time when Cousin Vinnie broke his leg right in front of us— the bone sticking out through the skin. Or, worst of all, when Bella left.

I stride on as if I know where I'm going. Ignoring the pinch of the ridiculous black satin shoes with the peep toes and the papery swish of the black dress. I walk past a fence with white roses. I walk past a car with yellow peeling paint and a wobbling, faded blue plastic Mother Mary on the dash. The tall, dark-haired woman inside opening the door. Looking like she wants to call out to me. I keep walking, get into my car, and turn the engine over. The hair dryer heat of the air-conditioning blasts my face.

I drive quickly through the city, Sunday-sleepy and quiet, and into the suburbs. Minutes pass like seconds. Buildings clustered, and then farther apart from one another. A woman stares from her kitchen window, squinting, pausing, gripping a handful of cutlery. A cat watches me from a porch as if I'm a mouse, its yellow eyes unblinking. A child on a swing, a mutinous stare. A dog follows for a way, wide grin, tongue hanging like a bookmark, as though he wants to go where I'm going. As though he knows where I'm going.

I don't. Not exactly.

I turn off the air-conditioning and open the windows, feel the world bear in on me. My phone rings. I stare at it on the passenger seat; I can't remember putting it there. It rings on and on, stops and then starts again. I imagine the questions at the other end: *Where? Why? How long?* And the pity: *Oh, darling,* cara mia, *please don't, I know.* But no one knows. Only I know. He was mine. And now he is gone.

I pick up the phone when it rings a third time and drop it out the open window. I don't hear it meet the road; it just vanishes, as if swallowed up by the earth, and then there is sweet quiet again. Just the sound of the motor, the air rushing past the windows, the wheels against the road.

Houses retreat like toy soldiers. Roads stretch out like long yawns. There is the whispering scent of the sea through the open windows. The earth cooling. Soon I will come to the forest.

The sun descends, inch by slow inch, settling into the clouds, to sleep. I drive slowly now, to find my way. Alex, blond, alive, and sure, is beside me, pointing out the way. Except that he's not. *You remember, Frankie.* And it turns out that I do. A left turn, then another; follow the signs. *Edison, WA.* Keep going.

Trees looming. Welcoming and warning both. Then, finally, the road becomes a driveway, becomes loose and crunchy and slows me down even further. Tree branches form a cathedral above me, like interwoven fingers. *Here's the church and here's the steeple, open the door . . .*

I stop the car and step out, leaving my pumps on the passenger seat. The light is weak now. The cabin rests in front of me. It is old but sturdy, small and perfect. The thick logs cut and arranged just so, by men who wanted it to stand a long time; Alex, the fourth generation of sons to find spiders in its walls, to pick at the surrounding Douglas firs to watch their resin drip, to walk the long path to the sea and swim when the water wasn't yet warm enough.

I walk around the back of the cabin, feeling pine needles pressing into the soles of my feet, the warm, damp perfume of the forest all around me. I run my fingers down the logs. The key drops on my foot, heavy and rusted.

I push it into the lock, then pause, leave the key as it is, and step back to sit in one of the two ancient Adirondack chairs out front. I wonder, for a moment, if it will break, as happened for Goldilocks, but the chair is made of stronger stuff than that. Instead it is my pretty, impractical black dress that snags on a piece of wood and tears a ragged hole.

Darkness eventually finds and cloaks me. The moon, through a break in the trees, is full-cream milk. Wind shimmies through leaves. Trees reach up to the stars, grabbing and waving. The stars peek, like diamonds, through their fingers. I am cold now and my skin brailles with goose bumps. I shiver.

Falling in love with Alex was easy.

I was a "late developer"; that's how Aunty Connie liked to put it. Or, as Aunty Rosa used to say over her espresso with too many sugars, pretending I wasn't there: "*Porco Dio*, when are the girl's bosoms coming in?" Bella never had the same problem; her breasts appeared one summer break when she was almost fourteen, and when she went back to school the boys couldn't keep their jaws off the floor. At the same age, I spent a lot of time in the library, hiding away from the mingling of boys with new, musky scents and girls with soft mounds of flesh rising from their T-shirts. The strange new laughter they made together, the pushing and pulling that went on—drawing each other in, pushing each other away, push, pull, push, pull—it made no sense to me.

But then it happened. Like a collision. Just at the moment my heart bloomed to the realization there were boys in the world to be loved; just as I noticed their voices had dropped and their chests had broadened and their eyes now darted sideways when I walked down the hallway; just at that moment, there was Alex.

When I think back, it was worse than a cliché. Worse than a cheesy movie. Me: putting books in my locker. Him: sidling up to the door. He was nervous. He glanced down at my chest and then further still, to his shoes, then back up again, took a quick breath and gave an awkward smile. I waited. Frozen and mute and hoping I wouldn't have to say anything. He was wearing a T-shirt with a Seahawks logo on it.

"Hey. You're Francesca, right?"

I nodded.

"Alex. Alex Gardner."

I managed a smile, but didn't say anything.

"You always have a lot of books."

I shrugged and smiled again, felt my cheeks burning. "Yeah," I said, throat thick.

"Yeah," he said back, glancing around. "Hey, I was wondering if you're doing anything this weekend?"

We started stumbling over each other's sentences, as if they were feet and we were trying to dance.

"This . . . ?"

"Like, Saturday night, or whatever."

"Oh. Umm . . ."

"No biggie if you're . . ."

"No, it's okay, I . . ."

"Jason and me . . . Jason Shannon, you know him?"

I nodded. Jason was two years older than me, the biggest guy in school, a six-foot walking wall of brawn. Alex's best friend.

"Cool. Well, we were thinking of going bowling or something. Or just hanging out. You know, taking it easy?"

His teeth were so white; I couldn't stop staring at them. I nodded again, then realized I should say something.

"Yeah. Yeah, okay. I mean, I'm free. Saturday." It felt as though my mouth was full of marbles.

Alex grinned. "Yeah?"

"Yeah," I replied.

We met at the bowling alley because I didn't want him to see our house. Not if he lived in one of those fancy places in Queen Anne like everyone said. I wore a tight white top because I'd read somewhere that white made your boobs look bigger, and I put on eyeliner four times before getting it to look even on both sides. When I got there, Alex had a green ball and I had a lilac one. He touched my hand when I went to pick it up from the ball return. We drank Cokes and chewed on the ice. Angela O'Brien sat on Jason Shannon's knee and they necked in front of everyone until Alex said, "Shit, guys, get a room."

That day at the locker was the beginning of everything. We were high school sweethearts, just like everyone dreams about but no one actually has, because that kind of thing only happens in the movies. Or back in our parents' time, when things were simpler or girls got pregnant and that was that. I didn't get pregnant and I wasn't in a movie; I was just lucky and I knew it. I knew right in my bones just how lucky I was. I knew everything was perfect, and did all the right things to keep it that way. Until now.

Until Alex called out from the bathroom in our apartment, "Hey, Frankie, think I'll go out for a surf."

And I said, "Okay." And then, lifting my head from the pillow, "You going to be long?"

And he had come into the bedroom and put a kiss on my forehead, right where superstitious people, young wide-eyed girls, and old and wary women say your third eye is. Not that I believe in all that. And he said, "No, won't be long. Back by lunch I'd say."

The day was just like this one had been: the sun bleeding into the clouds, the light as sweet and yellow as pouring honey. A perfect spring afternoon.

When my phone rang, my hands were in the sink. I'd made

*pitta 'mpigliata.* I don't know why; it wasn't Christmas, Alex rarely ate anything sweet, and tomorrow we'd probably be going for brunch at our favorite café. The apartment—our little home with our little things: pictures in frames, books on shelves, lists on the fridge—had been all mine for the morning, so I'd baked and lost track of the day. The place smelled of figs, raisins, sweet wine, cooked dough, and honey.

When my phone rang, I thought it would be Alex. But it wasn't.

"Hi, Francesca."

"Hi, Mrs. Gardner . . . Barbara."

Her voice was strange and wobbly, as if underwater. I couldn't understand what she was saying.

"Are you looking for Alex?" I said. "He went for a surf this morning. He should be home soon."

"Francesca . . ."

I don't remember the next bit. I can never remember the next bit. I was light and free and floating for a moment and everything was fine. And then I was Alice tumbling down the rabbit hole.

# Pitta 'Mpigliata

## SWEET BREAD ROSETTES
## WITH FRUIT AND NUTS

These stuffed bread scrolls originated in San Giovanni in Fiore,
Calabria, and are served at Christmas.

*Makes about 1 dozen small (about 6-inch-diameter) rosettes*

1 cup pecans
1 cup almonds
1½ cups raisins
½ cup dried figs
½ cup dates
¼ cup honey
½ cup muscat or other
   dessert wine
¼ cup extra virgin olive
   oil, plus more for
   drizzling

1 egg
⅛ teaspoon sea salt
2 cups Italian flour (type
   "00"), plus more if
   needed
7 grams or one envelope
   of active dry yeast
Powdered sugar, for
   dusting

### PREPARATION

Roughly chop all the nuts and fruits. Add the honey, mix well,
and set aside. Line a baking sheet with parchment paper.

In the bowl of a mixer fitted with a dough hook, combine the
wine, olive oil, egg, and salt. In a separate bowl, sift together flour
and yeast. Add the flour mixture and mix until a dough ball is
formed (add more or less flour if necessary). Let the dough rest for
15 to 20 minutes.

Preheat the oven to 350°F. Taking a piece of dough at a time,
roll into thin lasagna-like strips about 3 inches wide (the length is
up to you; once rolled the length of the strips will determine the

size of the rosette). Trimming edges with a pastry jagger or fluted pasta cutting wheel will give a pretty edge.

Add nut and fruit mixture down the center of the strip and fold in half lengthwise. Carefully start coiling the filled strip into a rosette/pinwheel shape. If you choose to make larger rosettes you can secure the coils with toothpicks pushed horizontally into the sides.

Place the rosettes on the lined baking sheet and drizzle with olive oil. Bake for 25 to 30 minutes, depending on the size of the rosettes, until they are golden brown and fragrant.

Dust the baked rosettes with powdered sugar or serve warm with ice cream if desired.

# Chapter Two

· · · ·

When I wake, I'm under an old quilt that smells like mothballs. The cabin is a womb. Its thick walls shelter me from both noise and light. There are no alarm clocks, no cars jostling to deliver sleepy commuters to work, not even children on their way to school, laughing, fighting with sticks, the slick sounds of their scooter wheels against the pavement. My feet touch the end of the short bed. I roll onto my back. Beneath me my dress rustles, and above there's the hum of a lazy fly. I open one eye. There it is, turning in slow figure eights and then gone. I open the other eye. The pale morning light quivers with dust motes. It's so quiet. There's only the movement of a bird taking flight, the creeping walk of the clouds. An entire community of leaves and sky and birds and insects beyond the four braided log walls, paying me no attention at all.

But then there's something else. The something that woke me. The scuffle of footsteps. Murmuring. A rap at the door, which stirs up more dancing of dust in the air.

I pull the quilt up to my eyes. It's on the bed sideways, so now my bare feet stick out at the bottom.

"Hello?"

I don't reply, breathing slowly, making myself as still as possible. It reminds me of Bella, of playing *nascondino*, hide-and-seek, with our cousins. Bella never won at hide-and-seek. Never. She breathed noisily, she started to giggle, and she took up too much space despite her small size. I hated playing with her, in that way all older siblings hate playing with younger ones. Especially when they crawl into your perfect hiding spot and give you away with laughter that just gets stronger when you try to shush it.

"Hello? Are you there?"

I look down at my body as if it might not be. But I'm still here. Stiff black dress with a hole, dirty shoeless feet, painted nails. "Hawaiian Sunset" the young woman at the beauty spa called the nail color.

"Who's in there, Dad?" A girl's voice, light but needling.

I peek out from under the quilt. There's the sound of footfalls among the leaves and detritus.

"Dad?"

A hand pats the back wall, searching for the key. I scan the wooden floor quickly, and then the blackened fireplace and the stool near it. There is the key, lying idly on its side. I feel myself exhale, but the quilt is still gripped firmly in my fingers.

In a game of hide-and-seek the trick is to think yourself invisible; that's what I tried to teach Bella. "Don't breathe," I'd hiss at her when she followed me into a hiding place, as if that were possible.

"Dad?"

Over by the sink, above a cupboard containing a few chipped

cups and enamel plates, a window has been cut. The frame is aging poorly, bullied by the walls, which are older and know better. The glass is warped. I stare at it, my body still and frozen, waiting.

A face fills the window. The man cups his hands by his cheekbones to peer in.

"Dad?"

"Stay there, Huia." His voice is steady and assertive, it has a hint of an accent. "Are you a Gardner?" he calls.

The question burns. My heart beats a little faster.

"This is a private cabin," he adds.

I am mute.

"Are you a Gardner?" he presses again, voice kinder, as though he can see me now and knows already that I'm not.

I lift the quilt over my face. I hear the little girl again, but can't make out what she's saying. The man taps on the window but I squeeze my eyes shut. The girl's calls become a shadow to his footsteps around the cabin, once, and then again the other way. He knocks on the door.

"Can you hear me? You're trespassing."

"Dad?"

"I'll have to contact the owners of the property—"

"Dad?"

"It is illegal to stay here without permission. I will be contacting the owners and, following that, the authorities, if you don't vacate."

My eyes stay squeezed shut. That's the other trick with hide-and-seek. Don't give up. Once you start thinking you've been seen, you stop thinking you're invisible, and someone will notice you. Don't give up till your cousin, tall and skinny with scraped knees, is tugging on your shoulder and smacking his forehead, declaring, "*Imbecille, sta stronza!*"—You idiot. Bella learned all the tricks in time, once we were well past the age for games. You could say that hiding became her forte.

When I finally get up, reluctantly, I pad across the floor to the window where the stranger's face appeared. As far as I can see, which is to the closest wall of trees—Douglas firs, western red cedars, western hemlocks, salmonberry bushes, ferns, green upon green upon green—the man and the child are gone. I feel myself shiver, and glance down at my bare arms and the black dress that is creased in a thousand places like an old face, then turn from the window to take in the cabin, scanning for food and clothes.

This was Errol Gardner's cabin, Errol being a direct ancestor of Alex's grandfather. It's been passed down through the family to Marshall Gardner, Alex's father, though he and Mrs. Gardner rarely visit. Mrs. Gardner can't stand the isolation, the bugs, and the outhouse. Especially the outhouse.

I bend to peer into the cupboard below the sink, clearing a grayed spiderweb. The sink and cupboard and the flushing toilet in the outhouse must have been added in the 1950s by Alex's grandfather, Henry—Hank, as he was known. The cupboard handles are silver and round, the top covered with mint-colored linoleum. There are a few old cans on a shelf—fruit, beans, one with the label peeled off that I decide to avoid. I find a can opener and a few pieces of mismatched cutlery in a resistant drawer and open a can of peaches. The pink-orange orbs bob about in silken syrup like flotation devices. I pierce one with a fork and pop it into my mouth, juice slipping down my chin. I remain standing by the sink and look around the room. It's a cabin for one, only a few pieces of furniture: a bed now covered in the soft, worn red-and-white quilt, a chair, an awkwardly leaning narrow closet, a small square table, a fireplace—if you consider that furniture—and a sparsely stocked bookshelf. Strangely, a child's coloring book lies open on the small table.

Outside, the forest is vast and towering, but inside the cabin is cozy and perfect. There is reassurance in its smallness and its age, and that nothing matches—red quilt, mint linoleum, large forks with small knives. A confused, broken, mismatched woman is not out of place here. A confused, mismatched woman can become invisible here by closing her eyes and practicing childhood tricks.

I walk to the closet where I'd found the quilt in the dark last night. The heady, sickly smell of mothballs fills the air when I open the door and it seems to lean even more. Like the cupboard below the sink, it doesn't contain much. An oilskin jacket on a crocheted coat hanger, a large pair of boots, blue rubber sandals. In one drawer there's a green Hudson's Bay blanket and starchy cream-colored sheets with a scattering of gray spots; in the other, a man's woolen sweater with navy stripes and three brown leather-covered buttons, socks that haven't dissuaded an opportunistic moth, a pair of well-used gardening gloves.

I unfold the sweater and put it on. The wool is coarse against my skin but quickly warms me. I glance at the wooden chair next to the little table, but decide to take my breakfast outside instead. The door gives a protesting screech as I push against it.

I have only visited the cabin a few times. It sits in a little patch of coastal forest near Chuckanut Drive between Seattle and Vancouver. The closest village is called Edison, which I only remember because of Thomas Edison and because we stopped there for coffee a couple of times. Coffee and a cookie from a place that only accepted cash. I long for a coffee now.

I glance around the clearing, which seems tidy, maintained even, though I can't imagine that's the doing of any of the Gardners. Alex hasn't been here for a long time, and his brother, Daniel, is neck deep in college study. He's going to be a lawyer, to the delight of his parents. I peer into the trees, searching for the man at the window, but can't see or hear him. I lower myself into one of the Adirondack chairs, place my can and fork on the arm, and lean back.

The trees here are giants, forcing the light to duck and weave between them, to reach around defiant trunks to throw rays across the cabin roof. All the tiny flying things, seeds, grit, and small insects, seem to pool in the radiant fingers. Despite the light it is always cooler in the forest, the trees drinking up most of the warmth from the sunshine before it drops through the canopy. The Caputos are always complaining about the cold in this country, the warm Sicilian blood in their veins offended by the Washington damp and cold, but I don't mind it.

I hear a car moving along the driveway and sit up a little straighter. I consider retreating into the cabin but it seems pointless; the man who came this morning already knows I'm here. The sound of a stereo grows louder as the car comes closer and I guess it can't be the police. Finally the nose of a white Ford comes into view, the music suddenly turned down. A young man unfolds his tall body from the driver's seat.

"Francesca?"

A voice just like Alex's. My breath catches for a moment.

"Daniel."

He sits down beside me and runs his hand over his face.

Alex's brother doesn't look a thing like him. Daniel looks like their father—brown hair and greenish eyes—where Alex looked like his mother. But their voices are so similar I sometimes had trouble telling them apart on the phone. It only got worse as they got older.

Daniel glances at me, silently taking in the knitted sweater and the black dress sticking out below it. When his gaze drops to my feet I remember I'm not wearing shoes.

"I thought you might be here," he says.

"Am I in trouble?"

He shakes his head and shuffles back a little into the chair. "For running away? I don't think so."

I might not be in trouble in his books, but I know, with certainty and a pang of guilt, Papa and the aunties will be worrying about me. I look at my can of peaches and imagine their horror. *You can't eat that for breakfast! Please, my love, my heart, come home. You'll fade away.*

"How did you know I was here?"

Daniel shrugs. "I thought about where Alex might go." He

looks at me and I notice how drawn his face is, how dark the circles under his eyes. "Why did you come?"

"Maybe the same reason. I wasn't really thinking. I just had to get out. I ended up here."

He nods. "Yeah, the"—he can't say it either—"was pretty . . . stifling. It's nice here, huh?"

We both look around.

"Yes. It's nice," I agree politely. Daniel has always been sweet but formal with me. I recall when I first met him. How old was he? Fifteen? He'd been playing guitar in the basement with a friend, and Alex and I came down the steps holding hands. He'd looked between us and then at our hands and his face had gone dark red.

Alex had cleared his throat. "This is Francesca."

I remember glowing inside, the way Alex said it, so seriously. Like I was important.

"This is my brother, Daniel," Alex had explained.

Daniel had kept staring. Then stuttered, "You're one of the Caputo girls." As if it was like being a First Lady.

"Yeah," I'd said, and he'd nodded, as mute and bright as Papa's tomatoes.

Even now, years later, Daniel looks uncomfortable, half-perched, half-slumped in the chair beside me. Somehow too tall, or not tall enough, like he's embarrassed about taking up more space than he deserves. He has always shown less confidence than Alex. I try to think of something to ask him, to talk about, but all I can think about is Alex. Alex, in his death, takes up so much space it feels like there's no room for anything else.

"I miss him," Daniel says in a choked voice, when the silence has gone on too long.

"I miss him too," I reply softly.

"I can't think of any one thing—like, stuff we talked about or the way he did things. People ask me, what do you miss the most? I don't know what to say. It's just everything, you know? How he spoke, the way he was—just . . . him."

I nod.

Daniel draws breath. "And the house feels different, even though he hasn't lived there for ages."

"As though there's a shadow in every room."

"Yeah."

"That's why I can't go home."

Daniel looks at me.

"He's everywhere," I say. "Everywhere and nowhere. In the kitchen, in the living room, in the bedroom. Sorry, but . . . all over the bedroom. There's a stack of surfing magazines that he never threw out, they always get tipped over, make a big mess. I was always on him to tidy them up or throw them out, and now I wish the whole room was full of them."

Daniel is silent.

"Sorry," I murmur.

"No, I get it. Sometimes I want to tell him to get out. Out of my head, I mean. And then I feel bad because I just want him back. It makes me feel . . ."

"Crazy," I say.

"Yeah, crazy."

Daniel pauses, then reaches over and pats my arm.

I look down at his hand. The gesture is unnatural for him, but he is trying. I appreciate that he doesn't ask me questions or tell me everything is going to be okay. He knows the world is changed and there's no way to repair it. I take a deep breath and try not to wish that he was Alex, try to be grateful instead that he's Daniel and the closest thing. Even silent, his presence is the most like Alex's. It's both comforting and torturous.

"He did love you," Daniel says firmly.

I look at him. He's gone pink again.

"I know you guys had been together a long time, and he wasn't always good at saying . . . I mean, it's a family thing. . . ."

I shift my arm away from under his hand. "I know."

"He may not have said it all the time. . . ."

"Often enough."

"And he took all that time to ask you to marry him . . . but he did—"

"It's okay," I interrupt. Daniel looks at me, concerned. "Thank you. I mean . . . I know he loved me."

"I wasn't suggesting—"

"We were going to be married."

"Yes."

Now, when the silence comes, it seems to cleave a gap between us. Daniel doesn't reach for me and I don't reach for him. I wish I could say "wife" in the certain, always way that Daniel gets to say "brother."

"I borrowed a sweater," I say, changing the subject, then nod towards the peaches. "And some food."

"Sure. That sweater was Granddad's. Alex loved it. He was

Granddad's favorite—you probably know that already." Daniel gives a small smile. "Granddad did everything in that sweater, including fishing . . . I don't know how often he washed it."

I shrug. "I can't smell anything but mothballs."

"That's Mom. She hates the bugs. I could bring you more clothes," he adds. "If you're staying?"

Despite not being able to bear the thought of going home, I haven't considered staying. Now I rapidly imagine my aunties back in Seattle, still wearing their dark clothes, heavy sobs shaking their shoulders. I imagine the phone ringing in our apartment— my boss, Alex's friends, my cousins. Explanations, commiserations, and condolences that feel foreign and empty.

Daniel studies me. "I'll call someone," he says, trying to be helpful. He's used to being the youngest, letting others make plans for him, without him. This is new. "Your sister . . . ?"

"Bella?" I almost laugh. What help would she be? I'm not even sure where she is. Somewhere in Portland, where she's been living since she left Seattle? I don't have a current phone number for her. Besides, you can't trust Bella with anything. Not even to come to your fiancé's funeral. "Papa will help," I say. "Are you sure it's okay for me to stay here?"

Daniel shrugs. "No one else is using it."

"You don't want to—"

He cuts me off. "I've got to be with Mom. My parents, I mean."

"Okay. Thank you, Daniel. I just need some . . ." But I can't finish the sentence and Daniel doesn't press.

"Hey?" I manage. He looks up. "Will you do me one favor?

Will you please call me Frankie? I feel so old when you call me Francesca."

He nods but looks away. "Sure."

I follow his gaze, but there's nothing to see but forest. Cedars, firs, brave ferns growing high on a fallen tree. A tiny bird effortlessly balancing on a new branch that bends and bounces like a high wire.

"Thank you," I say again. For coming. For patting my arm. For sounding so much like Alex that it feels good and burns all at once.

He nods again. "No problem, Frankie."

He stands, and moves towards his car, then turns back to me. "I'll call your dad," he promises, "and bring you some more clothes. There's a gas bottle in there somewhere—did you find it already? There's a camp stove."

I shake my head. "I'll find it. You go. Your mom will be worried."

"You don't want my phone?"

"No."

He stares at me a long moment before nodding.

This is the thing about grief: it allows you to be stubborn, even if it's irrational and impractical. People treat you delicately, as though you have a terminal illness, and grant you your unreasonableness. Except for my family, of course, the Caputo clan, who somehow become bossier and more prying. I know the aunties will be distressed that I'm missing, though Papa will do his best to reassure them. That's the way with the three of them: Concetta and Rosaria—Zia Connie and Zia Rosa to Bella and me—the two all-knowing, dictatorial, elder sisters; and Giuseppe, our father, Joe, the placating younger brother. Papa will tell them I'm okay, that I'll come back, not to worry. He will be worrying too, but he trusts me. He has no reason not to. The aunties will be whispering about Bella too—loud enough for Papa to hear, although he'll pretend not to.

"Call Papa straightaway, will you?" I call out to Daniel.

"I'll drop by," he reassures me.

He curls himself into the driver's seat and reverses. The ground is noisy beneath his tires. He lifts his hand in a wave. It reminds me of Alex leaving for work.

That's when I remember the man at the window. "Wait!"

The car slows to a stop. Daniel sticks his head out the window. I curl my fingers over the edge of the window frame. "There was a man here this morning. . . . He was talking about trespassing. About calling your parents. Do you know him?"

Daniel shakes his head. "Maybe Mom hired him."

We both look back to the cabin, the tidy ground around it, the weeds held back from crawling over the wooden walls.

"I'll talk to Mom," he promises.

"Okay." I uncurl my fingers and step back.

He surveys me. "Are you sure you're—"

"I'll be fine."

He nods slowly, disbelieving.

As his car drives away the music is turned up, blaring so loud it's as though he wants it to smother him. I hear it long after the car has disappeared from sight. When it's gone I feel cold again, as though a ghost has returned to stand beside me.

## Chapter Three

· · · ·

I find the camp stove in the sink cupboard, pushed to the back and covered in dust.

I stand taller, make a list of supplies in my head for Papa to pack. *Towel, washcloth, soap.* This makes me feel oddly purposeful. I scan the cabin again and notice things I missed in my first assessment. There's a small lump of soap, yellowed and cracked, on the windowsill. The open pages of the coloring book have been neatly colored in all the wrong shades. A purple sun, pink ocean, orange grass as if on fire. I run my finger along the spines on the bookshelf. A historical account of the Second World War, several *Reader's Digests,* four *Story Collections for Boys* from 1951, 1952, 1963, and 1966. My finger pauses on *The Swiss Family Robinson* by Johann Wyss. I remember the Disney film. The elaborate tree house, the handsome sons, the elegant, practically effortless way they all adapted to their new, lonely fate. I loved that movie. There's a purple hair tie on a hook on the back of the door and I use it to lift my hair into a ponytail. Alex liked my hair up. The ghost leans heavily against me.

I walk to the sink and run the tap, glancing out the window

before unzipping my dress. I let the dress fall from my shoulders and onto the floor before rubbing the wet bar of soap under my arms. Water splashes on the floor as I rinse it away and then lift water up to my face.

I'm standing in my underwear when I notice the shrubbery moving outside. I squint, wondering if it's a bird or an animal. A bear. I didn't ask Daniel about bears. Though an animal lover, Bella's greatest fear when we were growing up was bears. We'd seen a movie with a bear in it that opened its huge, dripping mouth and roared and shook a car full of people screaming. Bella had never forgotten it. In my crueler moments as a big sister I'd remind her, in whispers, of that bear from the movie and watch her face turn white, her bottom lip quiver.

It's probably just a bird, maybe a squirrel.

I pull up my dress and, on the way out of the cabin, pick up *The Swiss Family Robinson*. The cover is dusty beneath my fingers. I pull on the boots from the closet to protect my feet, though they are huge and loose. Then, instead of sitting in one of the chairs to read, I find myself stepping, as quietly as possible, around the back of the cabin. The cedar needles give off a lemony-peppery scent as I crush them with the heavy boots.

There's a rustle from one of the trees above. I freeze and feel my heart thumping in my chest, as though it wants to be free of my body. I glance up and spy a foot. Small, brown, and bare. A bird nearby takes flight in a squawking, urgent rush of feathers.

My gaze follows the foot up to a leg, a leg that quickly disappears behind a trunk that's forked in two. I step around the tree but still can't find the owner of the leg.

I clear my throat. "Hello?"

A rustle.

"Hello?"

A head appears. Small, with dark hair, and eyes that could belong to an animal. Black and blinking. I exhale a small sigh of relief. A girl, I'm guessing, not much older than eight.

I try again. "Hi."

The girl stares.

"Please, be careful up there."

She shrugs. She stares from my dress to the boots and back again. Assessing it all. "I'm not allowed to talk to strangers."

I recognize the voice now. The child calling to her father this morning. I glance around for any sign of him but it seems to be just her, all alone. The two of us stare at each other for a while. She's wearing a pink T-shirt with what looks like a Popsicle stain down the front and yellow leggings. As far as disheveled goes, we're an equal match.

"I can whistle," she says.

"Oh."

"My dad taught me."

"That's good."

I don't spend much time with children other than my cousins' kids, who are more like puppies than children, rushing at you from every side, kicking balls into your shins, dropping food on your shoes.

"Can you?" the girl asks.

"Whistle?"

She nods.

"Yes, I can whistle."

She looks unconvinced so I give a little whistle and it sounds so ridiculous I quickly stop. The girl gives an approving nod. She clambers quickly to the ground. She only comes up to my chest, her frame lean and lanky, and her curls dark and springy. Unbrushed. Whoever looks after her isn't like my aunties, especially Aunty Rosa, who insisted on ironed slacks and spotless, food-free cheeks.

"You live around here?" I ask.

"Yup."

"Close by?"

The girl pauses, tilts her chin. "Why are *you* here?"

The question is bold, the pleasantries decapitated from it. I pause before avoiding it. "My name's Francesca. What's yours?"

The girl looks at the palm I'm holding out but doesn't take it. It drops to my side, stupidly. She leans against the tree trunk, her leg jiggling, as though she might run at any moment.

"Huia," she says.

"Hi, Huia." I say the name slowly to get the vowel sounds right. *Hoo-ee-ah.*

"It's a bird."

"Ah."

"From New Zealand."

"That's nice," I say.

"A dead bird. There's none of them left."

She blinks her very round black eyes. I can almost see my face in them. Her chin is pointed, her forehead wide. I realize that the

night-black curls that wisp out this way and that remind me of
Bella's as a girl.

"People call me Frankie."

Huia studies me carefully. "Frankie's better."

I nod. She's right.

"Why are you here?" she repeats, more gently this time.

I consider my explanations. Something about Alex. Something
about the apartment where Alex's shoes are still in the closet, his
favorite mug in the kitchen cupboard. The place that now feels
too small, too crowded with memories I can't face. Something
about needing space. Adult explanations. A lie about a vacation.

"I don't . . . feel . . . very good."

Huia pauses, then nods. I'm surprised this explanation passes
the test. Another thought knits her brows together. Her gaze falls
upon the book, drifts over the cover picture: a man in a tree
house, shirtless, with ragged pants, scanning the horizon.

"You like to read?" she says.

"Sure."

"That looks good."

"I've only seen the movie," I concede.

Through the trees there's a loud whistle. It isn't a bird I've
heard before. Huia glances towards the sound. Stands straighter.

"You can borrow it," I start to say, holding out the dusty book,
but she shakes her head.

"I have to go."

"Okay," I reply, strangely disappointed.

Huia gives me a tiny wave and I return it. She disappears as quickly as she arrived, her body moving effortlessly, as though she's lived in a forest her whole life.

I continue to watch her dart through the undergrowth, towards something that's caught her attention, until I can no longer see her or her yellow leggings.

Somewhere, close by, there's a path to the ocean. I consider the dangers: I could get lost, I could be bitten by a snake, I could fall. But I'm less worried about snakebites and stumbles than ghosts congregating by the water.

I imagine Huia looking up at me with those animal eyes, then dashing off ahead of me. "Come on!" she might call, somewhere between encouraging and whining. Like Bella—unafraid of risks, wanting to try everything new. I remember the time Bella and Vincenzo found a rope swing by the creek and returned triumphant, eyes shining and clothes wet. I'd been too scared, too rule-bound, to follow them, and they'd had, by their own account, "the best day ever."

That seals it. I pick my way through the sword ferns, which swish coquettishly at my bare legs, to find the little path. It's narrow and covered with fir needles and rotting leaves—but I can feel the firmness of the ground beneath the heavy boots, the soil pressed down by generations of Gardner sons.

My breath catches in my throat. I move slowly, carefully, in the enormous boots and pull my dress away from snagging bushes. This is where he brought me. I was blindfolded, my eyes squeezed shut behind it, but I knew the forest by the smell of it and the birdcalls. Alex gripped my hand; I knew he was smiling.

I am tempted to close my eyes now, but that's stupid. I might fall, with no one to lift me up into his arms, to soothe me. I keep my eyes open and focused on the path, glancing up occasionally into the canopies of cedar and fir that soar above me, stretching out to one another to make a green and branchy patchwork in the sky. I was wearing jeans that day; I didn't feel the forest against me, shrub and bush reaching out for me as they do now. I only noticed the grip of Alex's hand, the skittery percussion of my heart that left me feeling thrilled and a little sick in my stomach. Alex laughed at me, my concerned face, my tentative steps, and I scolded him for being cruel, though I was giddy with happiness. This was it. This was the moment.

I opened my eyes and peered through the blindfold, the fabric thinned by the sunlight. I stared at his broad back and golden head, blond hairs catching the sunshine, and grinned. We had come to a little clearing and a flat, smooth ledge of rock. Beyond that, ocean. It was laid out like a beautiful silk sheet, just for us. It glittered as Alex removed the blindfold.

"I've never been here," I said, my voice cracking with nerves. I'd imagined he would take me somewhere we'd been before. Maybe our favorite restaurant, or the lookout where we made out so many times as teenagers. But *this*. This was better. My heart pounded.

"I know," he said.

He shook out the picnic blanket for me to sit on while he opened his backpack and pulled out food and a bottle of champagne. I peered inside the plastic containers and saw *arancini*, thick slices of salami, and green olives.

He laughed and shrugged. "Aunty Rosa."

Bread followed, a tub of strawberries. Then he settled back onto the blanket and sighed. We both knew what was coming next. I felt like I might explode.

Alex licked his lips. "Okay."

"Okay," I replied.

"Francesca."

I burst out laughing. He blushed and laughed too.

"Frankie."

"Yes?"

"I love you."

A lump formed in my throat, making me mute.

"We've been through so much together. It's been . . . years and here we are, just you and me, babe. In this special place. I don't want to be without you. I don't know who I would be without you. We make sense. You've stood by me. You've been so good to me."

His voice wobbled a little on that last sentence. I stretched out and touched his hand, but he withdrew it and reached into his pocket. It felt as though my heart was going to leap right out of my mouth. Alex rearranged himself so he was on one knee, a box in his hands. I put my hands over my mouth to keep my heart in my chest, urged my brain to remember every detail even as they were already scrambling away from me.

"Will you do me the honor . . . ?"

I started to cry.

Alex popped open the lid and there was my ring. Glinting.

"Of becoming my wife?"

I fell into his arms, nodding and kissing his face.

"Yes?"

"Yes!"

Then we tumbled together, onto the blanket, laughing and crying, and I thought *just like in the movies*. Alex kissed my hair, my eyelids, and my cheeks. I clung to him. Tears slipped down my face.

We both sat up and he slid the ring onto my finger. That's when I properly noticed it.

"Oh, it's perfect. I mean, really perfect."

A white gold ring, just like Mama's and Nonna's were. An oval diamond, and encircled around it were tiny diamond chips like stars. Simple and elegant. I had waited so long and so patiently for him to ask me, to have this token on my finger. My heartbeat fluttered; I wanted to laugh. It felt like relief. I wanted the moment, the minute, the hour, the day, to last forever. I twisted the ring around on my finger with my thumb, the diamond winking and glittering.

"Really?" he asked.

"Truly."

I pause from walking and stare at my finger. Did that happen? Just last summer? In this very place? Perhaps it was a dream. Something I saw in a movie once.

I take a breath. I can hear the ocean in the distance and the intermittent cry of a gull. The trees are thinning, as though they know they will soon be unwelcome, the soil too salty and the wind too battering. Beneath my feet the ground has become rock in patches. My feet are still, as if frozen in place. Much farther ahead on the path I think, for a moment, that I see a figure. Someone in jeans, a hat maybe. Too slight to be a man. Perhaps it's me, another version, coming back from the border of rock and water, of past and present.

A breeze finds me. It smells of salt and iron. Like blood. My stomach lurches.

If I walk just a few minutes longer, the ocean will be at my feet, swaying and blue. Somewhere within it, cradled in a dark, cold place, the ghost of Alex. Blond hair moving in the inklike water, eyes unseeing.

I had wanted being engaged to last forever. That wonderful beginningness of something so sweet. Childhood sweethearts sealing themselves to each other forever. It was a fairy tale. It was our fairy tale, and it was perfect. Now I will be engaged forever. I will never marry Alex. And nothing makes sense.

I turn and run. Running again, like I did from the wake.

I stumble in the oversized boots and trip, fall against the hard ground. The skirt of my dress is covered in soil, dark and dusty as cocoa, musty and pungent. My knees ache, my shin is skinned and bleeding. I lift myself up and cry; from the grief, from the pain of the fall, I'm not sure. Tears mix with soil as I try to brush them away with dirty fingers. I lumber on, letting my cries fly out into the forest, where the air becomes cooler and the trees crowd in again as if to offer comfort. *Shhh shhh shhh*, their leaves say.

Anger rises up in me. Anger at the ocean for claiming what's mine, anger that I believed things could last forever.

I have been so stupid.

The ferns scratch against the grazes on my legs and it is a strange pleasure to have validation of the pain on the inside match the wounding on the outside. My sobs are raw and ragged as I round the corner to see the little cabin waiting for me. I slow and walk now, limping a little, my breath slowing too. Safe now.

Sitting on the step at the front door, under the shallow eaves, is a woman in a long skirt. She hugs her knees, her sandaled feet just visible under the fabric of her skirt. She has an armful of bracelets and wears a T-shirt without sleeves. She lifts her head, covered in loose, dark curls, the tips dyed cinnamon, and gives me a careful smile.

Bella.

# Chapter Four

· · · ·

When my sister left, her hair was long and purple-black, the ends wispy and split. She wore black eyeliner so thick she looked bruised. She had recently pierced her nose and it was red, infected around the puncture. I was still living at home then, barely a year into my first job. I had bought a suit with my first paycheck. A little gray jacket with a nipped waist and matching skirt. Alex thought it was sexy. I'd wished I could wear it every day.

The night Bella left she crept into my room very late. I had my eyes closed but I wasn't asleep. I was sick of her by then. Tired of the mischief she caused, the worry she put Papa through. Trouble followed her around like a shadow, like a stray cat she knew she shouldn't feed but couldn't help herself. By then she'd been suspended from high school for being involved with a party before prom that had gotten out of hand; a boy had ended up in the hospital with alcohol poisoning, the talk of the local paper. She'd been barred from the neighborhood drugstore for stealing lipstick. Papa had found marijuana in her room. Then she'd taken Papa's car and driven it into a telephone pole. No one was hurt, or not much, thankfully. The police had arrived at our house with their lights flashing red and blue to report the abandoned, damaged vehicle, and Papa had lied—not for the first time, surely not for the last—to protect his baby daughter. I'd especially hated her for that, for making Papa lie. Papa told the police he didn't know who had been driving, that the car must have been taken by joyriders. His face had been pale; he'd looked ill as he made his false report. Everyone, including the police, must have guessed it was Bella.

We'd become exact opposites of each other; it seemed a miracle we came from the same gene pool. I didn't want a life like hers. I didn't want her around at all, as though I might catch whatever she was spreading.

"Frankie?" Bella whispered into the dark of my bedroom.

She tried again. "*Soru?*" Her voice was a bright, curling ribbon in the silence.

Her silhouette sat on the end of my bed. A tent of a person, fluffy hair falling to her shoulders, thick jacket meeting the top of the quilt. Just the shape of her, without her stupidly blackened eyes, the crooked little eyetooth, the small hands with chewed nails, the scar by her eyebrow from when she fell out of a tree she wasn't supposed to be climbing, drove me crazy. I wanted to tell her to leave me alone. To go to bed. To fuck off.

I didn't know that was exactly what she was doing, that there was a bag on the lawn and someone waiting in a car. She hadn't even finished high school; she was still a minor, a child, despite getting herself into adult-size trouble.

I heard her cough lightly, felt her lift herself from the quilt. I still said nothing. She came to stand closer and I squeezed my eyes shut again, before sensing her leaving the room.

"Frankie?"

The woman—the stranger—on the step stands, and I remember how tall Bella is. Tall and pretty, especially with her hair cut like it is. I look her up and down, as though she might be a figment of my imagination. She gives me another wary smile and I notice the nose piercing is still there. A tiny emerald-colored stud by her right nostril. I want her off my step.

"What are you doing here?"

"Frankie." Her voice is soft, coercing.

*Papa . . . can I borrow ten dollars? For the movies? Papa . . . you'll drop me at Valerie's, won't you? Frankie . . . I'm just borrowing your skirt . . . you hardly wear it. . . .*

"What are you doing here?" I ask again firmly. Willing her to get off my step, but she remains there, in her long skirt, with her pretty hair.

I lift a hand to my own hair, knotty and pulled into a ponytail. The shin of my right leg starts to throb.

Bella glances down at it, as though she can read my thoughts. "You've had an accident."

"It's no business of yours." My tone is clipped and prissy. That's the version of me Bella brings out.

"I might have something in my car." She looks towards the lemon-colored Datsun parked close to the cabin. The paint is peeling, like a cicada trying to rid itself of its shell. She's driven over shrubs as she parked, white foamflowers crushed into the soil.

"I don't need your help," I declare.

"Frankie, I—"

That voice again. I want to smack it out of her.

38

"Why are you . . . Who told you I was here?"

Bella looks at the ground. "Daniel Gardner came to the house."

"The house . . . You were with Papa?"

"I told him I'd come see you. I've got food in the car."

The thought of Bella coming instead of Papa—Papa who would bring the right clothes and coffee, my favorite food, even a couple of books—makes me feel hot and prickly all at once.

"You're staying with Papa."

"Just for a—"

"Since when?"

"Yesterday. I—"

Yesterday, the day of the funeral. The coffin, so impossibly shiny, gleaming, that it seemed wet. The pallbearers, grown men, Daniel, Alex's friend Jason, sniffing back tears, their faces pale and twisted with grief. The dark vacancy in the earth. The cucumber sandwiches.

"Yesterday. Right. We buried him yesterday, Bella."

She looks at her feet, at her chestnut-colored sandals, a silver ring on the top joint of her second toe. "Frankie . . ." Her voice is thin now, barely there.

"Yes?" I urge. "Frankie . . . what?"

"I . . . I'm sorry . . ."

"Sorry you weren't there? Sorry you're *never* there?" My voice is rising; I can't control it. "Sorry you never replied to my wedding invitation? Your own sister's . . . Sorry that Alex . . ."

I can't finish. I shake my head, lick my dry lips. My cheeks are hot; it feels as though I'm burning.

"Frankie, I didn't think you . . . Funerals . . ."

"Get off my step."

She blinks. Then she steps down and out of my way.

The key slides into the lock. I hear her cough, just like the night she left. A tiny, polite cough to clear the throat. To stop tears from falling. I don't look at her.

"Leave, Bella."

I push open the door, slip inside, and close it so hard it slams and rattles in its frame.

Bella doesn't leave until the light is draining from the sky. I sit on the lumpy single bed and turn the pages of *The Swiss Family Robinson*, barely reading a word, waiting for the sound of her engine turning over. I don't go to the window, don't go out to the bathroom, simply wait, restlessly, inside the dark cabin, remembering all the ways she has hurt me, let me down. I'm hot and jittery, almost breathless. Mad.

It consumes some time, recalling Bella-hurts. They can be twisted and turned and stared at from many angles. As sharp and hard as engagement-ring diamonds.

First there are the things she's wrecked, from when she was small to when she should have known better. The handle broken off a christening mug; the hair snipped from the head of my favorite Barbie doll; her name written, sloppily, in blue crayon inside one of my books; grass-stained T-shirts; shoes stretched from her larger feet; earrings with stones missing. She couldn't borrow something without damaging or losing it, and that made me possessive and territorial in response. She makes me ungenerous and petty, I fume, gritting my teeth. It's her fault and she couldn't care less.

I force myself to read about the shipwreck and the Robinson family, now ashore, finding ways to survive. I try to dive into the words, to stop thinking about my sister.

It isn't just the broken things. You can't trust Bella's word. She says she'll be somewhere and then she forgets. She is late, always late. Late and laughing as though it's no big deal you've been waiting in the cold or the rain. She isn't concerned about anyone else's life, anyone else's time. She's concerned about *her* life, and sometimes barely that. She's concerned about the last-minute invitation to a party; about the boy she's kissing, the latest one, who is different from the one before but really the same, who smokes cigarettes and knows about music and drinks liquor straight from the bottle wrapped in a paper bag. Like it's cool, like he doesn't look like a bum.

I was glad when she left five years ago, coming back home less and less over the years. If there was ever any closeness between us, it existed only when we were children, and then our paths forked. Her path, her life so distant from mine she seemed more and more foreign as time went by. But I'm still angry with her; that's never disappeared. I feel more angry with her here, now, than ever.

Papa would have driven to the apartment. He would have found the things I always wear: jeans and shorts, T-shirts, my green cardigan, sneakers. He would have packed the pajamas that are folded under my pillow and plucked my toothbrush from the cup in the bathroom. If there was a book open on the nightstand he'd pack that too. Papa would have remembered cotton underwear and socks in balled pairs. He'd bring my mail, and a bottle of sunscreen, just in case. He'd close the closet door on Alex's side, always left open, all Alex's empty shirts on hangers in a neat row. Shirts missing a body. He'd pause and breathe in and try not to cry, because he loved Alex too. Because I loved him. Because Alex had made his daughter happy.

I try not to cry now.

I will myself not to open the door and shout at my sister to leave, to stop ruining my life, because that isn't really the truth. But it's easier to hate her than to hate God, to hate a faceless, careless, callous Providence that puts young men into watery graves and too-young women into black grieving dresses.

There's a rustling outside, by the door, and my body stiffens. My breath quickens, my heart races, blood and anger pumping through my veins. I hear the little cough, which instantly enrages me, as if it's a curse, a cruel taunt.

"Leave me alone!" I want to shout, but don't, because I want to be angry and silent.

Bella is the wild, selfless, thoughtless one. If I am cruel it's her fault, and if I am cruel I will be elegantly cruel.

The broken things, the broken promises . . . and then there's the worst thing.

I was watching. I saw it all. On the edge of a party, Cousin Cristina's engagement party, in the half light, much like the light outside now. Such a big gathering of people: Caputos almost as far as the eye could see, even some of Mama's family; Sicilians and Calabresi and those who simply called themselves American; dark heads and loose mouths, arguing in the way that only people who truly love one another can. Two people together could go unnoticed in this kind of crowd, this kind of noise. Two people talking over paper plates, plastic forks in hand. Bella's lips as red as blood, her long hair loose over her shoulders, her free hand jammed under her thigh, her eyes doe-wide. Her teenage face forever imprinted in my mind as she leans in . . .

"Frankie?"

Her voice comes to me through the hinges of the door. All my muscles tense.

"Frankie?"

I wait. The door is unlocked. If she opens it, I will shout. I will throw my book at her head and scream all the things I've kept inside for all these years. All the tarry, poisonous things, the truth of it. I'll scream until I run out of voice. Till there is nothing left in me.

I stare at the door handle as though willing her in. *Just you try it.*

But she doesn't. She doesn't call my name again, doesn't turn the handle. There's the *shhh shhh* of cardboard moving against the front step, and her exhaling, and the crunching over stones and leaves to get to the car. I hear the car door open and close again, and finally, finally, the engine turning over.

Only when the sound of the car has completely disappeared do I get up and open the door. There, in the sunset, is a large fruit box. I see the tops of cans, smell coffee, see my pajamas folded on top of a neat pile of clothes.

I lift the box into the cabin and sort through the contents. T-shirts and jeans, a pair of shoes, a sweater. Mail that looks like bills, which I ignore. Pink- and blue-lidded Tupperware containers. *Arancini*, Uncle Mario's homemade salami, *cotolette* in aluminum foil, a bag of apples, sliced provolone, another bag holding half a loaf. Leftovers from the wake. No cucumber sandwiches. Aunty Rosa's cannoli. My silver coffeepot and grinds. Everything arranged carefully in the big box, like a puzzle. Now, with the contents littered all over the bed, it looks like Bella's bed did at Christmas. I always pulled each present from my stocking slowly, and arranged them in ordered piles, making the anticipation last as long as possible. And, if I'm being honest, to aggravate my sister. Her frustration at my neatness, my snail-slow pace, was a gift in itself.

I change into jeans and a T-shirt, clean underwear and socks. It's a relief to be out of the black dress, which I ball up and shove into the top shelf of the closet. I put the rest of the clothes and the sneakers in the closet next to the man boots, and the food and coffeepot on the counter by the sink. I leave the mail in the box. There is no toothbrush or toothpaste. I run my tongue over my teeth; they feel slick and dirty. I can't remember a time I went longer than twelve hours without brushing my teeth.

I wash my hands, and sit at the tiny table, and bite into the crust of a lukewarm *arancino*, wondering which relative made them. The rice is sticky and the filling salty and cheesy. I lick my fingertips, then fold slices of provolone into my mouth. This is Papa and Aunty food. Comfort food.

Afterwards, I find a flashlight that doubles as a hanging lamp and hook it up so the cabin has some light as the sun vanishes, swallowed by the forest. Soon the night noises will start. Owls;

creatures hunting for food to feed their furred or feathered families. I press down firmly on the Tupperware lids and put them in a plastic bag, the handles of which I knot together.

I curl up in bed with the book, knees to my chest and stomach full. As a child I read practically anything—classified ads, recipes on the backs of food packets, the bits of old Italian newspapers that lined drawers. I couldn't understand all the words but I traced my finger along the fat, rolling vowels, tasting out the sounds in whispers. I have always been in love with words. My earliest memory is of Mama reading me stories, stumbling over the English that sounded awkward and glassy from her mouth, her kisses pressed into my hair. I have only a handful of memories of her, and those are the most precious. Quiet times, full of love and words.

Elizabeth, the mother in *The Swiss Family Robinson,* reminds me of the aunties. Frank and resourceful, armed with cooking skills to transform any tropical island animal into dinner. Adversity does not dissuade her.

As the darkness bears in, and the owls start to call, as though mourning, I put down the book. I reach up to switch off the flashlight and lie awake in my clothes. That's when my body starts to yearn. I am learning that grief can feel a lot like hunger. Aching and dizzying.

Growing up in an Italian home I wasn't often hungry. Perhaps Italians know that hunger feels too much like sadness. They know that to love someone, to make them happy, means ensuring they are fed. Alex used to groan about how much food got eaten at our family dinners. He got heartburn from the thick, fatty salami and soft, warm *polpette*. He didn't understand our fawning over Nonna's secret *pasta al forno* recipe, stuffed with meatballs, cheese, pasta, and eggs. He couldn't believe we ate octopus and rabbit and, sometimes, mainly the older family members, pigs' feet. We fed him full of artichokes, macaroni, caponata made with capsicums and cauliflower and tomatoes while the cousins talked of breakfasts in Sicily—chocolate granita or gelato stuffed into brioche rolls. After dinner, Papa urged Alex to join him and the uncles for an affogato, vanilla ice cream with black-as-spades espresso poured over the top. Alex always gave me a pleading look as he went to join them. *Too much food!* Too much love was what he really meant. He wasn't used to it. His family was more reserved, sometimes seeming a little ashamed of strong emotion, of crying and cuddles and loud laughter. That was foreign to me. Our family was the opposite—love poured out and over, in all its various forms. As food, or criticism, or the tears Aunty Rosa shed as if on cue. Love in the tugging of a brush through your hair, Aunty Connie's spit on a tissue rubbed against your cheeks, hands thrown up when you walk into the room, tight embraces, advice you never asked for. However it comes, it comes—as with the bowls of pasta—in abundance. Lashings and lashings of it.

I long for Alex as if I am starving. I wish for my life as it was. Without confusion and guilt and grief. I ache past the point of mild discomfort, past the point of annoyance.

Often, these strange days, I find myself making prayers. They start out with *Please, God* and never seem to finish. *Please* is all I can ask for, because the rest is too hard. *Bring him back. Undo it. Make it right. Make it normal again.* These are the impossible things that cannot be prayed for. There is no saint for this. Not like when Aunty Connie can't find her purse and appeals to Saint Anthony. Not like when we take a long trip in the car and Papa whispers a Hail Mary, his fingers resting on the Saint Christopher medallion around his neck. There is no saint for this and no prayer for this. Instead, just *Please . . . please . . . please.* I close my eyes and don't move a single muscle while I make my impossible request, over and over and over. As if being still and quiet and keeping my eyes shut might make it possible.

Like hunger, the grief takes up my entire mind and fills my stomach and my heart with . . . nothing. I am drowning in nothing. In emptiness. In loneliness. I scramble through the deep forest darkness to find the tied plastic bag, and search out the edge of one of Aunty Rosa's precious, pastel Tupperware containers. I crack open the lid and feel the sugar-dusted tubes of cannoli with the tips of my fingers. I lift one to my mouth, press my teeth down through the crisp crust to the soft sweet ricotta sprinkled with chopped pistachio nuts. The cannoli tastes like home. But it doesn't make it all better.

"I loved him," I want to say. "And he loved me. He did. I know it."

I just want it to be how it was. Simple. Simple and unbroken.


After a trip to the outhouse, I stand in front of the sink and run a wet cloth over my body. I long for a bath, though it's not cold.

I daydreamed about the big claw-footed bath we would get when we had our own house. Four bedrooms—enough for us, two kids, and a study. A bathtub I could sink into. Deep enough and long enough to hold both of us. Alex loved being in any kind of water. He was a fish, his mother told me once, uncharacteristically wistful after three gin and tonics.

After prom, Alex and I had a bath together.

I told Papa I was staying at Angela's, and Alex told his mom that his mate Bobby was having a bunch of guys over. His story was at least partly true. We pooled our money and booked a motel. We'd talked about it for months. I barely remember the prom because I was already thinking about the motel and staying with Alex for the whole night without having to say good-bye. I knew we would make love that night. We'd talked about that too. A girl in my class, Janet Longhurst, told me she'd lost her virginity at a house party to a college boy. Who wants to lose their virginity like that? To some college boy you'll never see again. I didn't want that. I wanted it to be with Alex, for it to be sweet and honest and real. I wanted it to be with Alex for the rest of my life. Every minute of that long prom, I thought about waking up in his arms. And when he looked at me like he could see through my prom dress it sent electric waves up and down my spine.

We left the prom hand in hand, ignoring the teasing from his friends. Someone had tied cans to the back of his dad's car, like we were a bride and groom. I got out a mile down the road, in my long blue dress and heels, and untied them. Cars drove by honking, with guys hanging out the windows, whistling and carrying on. Alex raised his middle finger out the driver's window, but he was grinning; we both were.

When we checked in to the motel he put on a deep voice for

the receptionist. I was clinging on to his hand so tight I thought I might scream.

Alex unlocked the door to the room and let me go in first. The floor was carpeted in plush navy, and the bed was covered in a worn, floral bedspread that made Alex laugh out loud. "Grandma did the decor."

I pulled the blinds down and rushed into his arms, desperate for his lips on mine. We kissed until my face hurt.

On that navy carpet, my dress twisted up around my hips, Alex sat back off of me, a little breathless. "Wait."

"Wait?"

"I got something." He reached over to the backpack he'd brought in from the car, unzipped the front pocket. Tea-light candles tumbled out. He retrieved a couple of handfuls more, then dug around until he found a black lighter. He flicked it on and raised his eyebrows at me. "Come with me."

I pulled my dress down, stood, and followed him into the bathroom. The light was one of those long fluorescent bulbs. There was a bathtub with a showerhead over it, and a small sink with a mirror. I noticed my lipstick was smeared around my mouth, and the pimple on my forehead that I'd smothered with concealer was poking through in a raised bump. I wiped the lipstick off with the back of my hand before Alex snapped off the light. He lit the candles one by one, arranging them around the tub. I bundled up the shower curtain—floral again, with gray mold stains at the bottom—and slung it over the curtain rail before turning on the bath taps.

The candle flames flickered over the water filling the tub, and

I no longer noticed the worn linoleum or the chipped tiles. It was just Alex and me, the running water and dozens of little lights, dancing on their wicks.

I turned off the taps while Alex lit the last candle and placed it on the edge of the sink. We were surrounded. Then he came over to me, so close I could feel his breath against my cheek.

"Hey, baby."

"Hey." My voice came out deep and soft.

He put his finger underneath the strap of my dress and tugged it off my shoulder. He kissed down my neck. Then my other strap. He turned me around and kissed down the back of my neck. It was like a feather being skimmed over my skin. Incredible. Teasing. It felt like the room was spinning.

I heard the *zzzzhhhhh* of the zip and felt the dress go slack. I breathed out as it fell. His hands moved to my chest where the dress had been holding in my breasts. His palms against me, against my nipples, making me moan. He pulled me back against him and I could feel him through the fabric of his rented suit pants. I reached around and fumbled with his belt. He moved my hands aside to do it himself and I heard the pants fall to the floor on top of my dress. I turned around and cupped his face in my hands before pulling him to me and kissing him hard.

*My Alex.*

He was standing in shirt, tie, socks, and underwear. I yanked at his tie and he unbuttoned his shirt like the thing was on fire. My breasts brushed against his chest and he groaned through our kiss. He pulled at the side of my underpants, then crouched down to drag them down my legs. I stepped out of them as he pressed his face against me. I'd never felt anything like it before. My whole body seemed to crumple in on itself, and then I was on top of him and he was underneath me on that linoleum floor and we didn't care.

His underwear got caught on him. He sat up and maneuvered them off, then patted around on the floor till he found a small packet. I watched as he put the condom on, his hands shaking, but he was quick, as if he'd practiced.

We both paused, as if the floor was going to fall through. This moment we'd been thinking about for so long. Planning. The room came back into focus; tea-lights, like a thousand stars, white flames flickering around us. Alex, in the shadow of the bathtub, his face pink and his eyes wide.

He inched inside me, slowly, slowly. It hurt, but not as much as Janet Longhurst had said it would, and then it felt good. It felt good that Alex was groaning and saying, "I love you. Oh, God, I love you. Oh, God."

I blinked fast in the darkness, noticing every sensation. My knees against the linoleum, the cool air grazing my nipples, Alex's fingertips pressed into my buttocks.

He grasped hold of my hips and moved me back and forth until I got the hang of it, and he was pressing himself up and into me. Faster and faster.

"Oh, Frankie . . ."

His whole body went rigid, his breath caught in his throat. Tea-lights twitched. Then I felt him shudder beneath me and his head tipped back. His body seemed to slump.

I lay down on him, all of my skin against all of his, and he kissed my forehead.

"Was it okay?" I whispered.

"Yes. God, yes." Another kiss. He was holding me to him, his arms looped across my bare back. "Are you . . . all right?"

"Yeah. Yeah, I'm good."

I kissed him and felt a smile on my face. It felt like he was still inside me; I could feel him in the muscle, in the tissue. I ached, but it wasn't bad.

Alex sat up a bit, took off the condom as I glanced away. I crawled off of him and he stood to check the bathwater. My knees were pink. He pulled the plug to let out some water, and then got in, carefully holding my hand. He bent his legs so we could both fit, and we sat, one at each end, smiling at each other.

"We did it, Frankie."

I stared at him, smiling, and then at the water and the lights swimming on its surface. I begged my brain to remember it all and never, ever forget.

# Affogato

## ESPRESSO AND ICE CREAM

The word *affogato* means "drowned" in Italian because the ice cream is drenched in espresso.

*Serves 4*

Good-quality vanilla ice cream

4 shots (about ¾ cup) hot, strong espresso

OPTIONAL EXTRAS:

Good-quality dark chocolate (broken into pieces then stirred into the hot espresso so it melts)

Frangelico (a nip added to each serving)

Whipped cream (a tablespoon on top of each serving)

Amaretti cookies (1 cookie crumbled on top of each serving)

## PREPARATION

Scoop a generous serving of ice cream into small bowls or glasses. Pour a shot (about 3 tablespoons) espresso over each. Add the extras of your choice.

# Chapter Five

· · · ·

Papa is outside, waiting in one of the chairs, when I get up in the morning. He's a small man, bald, with sagging cheeks and round glasses. He lifts his hand in a wave when I walk out to greet him. His fingertips are stained black from his work as a mechanic.

"*Principessa*," he says.

"Hey, Papa. Daniel told you I was here?"

He nods. I sit beside him and he smiles at me.

I had been living with Papa for two weeks before the funeral. He insisted on sleeping on the couch, waking before I did every morning and making me coffee. As the days slid by and fell over one another like skittles, Papa stopped just short of dressing me and propping me up on the couch before he left for work.

Papa works for his brother Mario, and even if Zio Mario had insisted he take time off to be with me, which, let's be honest, is unlikely, Papa wouldn't have. He takes his work seriously. I've never figured out if it's an immigrant work ethic or just the way he's made. Perhaps both.

He reaches out for my hand now, and frowns. "I can't stay too long, *duci*."

"It's okay, Papa. I know."

I give his hand a squeeze. I'm willing to endure a little loneliness for the solitude and peace, for the distance from the empty shirts hanging in the closet.

Papa glances around, up into the trees, at the sunlight falling like confetti through the tiny gaps. He looks out of place here, with his leather shoes and pressed, short-sleeved shirt. We never went camping as children.

"Have you enough food?" he asks.

I nod. I don't mention Bella.

"I didn't want to think of you hungry. You are eating, aren't you?"

I nod, and watch his chest fall with relief. Grieve, wallow, sleep till noon, tear your hair out by the roots if you have to, but *mio Dio*, don't stop eating.

"Good . . . good," he murmurs, and glances at the forest again, the cabin.

I know he will report back to the aunties. He will tell them I'm fine, that I'm taking a little break and will be home soon. That the cabin is very nice and trim and well cared for. He may even tell them it's more modern than he imagined, and won't check inside in case this is a lie. He doesn't lie well to his sisters. He looks towards the outhouse and away quickly. He won't tell them about that. He'll tell them about the food, tell them I'm eating. I'm glad I'm not still wearing my black dress and the boots I found in the closet.

"Bella came," he says, a little like a question, more of a statement.

I shrug, thinking of her on the step. Cropped hair, long skirt, skin the color of espresso *crema*.

"Do you want coffee?" I offer, remembering my pot and grinds, wanting to change the subject.

Papa frowns but indulges me. "No, I should go soon. I just wanted to see you for myself. Bring you some things. Mario will be expecting me. I shouldn't be late."

Papa is never late. Like me. Not like Bella.

"I will come back again soon, to see you are okay."

"Thanks, Papa."

He stands from his chair. "It's a nice little cabin," he says, gesturing to it.

"It was Alex's great-grandfather's."

Papa cocks his head. "Do the Gardners, Barbara and Marshall, know you are here?"

"Daniel does. They're not using it."

Papa's question makes my stomach jump a little. I can't go back to the apartment yet.

"No," he says, reassuring, giving me a smile. "You just have a little rest, Francesca, and come home when you are ready. Vincenzo has his birthday in a couple of weeks. You remember?"

"Of course," I say, though I'd forgotten. I can't plan beyond each day, sometimes each hour. That my cousin is turning twenty-two is of no interest to me. He is closer in age and personality to Bella. Alex never thought very highly of him.

Papa's face registers relief at my lie. It has been hard enough having one daughter who doesn't come to family functions, let alone two. That makes me think of Bella. I spent years making up for her absence. She's home now; she can go to Cousin Vinnie's birthday party. She can make a dish the size of a side table—meatballs and *sarsa semplice*, or something sweet like ricotta cheesecake with chocolate and cream and glacé cherries— and kiss cheeks and fill the family in on her life.

"Your sister is staying a little while," Papa says.

"Uh-huh?" I try to sound casual, though it comes out waspish. "How long?"

"I don't know, *cara mia*." He presses his lips together, pauses. "I think she would really like to talk to you."

"Uh-huh," I say again, looking at the ground. "Will you tell Aunty Rosa thank you for the cannoli?"

"Francesca?"

"It was very kind of her and—"

"Francesca, will you talk to her?"

I fold my arms across my chest.

"You should give her a chance."

"You give her enough chances for the both of us," I want to say. And, "You don't know." Instead I keep my mouth shut.

"Well," Papa says with a little sigh.

We walk to his car, which he's parked quite a way up the drive, as though he didn't want to wake me with the sound of the engine. I wish I'd put on the boots now; the roots and stones press into my feet.

"Do you want me to call the council?" Papa asks. "Mrs. . . . ?"

"Fratelli," I answer softly.

My work. The tiny cubicle with pinboard partitions around three sides, making a little fortress. I've been there for years—working earnestly; complaining about my boss, my colleagues, and the bureaucracy; going to the office Christmas parties; fighting off lecherous Darren Forthe like most of the other admin girls, bar Bertha Robinson who's in her fifties and has a fine, dark mustache that seems to catch the light; poring over Christal's wedding photos and Amy's baby photos; pondering which skirt to wear with which shoes; dreading Mondays and celebrating Fridays. Now it all seems pointless.

"Yes, please," I finally answer.

I realize I don't care if they keep my job open for me or not, though I'll have to figure out how to pay our rent at some point. Have to return to the city someday. Not now. It's best not to think too far ahead, lest I notice the large and terrible Alex-shaped hole punched into every day.

"Okay, I'll call," Papa says gently. He gives me a firm kiss on my cheek and draws me into a long hug, pats my back. "I'll be back soon, darling."

"Thank you, Papa."


I make myself a breakfast of fruit and a half container of yogurt, wish for honey, and top it with pine nuts. I get dressed in my jeans and sneakers and stare at *The Swiss Family Robinson*, drum my fingers on the little table and glance out the window. Then I slip the door key into my pocket and go out for a walk.

I avoid the path to the ocean, the thought of it causing my

heart to race; instead I head in the opposite direction. It's the way that Huia went, but there isn't a clear path, just ferns and shrubs around knee height to negotiate. I amble along, not caring if I get lost, listening to birds singing both warnings and love songs.

Only a few weeks ago, Alex and I were working on our wedding vows. We'd left them to the last minute, after selecting flowers and napkins, after picking up the rings, after organizing where his aunt Elizabeth and uncle John would stay the night. The wedding had become a kind of job. I was sitting at the table with a pen and paper; Alex was slumped on the couch. I had to beg his attention while he watched end-of-season ice hockey on TV.

"We can go with the traditional version—love, honor, and obey—though I'm not sure about 'obey.' Do you think it's a bit . . . old-fashioned?"

"Hmmm?"

"Obey, as in 'love, honor, and obey'—is it outdated?"

"Nah, I like it. Bring me some chips?"

"Huh?"

"Chips. I need potato chips. Obeying should start now." He threw his head back and laughed.

I frowned. "You're not taking this seriously."

I flicked through the papers on the table. I'd printed out several versions of vows I'd found online. I'd thought it would be an easy decision but there were so many options. Some more religious than others; some funny and lighthearted; some till-death-do-us-part serious. I plucked out a relatively nonoffensive version and scanned the words.

Alex lifted himself from the couch and walked behind me to the kitchen. I heard him open a packet of potato chips and then he was standing over me, his hand rustling in the bag. "Let's have a look."

He leaned over my shoulder and I smelled the salt on his fingers as he placed his hand on the table. His cheek was close to mine, his jaw working noisily. He read and then straightened.

"Well?" I said.

He shrugged. "Looks fine." He headed to the couch and settled back to the game.

"You've got to help me," I whined.

"They're fine," he said again, halfheartedly. "Just choose whichever one you like, Frankie. You know me; I'll say whatever you want. It doesn't matter."

I stood and went to the couch, took a deep breath. Tried not to be too Italian. Too dramatic. "It *does* matter."

It mattered because you have to mean what you say, especially in church. Though I'd said all sorts of things in church I might not have meant, made promises I hadn't even thought about. No sex before marriage, for one.

I softened my tone. "Is there anything you don't want to say?"

He shrugged again. "I don't know. I mean . . . do you really want to know?"

"Yes."

"Okay. All that forever stuff . . . it just seems so . . ."

"So . . . ?"

"It's not realistic, is it? Forever. What does that even mean?"

"Forever? Forever means you'll love me forever," I said.

He glanced at me, then put his hand back into the bag, popped chips into his mouth. He swallowed before answering. "Isn't it actually impossible? Who can promise forever?"

"I can promise forever." I felt my throat tightening. "You can't promise forever?"

I tried to keep my voice even. I had other things to get done before the wedding, a thousand things. Aunty Connie hadn't finished stitching the beading on the bodice of my dress and I couldn't ask anyone else to do it or she'd be offended. Mrs. Gardner was asking, again, about the food, wondering whether it was a little too exotic for the guests she'd invited. And I hadn't heard from Bella at all. A sister was supposed to help with this stuff. A sister was supposed to be forever. Forever, like a husband. I tried not to start crying.

Alex frowned, unconcerned. "It's not about me. It's the concept. Forever. Who can promise that?"

The lump in my throat seemed to expand till I felt like I couldn't swallow. Tears pricked at my eyes. "*Bedda Matri,*" I swore under my breath, sounding like one of the aunties, wishing the tears away.

Alex looked at me with alarm. "Oh, Frankie, I didn't mean . . ." He sat up and pulled me to him.

I was angry at the falling tears. The wedding was much more work than I'd expected. The girls at work had warned me, but I hadn't believed them. How could it be, when in their photos they'd all looked so beautiful, so radiant, so happy? Besides, I was organized; it would be different for me. My wedding would be a piece of cake.

Unbidden tears continued to pour out of me. I swore at them again. Alex was shushing and cradling me.

"We'll go with those vows. It's okay. I didn't mean to upset you. Hey, don't cry."

I tried to stop but the tears just keep coming.

Alex brushed them away with his thumb. "Don't cry, baby."

I sniffed, drew in a deep breath. The roar of the hockey crowd distracted us for a moment; we watched as the puck flew into the goal and the players swooped around the ice raising their sticks, grasping each other in clumsy, padded embraces.

Alex pulled me close and whispered, "I'm sorry. We can have whichever vows you like, okay? Whatever you want." He planted a kiss on my forehead.

"But you don't want . . . forever. . . ."

"Don't listen to me. I'm no good with this stuff. You know that. You choose, Frankie, I'll say whatever you want. Forever and ever and ever and ever, amen." He looked into my face and winked. "Love you." He kissed me.

I wiped my face and pulled away from him a little. I wasn't going to be "that girl," the needy one, the whining one. I just wanted the day to be here right now. To be standing in my dress, to have Alex looking at me like he was now. To be saying "I do" and becoming Mrs. Gardner.

"Whatever you want, babe, truly," he said again.

We both looked back to the game. I broke my pre-wedding diet and took a handful of chips. The grease and crunch of them, salt rough against my tongue, was somehow soothing. I curled up against Alex's shoulder and he wrapped his arm around me. I would be Mrs. soon enough. I'd waited for this and nothing was going to spoil it. I changed the subject.

"When we get married I'll be a Gardner."

"Too right, babe."

"People won't know I'm Italian," I murmured.

Alex nodded, but his eyes were following the puck. "That's good, right? You always say people judge you when they see your name."

"I guess."

"You can be American."

"Yeah."

The opposing team scored a goal. Alex smacked the side of the couch and I reached for more chips.

I pause, blinking, coming back to the present. The memory leaves me feeling a little sick. I almost hope to feel a ghost arm around me, but there's nothing other than the breeze.

The forest seems to be thinning a little, and ahead of me there's a road, surely connected to the cabin's long driveway but heading in the opposite direction from Edison and Seattle. The road looks like an unnatural dark river winding out of the green and I find myself following it.

I walk past faded mailboxes and driveways that lead to places I can't see, though I guess, by the state of their mailboxes, they're probably summerhouses or cabins much like the Gardners'. The sun is biting by the road, away from the tree canopies that act as parasols. Spring is stretching out her arms and reaching into summer. I scratch my shoulder and wish for shorts and sandals rather than jeans and sneakers.

Ahead, a house sits close to the road: a small, single-story place painted mint green. Ivy grows up one corner and onto the roof, the green tendrils swaying like a girl's hair let loose from a braid. In front there's a full and busy vegetable garden, with plants jostling for real estate and bees making a steady, low, collective hum. It reminds me of the aunties' gardens, and my nonna's when I was a kid. Tomato plants twist gently skywards, their lazy stems tied to stakes. Leafy heads of herbs—dark parsley, fine-fuzzed purple sage, bright basil that the caterpillars love to punch holes in. Rows and rows of asparagus. Whoever lives here must work in the garden a lot. It's wild but abundant, and I know it takes a special vigilance to maintain a garden of this size.

The light wind lifts the hair from my neck and brings the smell of tomato stalks. The scent, green and full of promise, brings to mind a childhood memory—playing in Aunty Rosa's yard as Papa speaks with a cousin, someone from Italy. I am imagining families of fairies living in the berry bushes: making their clothes from spiderweb silk, flitting with wings that glimmer pink and green like dragonflies'. I am humming to myself. Happy to be close to Papa, close to adult conversation, while Bella plays elsewhere—probably with the boys, probably tearing a sleeve, her shoes kicked off. I turn over leaves and find ladybugs as the cousin speaks to Papa in that rolling, secret, family-only language. "*Brava carusa*," she's saying, looking at me. "Good girl." *Brava carusa, brava carusa, brava carusa*—I add it to the tune I'm humming. Two feathers, now characters in my hands, climbing a vine. Sisters. One white feather and one brown with spots. "*Brava carusa*," the cousin says of me, and then something else about Bella that has my Papa frowning and which I now can't remember.

"Hello?"

It's a sweet voice, full of melody, startling me out of my day-dreaming. A woman by the door of the house, cradling a mug. She lifts her hand.

"Oh, hi," I say. "Sorry . . ."

Her hair is red, as red as a pepper at the roots, and then curling and fading to a luminous dark orange at the frayed tips. A bee lands on her, crawls along a strand of hair, then flies away, disappointed she's not the flower it expected. She wears harem-style pants, black with bright splashes of color, and a singlet top.

She steps towards me, her feet bare. "I'm Merriem."

"Francesca . . . Frankie," I offer in return. "Sorry, I was just walking and . . ."

She waves away my apology and comes to stand near me, both of us staring at her tomato plants. Her cheeks are round and smooth, covered with freckles.

"I finished all my harvesting yesterday so it would be done by the third quarter, and today I'm at a bit of a loose end," she says with a shrug, then tips her mug at me. "Want a cup of tea?"

"Oh, no, I should be . . ." I gesture back towards the forest.

"You're staying in the Gardner cabin."

"Yes. How did you—"

She thumbs towards one of the driveways I passed. "Jack Whittaker."

"Jack?"

"Looks after the place. Looks after a lot of places around here."

"Oh, I thought he must. He has a daughter?"

"Huia. You've met her?"

I nod.

"She's a forest sprite, that one. Probably on a first-name basis with most of the animals and birds and bugs in there. You're not a Gardner, are you?"

She studies me curiously. I shake my head. *Could have been*, I think.

"Jack says you were playing a little hide-and-seek yesterday?"

"Oh, well . . . no . . ." I start to explain unsuccessfully.

"It's a good place for a bit of hide-and-seek," Merriem says wistfully. "That's what got me out this way. Didn't think I'd be here long and then . . . sixteen years." She gestures to the house. "It's the garden that keeps me here. Verdant little temptress."

She laughs and it's loud and deep, almost a man's laugh. The kind of laugh that could set a whole room full of people laughing. We look back at her vegetable garden.

"I've just had to cut a lot of my asparagus and scapes, of course, sorrel. . . . Yesterday was a dry sign, Leo, and I was running out of moon." My face must be blank because she adds, "Vegetables harvest better in the third and fourth quarters of the moon."

"Oh."

"It's the rhubarb that's the worst. Even I'm getting sick of eating rhubarb. Come winter I'll be thinking about it again. I'm going to turn into rhubarb one of these days."

I find myself smiling. She has a calming way about her, despite the wild hair and the singsongy voice. She's at ease with herself.

"I can talk about gardening all day," she says. "It gets like that, you know?"

There's not a single potted plant in our apartment, but I nod.

"I lived in Rome a while—long story—but I even managed to garden there . . . on a four-foot-square terrace," she says proudly.

"My family's from Italy."

"Whereabouts?"

"Mama's family was from Calabria, Papa's are from Sicily. But my parents met here, in the States."

I think of my family, all together at a feast for one of the festivals. They speak in Sicilian dialect with the older generation, or to swear, and in Italian with the Calabresi or other American-Italian friends. English for Alex, of course. We're a mixed bunch—diverse as orphans, thick as thieves.

"Like Cyndi Lauper," Merriem says.

"She's Italian?"

"Her mother's Sicilian."

"I didn't know that."

I think of Bella and me, an infinitely long time ago, hopping around to "Girls Just Want to Have Fun," ponytails bouncing, TV and stereo remotes as microphones.

"A lot of Italians garden using moon charts like I do," Merriem says. "You'd think it wouldn't sit so well with the Catholic side of things, but it seems to. Food must be too important to get messed up in religion."

"We love our food. That's no myth."

"It works. I get tomatoes that are as big as footballs." Merriem winks at me. "Besides, it's not as kooky as it seems. The sun and the moon make the tides, and the tides affect water. What do plants need most? Or seeds, I should say. Moisture. Right at the surface of the soil where they can use it best. There are also tides in the air, lunar winds, and even earth tides—the soil rising and falling inches in a day."

"Really?"

"Yup. It's old stuff. Planting calendars have been around for centuries. Waxing moons and waning moons are good for differ-ent things, and when you put that together with the signs you can figure just the right date for planting. Or picking."

When Merriem smiles her freckled cheeks rise up and her eyes almost disappear, like vanishing moons themselves. She shifts her weight from foot to foot, her limbs lean and her back straight, graceful and yet full of latent energy.

"It's a waning moon now," she says. "Could you tell? It's pretty black at night. Can take some getting used to when you're accus-tomed to regular light switches and all the rest."

I nod, thinking of our little apartment with every comfort and convenience. At the cabin everything takes a lot more effort—cooking, washing, going to the bathroom.

"Makes you realize just how much of a human hand there is in every single thing we do, everything we touch. We've made living so easy it's hard to know who's in control. Nature or us? Sure feels like us."

"Not here," I say.

She nods. "No, not out here in the forest. Here we're in God's palm."

It's something Papa or the aunties would say. The thought makes me shiver a little: how limited the control we have over the things that matter is. My generation expects the world to yield to our command, to do as we bid it. How naive we are.

I walk back to the cabin through the dappled light and duff that smells both sweet and rotting. I'm carrying a basket filled with spears of asparagus and two big jars of pretty, pink, stewed rhubarb.

Coming along the path the other way is a woman, looking at her feet as she walks. She's wearing jeans, a big shirt, and sneakers that were white once. She has a hat over the top of long blond hair. When she lifts her head and sees me she stops walking. I must have startled her; she looks pale.

"Hi," I say. She seems familiar. "I'm—"

"Frankie," she says.

"Frankie, right." I stare at her a little longer. Her eyes are light and grayish blue, her eyelashes a collection of blond and brown, like pieces of sand. "Sorry . . . Do I . . . ?"

"Summer," she says. Her voice is tight. She clears her throat. "Summer Harrison. I'm just on my way to Merriem's."

"Oh, you know Merriem, okay." We stare at each other a moment longer. I feel like I ought to know who she is. "Well . . ."

She steps off the path to allow me past, then says, "Are you staying here?"

I turn. "Yes. Well . . . for a while."

"For a while," she echoes. It makes me feel a bit disoriented.

"Maybe I'll see you around?" I say.

"Yeah. Bye, Frankie."

# Chapter Six

· · · ·

When I get to the cabin, there's someone else new, a man, waiting. He's tall, his shoulders broad but slumped a little, his skin
tanned. He's fingering a piece of paper folded lengthways, and he
clears his throat as I approach. I walk more slowly.

"Francesca?"

I press the basket closer to me. "Yes?"

"Jack." He holds out his hand.

I look at it but don't take it. He pulls it back, frowns, scratches
his head. His hair is black and coarse with just a few grays. It
reminds me of the coat of an old dog belonging to a relative in
Sicily: *Aragosta*, they called him; Lobster. He's probably dead now.

"I work for the Gardners," Jack explains.

I blink at him. His eyelashes are dark and long. His voice
has an accent I can't quite place, but I know he's not American.
"You're Huia's father."

Then I remember Huia telling me her name came from New
Zealand. A distant cousin of Papa's once told me that if you
drilled down through Italy, through the center of the world, you
would come out in New Zealand. I'd never forgotten that. The

cousin had a straggly mustache that was long at the edges of his lips and he was too lean for an Italian man, especially a Sicilian; the aunties always said you couldn't trust a man who wasn't well fed. Years later I found out that what he'd told me wasn't true. It's Spain that's supposedly opposite New Zealand on the globe.

Jack nods.

"Merriem told me," I confess.

"You've met Merriem already?" He glances at the basket. "Oh, the rhubarb. It's good."

I say nothing, and try to step around him but he's in my path.

"Sorry, I have to . . ." He waves the piece of paper like a little flag. When I don't take it, he places it in the basket. "From . . . ah . . . the Gardners."

"What is it?"

He looks uncomfortable. "They . . . they might put the property up for sale."

"Sorry?"

"The cabin. They're thinking of selling it. Maybe."

"Selling . . . What? No, they can't."

Jack shifts his weight from one foot to the other. He's wearing khaki shorts that are frayed at the hem. *My aunty could fix those for you*, I think, then remember the beading on my wedding dress.

"It's Errol Gardner's cabin. It's been in the family for generations," I say instead, confused.

"Yeah. I don't really know if they want to . . ." Jack gives a small sigh. "Sorry." He moves out of my way.

"I don't understand."

He points at the letter, white as a gull's wing in my basket of green asparagus arrowheads. "They don't want you to stay," he says softly. "I don't . . . I mean, it's my job, so I have to . . ." He shakes his head, seems to shore himself up, but then all he says, again, is, "Sorry."

"Sorry," I repeat dumbly.

Jack nods his head in a good-bye. I stare at his back as he strides away.

Attention: Ms. Francesca Caputo

Re: Request to vacate property

Dear Ms. Caputo,

Please be advised that my clients, Mr. and Mrs. Marshall Gardner, owners of property "Gardner Cabin," Flinders Way via Chuckanut Drive, WA 98232, have informed me that consent has not been granted for your occupation of their property. They kindly request your swift vacation. Should you not vacate the property in a timely manner, trespassing procedures will ensue.

Sincerely,

J Whittaker

Property Caretaker

I stare at the dark type and the logo in the top right-hand corner: a tree in a circle, the roots and branches reaching out, a tiny bird in a central fork of the branches.

*Trespassing procedures.*

I stand in the dim light of the cabin with the fresh, grassy smell of asparagus and dust all around and find myself shivering, though it's not much cooler inside than out.

*Swift vacation.*

The word vacation has me remembering the envelope in our apartment, on the narrow hall table. The one with plane tickets inside.

I drop the letter on the table and take the jar of rhubarb over to the counter by the window, lift a spoon from the drawer, and unscrew the jar lid. I dip it into the contents of the jar. Pretty and pink, like a jewel, the color of hibiscus. The color of the bikini I was going to pack. Into the suitcases the Gardners bought us as an engagement present. As I bring the spoon to my mouth, my ring sparkles like tinsel on a Christmas tree.


"Merry Christmas, Francesca." Mrs. Gardner kissed my left cheek and passed me a glass of eggnog.

"Merry Christmas. Thank you."

She'd given me a gift of tea towels and a mug with a print of a flower on the side. Alex and I bought her wineglasses. As I held the eggnog in its cut-crystal tumbler I knew we'd made the wrong choice. Our glasses weren't crystal and Barbara Gardner surely owned dozens of wineglasses.

The eggnog was strong and caught in my throat. I automatically looked around for Alex but he'd gone into the kitchen. Daniel was in a lounge chair, flicking through a book we'd given him, the biography of a famous hockey player. Mr. Gardner had a glass of whiskey in his hand and was leaning back in his favorite chair, his eyes closed. Neither of them paid us any attention.

Mrs. Gardner leaned in. "Do you have eggnog with your family?"

"Oh, no."

"I imagine there are a few more people than this."

I nodded. Our Christmases were big and loud and chaotic. Except during grace when we gave thanks for the feast. For that children were dragged onto laps and shushed and gossiping ceased. But not for very long.

"Just our little four. Mustn't be very exciting for you," Mrs. Gardner added.

"Oh, no, it's . . . lovely," I said. "Quiet."

She gave me an odd smile.

"I mean peaceful."

Elvis was singing Christmas carols in the background, his voice deep and quavering.

"Hmmm," she said in reply.

There was a full glass of eggnog on the silver tray between us.

"For Alex?" I asked.

She nodded.

"I'll take it to him."

"Thank you."

I took a big breath as I stepped out of the pants. Perhaps I could tip my eggnog down the kitchen sink and pretend I'd drunk it. I was used to sips of *moscato* or *rosolio di arancia,* nothing as thick and muddy as eggnog. In this house I felt horribly homesick, even though I was minutes from home and I'd been with all my family for Christmas Eve. Aunty Connie scolding Aunty Rosa for not slicing the vegetables exactly as Nonna used to; Aunty Rosa scolding me for not keeping my nails tidy; both of them whispering about Bella when they thought I wasn't listening. All the cousins arguing about politics and discussing their next vacations. Uncle Mario and Papa smoking cigars; Cousin Vincenzo getting drunk; Cousin Cristina's baby, Emma, crying and being passed from person to person. The smell of espresso mixed with pine needles, tobacco, icing sugar, and almonds. The winking of Christmas lights, the tiny and perfect *presepi*—nativity scenes—with real straw and miniature donkeys.

I walked down the hallway towards the kitchen. It was cold. Family portraits lined the wall. Grandparents' black-and-white wedding photos, with stiff faces and dresses; Alex and his parents at his christening; his high school graduation photo. Ice clinked against crystal as I walked. *You don't belong here*, it seemed to chime. I couldn't understand why Mrs. Gardner seemed to dislike me so much, but it was clear I wasn't what she had planned for her son. She looked at me with a mixture of displeasure and pity. I guessed it was because I was too different, too Italian. And my family was not of the same class, if such a concern still existed. Alex said his mom was like that with everyone. But I didn't believe she looked at everyone the same way she looked at me. She looked at me like I was in the way; a dandelion head full of fluffy seeds among her roses; an annoyance. Like something that if left unchecked would spread and disrupt all her well-laid plans.

Alex had his back to me in the kitchen, slicing something on a chopping board. I placed the glasses of eggnog on either side of the board and wrapped my arms around him.

"Hey," he murmured.

"One of those is for you."

His waist was slender. My arms went all the way around. I rested my cheek on his back.

"Your mom doesn't like me."

"You always say that."

"That's because it's true."

"You shouldn't take things so personally."

His voice was gentle but dismissive, and I pressed my lips together so I couldn't reply and disagree. I'd never understood not taking things personally, especially someone not liking you. Wasn't that personal? I reminded myself that it was Christmas.

"What are you doing out here?" I asked him.

He laughed. "Slicing lemons for drinks."

"But we're having eggnog."

"Exactly."

I smiled against his back.

He laid down the knife and the fruit and turned around. "I never wished you a Merry Christmas."

"No, you didn't."

"Merry Christmas, Frankie." He kissed my forehead.

"Merry Christmas, Alex," I said, curling into him. My palms were pressed gently against his chest.

When he pulled back he picked up my hand. "Look at that."

"What?" This was a game we had played before.

"We should put a ring on there sometime."

I dutifully rolled my eyes. Acting playful, though I was longing for him to propose, had been for years.

"You'd think so, wouldn't you? After all this time?"

He pulled me back into him for a long kiss. It made my heart race.

Daniel came into the kitchen. "Keep it G-rated."

We pulled apart, laughing. Daniel stood aimlessly, arms at his sides.

Alex nudged him. "You looking for something, brother?"

"Nah. I just wanted to get out of the living room."

"Want my eggnog?" I held up the tumbler.

"No way. I hate it."

"Me too," I replied.

Then we were all giggling, hiding out in Mrs. Gardner's kitchen. Soon Mrs. Gardner would come looking for us. Mr. Gardner would wake up. We'd have to eat Christmas candies and talk about the weather, Mr. Gardner's golf, or the accounting firm they thought Alex should work for. Alex pinched my butt, and Daniel told us we made him sick, before dropping a lemon slice down the back of Alex's shirt.

It's the one part of that Christmas Day I remember. I've forgotten almost everything else, even what Alex gave me that year for a present.

I press the letter roughly into a ball and toss it across the cabin. It rolls through dust into the corner by the bed.

When I step outside, a bird breaks out into gentle chiding. *Shook shook shook shook shook*. It reminds me of the aunties—insistent and lyrical. It makes me wonder if I'm close to a nest.

The scent of dark, wet soil being warmed comes to me. My finger is pressed between the pages of my book. I pause.

*Shook shook shook shook shook*. Always in sets of five.

"Hello." The dark-haired girl stands among salmonberry shoots that reach up towards the light. She is wearing a green dress and green-striped leggings. The forest sprite. I can't see her father.

"Hi, Huia."

"Can I . . . ?"

"Sure."

She steps over to me, and stares, again, at the cover of my book, as if dying to reach out and touch it.

*Shook shook shook shook shook.*

She turns her head towards the sound. "Steller's jay."

"Pardon me?"

"The bird. It's a Steller's jay."

We both peer into the forest.

"There." She points.

A few trees away, its black eye staring straight at us, is a blue and black bird. The feathers on its head stand to attention like a punk Mohawk. The style suits it. Defiant. *Shook shook shook shook shook.*

"He's handsome."

"Yeah. And he can do cool sounds. Dad calls it something . . . mimicking? Is that it?"

"Making sounds like something else?"

"Yeah, like hawks and squirrels. Dad says they can even meow like cats or bark like dogs."

"That's pretty neat."

We both watch as the Steller's jay flies from its perch, taking its song with it.

"Do you always see those birds here?" I ask.

Huia blinks at me as if to test whether I'm joking. "Yup,

they're here all the time. Not like the birds you only see in spring or summer, like hummingbirds or tanagers. I guess they don't wanna be cold. They leave in winter."

Hummingbirds, I know. Tanagers I have no idea about.

"I don't know anything about this place," I mumble, mostly to myself.

Huia glances up at me. A gust of air ruffles her hair so it stands up for a moment like the Steller's jay's feathers. Her feet are still shoeless, her skin dark as bark, soil under her nails.

"I know everything," she says simply. "Well, a lot," she revises. "I could tell you things. If you want me to." She doesn't look me in the eye as she makes her offer.

"Tell me things?" I repeat.

Her voice softens. "If you had questions . . . or something."

"Oh, well, I don't know how long I'll be staying."

I pause, thinking of Mrs. Gardner's letter balled up on the cabin floor. Then I am back in our apartment, standing in our kitchen, at the beginning of the day. Standing over the sink with my espresso in hand. Another on the counter in front of me. Fronds of steam stretching up towards me. Alex reaching around me to take the cup. The blond hairs on his arm brushing against mine. Turning to face him . . .

Huia presses her toes into the soil, still not looking at me.

"Yeah, that would be great," I say.

She gives a broad smile. She has bright, white teeth, small and straight.

"Does that mean you might be staying a while?"

"Maybe," I say, more firmly than I expected.

"Cool." She finally lifts her eyes to mine. "Dad said you couldn't, but I knew you would."

I shrug, trying to be nonchalant. "I think I can stay a bit longer." Then, changing the subject, "How come you aren't in school?"

"School's finished for today."

I blink, puzzled at how quickly time passes in this place. "Of course."

"Do you go to school?" she asks.

"Oh, no. Not anymore."

"Are you on vacation?" Her eyes are wide.

"Well . . ."

I am guessing that Mrs. Fratelli, my boss, will have heard from Papa by now. They went to school together, Mrs. Fratelli and Papa, before she was a Mrs. She knew my mother. Not that she ever mentions her to me. Very few people do, bar the aunties and older family members. I think Mrs. Fratelli once had a crush on my father.

"Sort of," I say to Huia. "I'm taking a kind of break." *From life*, I don't add.

She nods, satisfied. "Dad looks after a lot of the cabins around here. People come for the summer, not even for very long, and then don't come back for ages. Looking after the places isn't his real job, though."

"Yeah? What's his—"

"Do you like foraging?"

"Pardon?"

"Foraging—getting things. You know, to eat?"

"Like gardening?"

Huia laughs. "No, no, no. *Fo-rag-ing*. Getting things out of the forest to eat. My friend is teaching me about it."

I think of the warnings issued to us in school about not eating certain berries and plants, the urban myths about children mistaking poisonous berries for raspberries and dying. The forest always seemed a pretty dangerous kind of place when I was young. Even now I'm more comfortable with houses and yards, streetlights and zebra crossings.

I shake my head. "No, I've never done that."

She grins. "You should try! I'll tell Merriem. We can show you."

"Merriem, she's your . . . Oh . . . I don't know if I'm really—"

*Shook shook shook shook shook* interrupts us. We both turn quickly to spot the Steller's jay perched just branches away from us, its blue tail swiveled in our direction, showing off its rear end. Definitely a male, he's so cocky. Huia giggles and I can't help but join in.

"Cheeky fella," she says to me, her smile bright.

A man's voice calls out. "Huia?"

Huia fills her lungs before bellowing, "I'm . . . here . . . Dad!"

She's so loud the Steller's jay takes flight in a flash of black and blue.

Jack appears around a Douglas fir. "Need to shake the leaves off the trees?"

Huia turns to me. "Dad reckons I'm loud."

I smile at her.

"I thought you were behind me, bub," Jack says. He frowns and places a hand on her head. "Sorry." This last comment is directed to me, the fourth apology from him today.

"It's okay," I reply.

Huia reaches for his hand and hisses, "I asked, Dad. She said it was okay."

"Frankie," I remind her.

"Yeah, her, *Frankie,*" she tells him.

"Okay. But it's dinnertime soon so we should leave Frankie alone." Jack gives me a cautious smile.

"She wasn't bothering me," I say. "She was teaching me about the birds."

Huia nods, then lets go of her father's hand and wanders off to examine a shrub, crouching down by its roots. We both watch her, lanky legs bent to hunker down, black hair falling across her face.

Jack clears his throat. "You read the letter?"

I nod.

"I . . . Look, I probably shouldn't know about this, but I saw the news . . . about . . ."

Huia has a stick and is poking at something in the soil. We stare at her rather than each other.

"Alex," I finish for him.

"Right." He nods.

"He was my fiancé," I murmur.

"Yes. I read that too."

Silently I beg him not to say he's sorry, and he doesn't.

Huia lets out a scream. "Dad, I found poque!"

Jack frowns. "I don't think so, bub. Poque should be closer to the sea."

I feel a tightening in my stomach when he mentions the ocean.

"Oh." Huia picks up her stick and moves to another shrub.

Jack glances at me. "I think you've got at least a few more days."

"Yeah?"

"I'd say so."

"I just need . . . a few days," I reply, but it feels like a lie.

"There you go," he says reassuringly. "If you need anything we're just up the road. Before you get to Merriem's. It's the bashed-up mailbox with a sunflower on the side, you can't really miss it." He lowers his voice. "It's the worst mailbox on the street. Don't tell Huia—she painted the flower to cheer it up a bit."

"Thank you," I say.

We're silent for a moment, watching Huia flitting about. I can't imagine her inside a house; she seems to belong outdoors.

Jack speaks again. "You didn't happen to see a coloring book inside, did you?" I turn to him. He looks worried. "My work . . . it's . . . Childcare's expensive and Huia loves it here with the trees and birds. Sometimes she comes with me when I do my rounds. I didn't know you were coming."

I nod. "I won't tell them."

"Thanks," he says gratefully. "I hope that's all right. It's just difficult with . . . Well, the Gardners can be . . ." He regards me with sudden concern. "Sorry. I didn't mean . . ."

I think of Mrs. Gardner among her roses. Studying them with disdain, seeking only perfection. "They require firm-handed pruning," she told me once.

"Alex wasn't like that," I say. "Like them."

"Oh. I'm sure. "

"Dad?" Huia interrupts.

"Yes, bub?"

"What's for dinner?"

"Ah . . . Beans and bacon."

"With Merriem's bread?"

"With Merriem's bread." Jack looks at me. "Merriem looks after all of us out here."

"Her rhubarb's very good; you were right."

"Everything out of Merriem's garden is good. If you don't want to be tucked under her wing, you might have to speak up now because it's where we all end up."

"It doesn't sound too bad," I say.

Jack laughs. "No, it's not."

"Okay," Huia calls out, "let's go have dinner then. You coming, Frankie?"

Jack looks to me.

"Oh, no. Thank you," I say. "I'm okay here."

"You've got plenty of food?" he asks. Like a Caputo.

"Yes, thank you, I'll be fine."

"We'll come check on you!" Huia sings.

"Yes, we'll come check on you," Jack says, taking his daughter's hand. "Thanks, Frankie."

By the earnest tone of his voice I know he is talking about bringing Huia to work with him and the coloring book left in the cabin. About keeping his secrets safe.

"That's okay."

They move away through the forest, back to where I know the road to be, Huia skipping and Jack lifting her by the hand over low bushes. She turns once and waves, flashes a paper-white smile, and I lift my hand in reply.

# Chapter Seven

· · · ·

This was the wedding menu.

**Starters**
*Rounds of* Grana Padano
*Breads*
*Seafood platters*
*Prosciutto with melon*
*Prawn cocktails*

(The prawn cocktails were at Mrs. Gardner's insistence. She said she'd never heard of prosciutto and was dubious about meat served with fruit.)

**Entrées**
*Chicken with white wine sauce and vegetables, or*
*Beefsteak with mushrooms and béarnaise sauce*

(Alex's requests. We copied them from the menu of his favorite restaurant.)

*Dessert*

*Platters of cannoli, cassata,* biancumanciari, setteveli, *and almond cookies*

The desserts were my wish list. Traditional and Sicilian, just the way I wanted them. Mrs. Gardner said she wasn't "a sweet tooth" (in a way that made it sound like a kind of tribe), and Alex couldn't care less about dessert. I thought of these desserts when I went to aerobics classes, trying to lose weight before the wedding—imagined the smooth filling of the cannoli, the cool velvet of the cassata, and the toothy crunch of the almond cookies.

I think of them again now as I warm meatballs in sauce on the camp stove. This is Aunty Connie's recipe, using pork mince and pecorino. The simple tomato sauce is so cluttered with meatballs you could stand the spoon up in the bowl. Aunty Connie's theory is that meat should be included in every meal to help children grow, and whenever we visited her as kids we came home with our stomachs at bursting point. She makes beautiful veal dishes, such huge piles of pasta they threaten to break the serving dishes, prosciutto sliced thin as lace so you can see through it, and *polpette*. Meatballs, meatballs, meatballs.

I flick off the camp stove. The pot sends up curls of steam and the scent of pork and fennel and tomatoes simmered till sweet. I breathe it in, pushing cannoli, cassata, and cookie fantasies to one side.

When the pot has cooled a little I take it to the table and lift spoonfuls to my mouth. I glance up at a scurrying on the roof. A raccoon perhaps. Maybe not that big, maybe a squirrel. Maybe a ghost.

I find myself wondering about Huia and Jack, whether they eat in front of a television or at a table. Table, I decide, with Huia barely able to stay still in her seat and Jack admonishing her for sending beans flying. Crumbs from Merriem's bread in their laps. Talking with their mouths full.

I place my palms against my full stomach. I'm tired. In this place I feel tired as soon as the light starts to disappear, as though I am becoming more and more animal, less and less human. Circadian rhythm, I remember from science class. I am synchronizing with the inhale and exhale of the forest. I am becoming a bird or a butterfly or a beetle. I feel safe here and don't want to leave.

I hear car tires on the driveway and then an animal running on the roof. The percussion—*pup pup pup pup*—travels the length of the roof and then ends, the animal presumably returning to the dark of the forest.

The sound is replaced by someone peppering the door with light but rapid strikes. I know who it is before she even speaks.

"Frankie. Open up."

"I told you to leave."

She whispers, "I did . . . and then . . ."

I snort. "Cute. I don't want you here."

"Let me in."

"Go away. I told you to go away. You don't belong here."

There's a hesitation before, "Technically, neither do you."

My chest tightens, my fingers make a fist. "*Vaffanculo*, Bella!"

"I just meant—" Now there is apology in her voice.

"I don't want to hear it!"

"I just want to talk to you—"

"I don't want to talk to you!" I'm shouting now. And hating myself for it.

I wrench open the door and Bella staggers back. Her eyes are full and round. They remind me of another time, when we were children. A summer's day and a house full of people wearing dark clothes and speaking Italian. Women with lace-edged handkerchiefs, men with bitter-smelling cigarettes. Sliding under a bed to hide, the smell of heat and dust, pulling pins from my hair. Bella came into the room and saw me there and I raised my finger to my lips. She was only four, and tiny; she didn't look bigger than three at most. She'd said nothing, just wriggled under the bed with me, looking out at the stripe of light and reaching for my hand across the carpet.

"Frankie . . . please . . . why are we fighting?" she says now. "It makes no sense. Come on."

"No," I manage in an almost normal voice. "No. I don't want you here. I don't want to talk. I want to be alone."

Her eyes shine in the dim light. "Maybe I can help. We could set things right between us."

"Maybe you can help? You have never helped. What do you want?"

Bella straightens. "Nothing. I mean . . . I want us to be sisters again. Friends maybe."

"Because?"

She's frowning. "Because nothing. Because we're family."

"You need money. You need a place to stay."

"No." She reaches out but I lean away from her. "Oh, Frank—"

"I don't believe you."

"*Soru* . . ." Sister.

"Don't speak to me in Sicilian like you're suddenly as Caputo as they come!" My voice is loud again. I am holding tight to the doorframe.

Bella's face hardens. "I *am* Caputo, Frankie. As much as you. I know I haven't been around much lately but that doesn't change the fact. And . . . I've had my reasons."

"Yeah. You and your reasons. Go away."

I push the door closed, but Bella lifts her palm and stops it from shutting.

"Move your hand," I say.

"No." She is calm.

"Move your hand."

There's an eight-inch gap between the door and its frame.

"Move. Your. Hand."

"I'm not leaving, Frankie. Not anymore."

I see her again as she was back then. Dark head leaning in towards him, hand pressed coyly underneath her thigh. Red lips seeking out that which wasn't hers.

"Move your hand or I'll break your fingers."

As soon as she removes her hand, I slam the door shut.


I sleep fitfully, kicking off the covers, waking up cold, burrowing back down under the dusty quilt and then waking again, hot, my skin slick with sweat. When morning comes I feel more tired than when I went to bed. When I hear two voices talking outside the cabin I am confused before I am irritated.

"A farmer from Edison. He brought me here, and when he left I stayed. A good thing too. The place is nicer without him in it."

A bellowing laugh.

"A senior citizens' home," Bella says. "About five years now. It's good work."

"Yoga . . . it keeps me centered."

"Oh, I paint too!"

They talk of artists I've never heard of and the conversation becomes hurried and punctuated by more laughter. They talk over each other, chattering like squirrels.

"Wasn't he wonderful? Such use of color. Wild."

"They were his muses, of course."

"The skin . . . the hair . . . It makes your heart sing."

I get to my feet and open the door. Bella is sitting in her car, hair messy and face tired but smiling. She's turned sideways so her legs hang out of the door. Merriem stands with a bag cradled in her arms.

"Frankie! Morning!" Merriem sings out when she sees me.

Bella looks up, but her smile fades when I return it with a glassy glare.

"I was just meeting your sister, Isabella."

"Bella. People call me Bella," she interjects.

"Beautiful. That's what it means, right?"

Bella nods.

"You both are. The beautiful sisters." Merriem points between us. "I can see the similarity. Your mother must be a beauty too."

"We're very different," I say immediately.

Bella stares at me.

Merriem glances back at Bella. "Uh, well, that's good too," she says slowly. "Frankie, I brought more vegetables. Did you eat the last lot?"

"Almost. Hang on, I'll get your basket."

I step back into the cabin and place a jar of rhubarb on the counter before carrying the empty basket outside. Bella is already taste-testing sorrel from Merriem's new offering. She looks slightly guilty and I'm glad. I'm surprised she stayed the night; I expected her to run away. As she always does.

"Thank you," I say to Merriem, passing her the empty basket.

"My pleasure, honey, truly. It's nice to share them with another human or two. Huia doesn't love rhubarb and I think Jack's sick of it."

"Oh, no, he told me he likes it," I reply.

Bella lifts her eyes back up to me.

Merriem sighs. "Bless him. He's kind to me."

"Your . . ." Bella asks Merriem, insinuation lifting her voice.

"Oh, no!" Merriem laughs. "He's got to be almost twenty years younger than me. More your girls' age and type, I'd say."

"Oh?" Bella says.

"He has a daughter," I say tersely, hating Bella for being such a flirt. I never had it in me; she seems to have been born with a double dose. *Don't think I didn't see you.*

Now they're both staring at me. Merriem changes the subject.

"He said he had to give you a vacation notice?"

I nod and shrug.

"Barbara Gardner," Merriem says, shaking her head.

Bella frowns. "What does she—"

"She doesn't even like it here," Merriem continues.

The Gardners' cabin isn't in a trendy, luxurious location like Orcas Island or Lake Wenatchee or Lake Washington. Every year Mrs. Gardner rented a beautiful house on one of the San Juan Islands, right by the ocean, and took pictures of her beautiful sons standing shoulder to shoulder by the water, arms crossed, hair thick, teeth as white as a photograph in a Ralph Lauren catalogue.

"You know her?" I ask Merriem, who nods.

"Not well. But I've lived here long enough to have bumped into her a few times. I've been around when she's been giving Jack his orders. He does a good job for her, above 'n' beyond what she pays him—or what she deserves—mainly because he cares so much about this place. Not that she'd notice—" She cuts herself off. "I'm speakin' out of school."

"The Gardners want you to leave?" Bella asks me.

I ignore her.

"You girls should come to my place for dinner one night," Merriem says, changing the subject again. "In fact, I've got another new friend popping over tonight. Why don't you come too? I can ask Jack and Huia as well. Lord knows I have too much harvest for just me."

"Oh, no—" I begin.

"That would be great," Bella says, beaming.

Merriem smiles back. "Good."

I try again. "No. Thank you, but—"

"Can we bring anything?" Bella asks.

"No, Bella—"

"Ah. No, I don't think so," Merriem says, musing.

"Wine?" Bella asks.

"Okay, wine. Perfect." Merriem looks pleased.

"Wait, no, Bella isn't staying," I say, but they're still looking at each other.

"Do you think I could be so rude as to ask . . . ?" Bella licks her lips. "Our father, Joe, he'll be home by himself . . ."

"Bella!" I hiss.

"Of course!" Merriem says. "The more the merrier."

"Merrier Merriem," Bella replies with a smile.

"That's what they say."

Then they're both laughing and I feel as though I could be a mile away.

"Bella, no," I whisper urgently.

"It's okay, Frankie." Merriem pats my arm. "I love to host. And I need to get rid of some of my vegetables. It's a great solution. Truly, no trouble. Quite the opposite. Being busy keeps me out of mischief." She picks up her basket. "I'll see you tonight around seven. Does that suit?" She's looking at me.

"Thank you," I stutter.

"Thank you, Merriem," Bella says smoothly.

I can hardly bear to look at her. Ruffled, cinnamon-tipped curls, wide smile, sparkling nose stud, a picture of perfect trustworthiness. Almost elegant. Charming. She is a snake. I turn away from her. "The aunties are coming," she calls to my back.

"What?"

"The aunties are coming. I thought you should know." She sounds a little apologetic. "And . . . I'm not leaving, Frankie."

"Perfect," I mutter. "That's just perfect."

I clean the cabin angrily. Soak cutlery in boiled water; take a hot, wet cloth to all the surfaces, even the inside of the closet. The omnipresent dust is thick and gray and furry. I tuck the coloring book and crayons into a drawer, and hang the red-and-white quilt over the back of the chair to air. Then I eat rhubarb and yogurt and a hunk of bread, make myself a coffee and drink it standing near the window, watching Bella doing yoga.

She bends and stretches like a cat, long and fluid, as if her limbs are simply strung together. Her skin is as golden as it was when we were kids, spending our days outside, and she's lost her teenage softness. Her face is sharper, her arms leaner. She moves languidly, as though nothing has happened, as if she's always been here, as though no one was just about to be married, as though no one has died.

I want to shout something cruel: "You look ridiculous!" Or reel off the colorful mean things Sicilians would say.

But I don't. I don't want her to see me watching her. I don't want her to try to talk to me.

She rolls up her yoga mat and tosses it into the back of her car. Then shakes out her legs and walks into the forest as if she owns the place. As if she's in an activewear commercial.

I stare into the trees long after she's gone from sight, sending wordless curses after her.

# Polpette al Sugo

## MEATBALLS IN SIMPLE SAUCE

A typical Sicilian dish to serve family for lunch or dinner

*Serves 4*

1 teaspoon fennel seeds
4 garlic cloves
1 handful flat-leaf parsley
12 ounces ground pork
   (or 6 ounces ground
   pork and 6 ounces
   ground veal)
¼ pound pecorino
   cheese, grated
½ cup fine dried
   breadcrumbs

1 onion, finely chopped
Sea salt and freshly
   ground black pepper
2 eggs, beaten
All-purpose flour
2½ tablespoons extra
   virgin olive oil
1 can (14 ounces) diced
   tomatoes
A pinch of dried oregano

## PREPARATION

In a small bowl, soak fennel seeds in a little water (about 2 teaspoons). Finely chop 2 of the garlic cloves and set aside. Take the 2 remaining garlic cloves and the parsley and chop together so both are finely chopped and the flavors are combined.

In a large bowl, combine the ground pork with the parsley-garlic mixture, pecorino, breadcrumbs, half the onion, and the soaked fennel seeds. Season with salt and pepper, then mix in the beaten eggs.

Spread some flour on a plate. Using your hands, form the meat mixture into balls (about the size of a golf ball). Flatten them slightly, dust with flour, and shake off the excess.

To make the sauce, heat 1 tablespoon of the olive oil in a

heavy-bottom saucepan. Add the chopped garlic and remaining chopped onion and cook gently until softened but not colored. Add the tomatoes and oregano and season with salt and pepper. Cover and cook over high heat until the tomatoes have reduced to a sauce, about 10 minutes.

To cook the meatballs, heat the remaining 1 tablespoon olive oil in skillet. Add the meatballs and cook until golden brown all over. Transfer to the saucepan of sauce, cover, and simmer over low heat for 10 to 15 minutes longer.

Serve the meatballs with the sauce or, for a typical Sicilian meal, remove the meatballs and serve the sauce over pasta, then present the meatballs as a second course with vegetables or salad.

# Chapter Eight

· · · ·

"Francesca?"

Piercing, rolling voice. European inflections. Zia Connie.

Both aunties are getting out of Papa's car, Papa helping Aunty Rosa, and Aunty Connie already standing, squinting, frowning, and calling out.

"Where is she? I can't see her. Where is she, Giuseppe?"

I hear Papa mumble in Italian: *Wait, sister*.

Aunty Rosa is wearing a silk head scarf with big dark glasses, as though she's Elizabeth Taylor. She's beautiful for her age, and knows it too, though she's bigger and softer than she used to be. In black-and-white photographs her little waist is nipped in, forming impressive triangles down to her hips and up to her bust. Now, two children and three decades later, her middle section is fleshy, filled in. She is holding a bag that I know will be packed with home cooking.

A dark-haired young man gets out of the backseat and yawns, stretches, and looks around. He's wearing a tight black T-shirt and denim shorts. Vincenzo, my cousin, Aunty Rosa's son. He appraises the cabin, peeking over the top of his sunglasses, and sees me. He gives me a wink and a grin.

"Francesca?" Aunty Connie again.

I shrink back into the dim light of the cabin.

Aunty Connie has glasses too, but they are prescription rather than sunglasses. She is the eldest, and has never married or had children. Her brother Pietro, the youngest in the family, died when he was very little, of polio, back in Sicily. Soon after, Nonna and Nonno moved to America with the four remaining children: Concetta (Aunty Connie), Rosaria (Aunty Rosa), Giuseppe (my father, Joe as most people call him), and Mario. Nonno said they left Sicily because it was too poor—beautiful, but like a prison.

Aunty Connie is wearing a neat jacket and matching dress in conservative green-gray, the same color as her eyes. Her figure has never had Rosa's curves. It's straight, columnesque, like a Douglas fir.

"Are you in there? Good Lord, is she in *there*?" Rosa asks.

"Rosa . . ." Papa again.

There's a short silence, then a shrill retort from Aunty Connie. "Get your hands off me, Giuseppe. Francesca? Francesca, come out here and look at me right now."

"Francesca?" Papa's voice sounds tired. Tired and full of love. "Will you come out for a moment? Your aunties want to see you, darling."

I hear Aunty Connie muttering, "You always babied her, Giuseppe."

I finally go to the door. Connie has her hands on her hips, Papa is frowning, and Rosa is brushing something from her skirt. Vincenzo is still grinning, his muscular arms folded across his chest, his sunglasses now folded and hanging from the collar of his T-shirt.

"Francesca Theresa Caputo." Aunty Rosa sighs, coming towards me with her arms wide.

"I'm sorry, Zia, I—"

"Are you okay?" Papa asks.

"I'm fine," I say, trying to sound reassuring.

"See, I told you she would be safe," Papa says in a slow, calming voice.

"Oh, for God's sake. Look at her! She's not fine. She looks like . . . like . . . a *homeless* person," Aunty Connie splutters.

"*Bedda Matri*, she does," agrees Aunty Rosa sadly.

Vincenzo places a hand against his mother's back and soothes, "*Mammina*."

I run a hand over my hair.

"She is perfectly . . . safe here, just as Bella said." Papa is careful with his words, as always with his sisters.

Vincenzo looks at me. "Where is Bella?"

I shrug.

He steps away from his mother to scan the surrounding forest.

"Look at her hair. What is she wearing?" Aunty Rosa talks as though I'm not there, her voice breathy and appalled. "And no makeup! Like a hobo."

"Everyone will think she is mad," Aunty Connie agrees.

"Zia Rosa, Zia Connie, I'm okay." Although being referred to as mad has me reeling a little. "Please, come in. Have a look around."

The moment I make the offer I regret it.

Papa reaches around Aunty Rosa's shoulder to offer reassurance, patting her back and shushing her. "Francesca isn't mad," he says with that gentle voice of his. "Come on, let's have coffee together."

"In there?" Rosa is sniffing. She digs in her purse, drags out a little purple plastic packet and tugs a tissue from it, carefully dabs at the corners of her eyes.

Aunty Connie crosses her arms and gives me a disapproving frown.

"I have a kettle, an espresso pot," I say, feeling embarrassed. "It's quite comfortable."

It's confusing having the aunties here. They had been at our apartment just a couple of weeks before. They thought it was just lovely and told Papa so. They were proud of their niece with the nice home and the nice man. I relished hosting them in the place I'd made into a home; the result of weekends spent at Home Depot and Ikea when Alex went surfing. Cushions and throw blankets, lamps, flowers in glass vases, prints in frames.

"I'm going to look for Bella," Vincenzo says.

"Is she staying here too?" Rosa asks, incredulous, stepping warily into the cabin.

I don't tell her that Bella slept in her car last night.

"She's probably just gone for a walk," I say to Vincenzo, who waves as he heads up the driveway.

The rest of us squeeze into the tiny cabin. Aunty Connie pushes at something, a dead moth perhaps, with the tip of her pump.

Papa clears his throat. "Sit down, everyone. Connie, you take the seat. Rosa, next to me on the bed here." He presses down gently on Aunty Rosa's shoulders.

"I'll get the espresso," I mumble.

"I won't have one, *cara mia*," Papa says politely.

I give him a grateful glance. It will take me some time to make everyone a cup using the little coffeepot.

I light the camp stove while Aunty Connie and Aunty Rosa watch in silence. One of the few silences I've ever experienced with my aunties. I find myself babbling.

"This was Errol Gardner's cabin; he was Alex's great-grandfather. He built it with some other settlers by hand. So it's one of a kind. Alex's grandfather, Hank, spent a lot of time restoring it. Alex's father has been less . . . Well, Alex loved it here." My voice drifts off as the pot starts to steam.

"It has been in the family for many generations," Papa adds supportively, nodding at his sisters.

I pull out two cups, relieved that I spent the morning cleaning.

"Sugar?" I ask Aunty Connie, who replies with a sour expression.

"That's Rosa. You know perfectly well I don't take any."

"Sorry. Zia . . . ?"

"*Due*," Aunty Rosa replies, holding up two fingers. Her nails are painted with bright pink polish; many sparkling rings are tight on her fingers. She leans over to touch the quilt hung over the back of the chair Aunty Connie is perched on. "Barbara Gardner made this?"

I pour the hot coffee into the two cups and add sugar to Aunty Rosa's. "I don't think so. Perhaps Alex's grandmother. I'm not sure."

I notice Aunty Connie is peering at the bookshelf as if appraising its contents.

Aunty Rosa sniffs. "It's good work." She is a very good sewer and avid quilter.

I pass the cups to the Aunties, the fragrance of coffee filling the tiny space. It makes it smell better, more familiar. I watch Aunty Connie's shoulders relax a little. They lift the cups to their lips and blow the *crema* into eddies and swirls.

Aunty Connie sighs and tuts. "Running away . . . not telling your father where you are going . . ."

"It's okay, Concetta, she is here," Papa cajoles.

"Running away," Aunty Connie repeats, taking a sip of her espresso. "Not something I'd imagine *you* would do, Francesca. More like—"

"We worried," Aunty Rosa cuts in. "After the funeral. You should be with family, Francesca. Your blood. Family look after you."

I glance to Papa to support me, but he's looking down at the bed, silently agreeing with the aunties. This is Caputo lobbying: loving but persistent, a generous dose of guilt.

"I'm fine, really I am. I just need a little time."

Aunty Connie snorts, as though I'm being ridiculous, and looks around the cabin with disapproval.

"Come home with us, darling," Aunty Rosa coaxes.

I shake my head slowly and she looks wounded. My chest is tight and I can barely swallow. I can't remember the last time I disobeyed the aunties. Or Papa. I can't say what I need to—that I can't bear to go back to our apartment. I can't bear for Alex to be dead. I can't bear the whisper of strange relief inside that makes me feel so dreadful. I can't bear to be anywhere but here, where everything is green and simple.

Papa lifts his head to me. *Please understand*, I beg him with my eyes. If anyone can understand, it is Papa.

"*Si tistuni*," Aunty Connie mumbles, meanly. *Stubborn*.

Vincenzo sticks his head into the cabin. "Look who I found."

Bella steps past him. She gives me an awkward smile, then glances around, seeing the interior of the cabin for the first time. She is still wearing the clothes she was doing yoga in: leggings and an orange T-shirt.

Aunty Connie studies her. "*Buongiorno*, Isabella." Her tongue serves up the syllables in Bella's name in sweet parcels: *Ee-sah-bell-ah*.

"*Buongiorno,* Zia Connie, Zia Rosa." Bella goes over to give them kisses.

"Nice digs," Vincenzo says with a laugh, glancing around. He peers out the window, hands on the counter. "Could use a hot tub."

"Francesca won't come home," Aunty Connie says flatly.

Bella looks at me but says nothing.

"I will, Zia," I reply, feeling hot. The cabin seems crowded. "Just not right now."

Vincenzo pokes at the linoleum countertop. "How *old* is this place? *Cuscinu*, it's a hundred years old. Seriously. It's kind of a dump."

Everyone ignores him.

He's a good-looking young man, Cousin Vincenzo: muscular, well-groomed, a good head of thick, dark hair. Aunty Rosa thinks he's heaven on a stick, but he's lazy and mischievous. He and Bella were always close growing up. Once they got caught shoplifting from the local drugstore. Vincenzo told his mother they'd meant to pay for the lipsticks, deodorants, and eye shadows they'd swiped and Aunty Rosa believed him. He's the apple of her eye. These days he works in sales for an electronics store. He always has the latest sound system and the latest phone. He still lives at home with Aunty Rosa and Uncle Roberto, posters of glossy-lipped, long-haired girls in bikinis on the walls of his room.

"Are you eating here?" Aunty Rosa suddenly asks me, her voice accusing.

"Yes, what are you eating?" Aunty Connie demands before I can answer, lifting her chin at me.

"Papa and I brought some food," Bella pipes up. "Didn't we, Papa?"

Papa is looking downcast, but at this he nods.

"And there's a neighbor, Merriem—she grows the most incredible vegetables, doesn't she, Frankie?"

"Yes." I'm surprised my sister seems to be sticking up for me.

"Asparagus, rhubarb, herbs—enough for a big family, Aunty Rosa. She has a vegetable garden just like yours, Aunty Connie. Well, not as good as yours, of course, but she's a very keen gardener." Aunty Rosa and Aunty Connie are staring at Bella now. "In fact, she invited us to dinner tonight. There's quite an active local community out here. Merriem, Jack—"

"I don't know if we're going," I interrupt.

"Merriem invited you too, Papa," Bella says.

Aunty Rosa's face lights up. "She invited Giuseppe?"

"How old is this woman?" Aunty Connie wants to know.

"I don't know. Fifties maybe? She has quite a youthful disposition, don't you think, Frankie?"

"What does that mean, youthful disposition?" Aunty Connie asks, still suspicious.

"It means she's a cougar," Vincenzo says with a belly laugh.

I watch the corners of Bella's lips twitch.

Aunty Connie's frown deepens. "What does that mean?"

"I just meant that she's fit and healthy," Bella explains. "She has a positive outlook on life."

Aunty Rosa nods. "Well, that's good, isn't it, Connie?"

"She sounds like a flake," Vincenzo says, shrugging.

Bella elbows him and he winces.

"I think she sounds nice," Aunty Rosa says hopefully.

Papa's looking around at us all, till his eyes fall to me. "What is this, Frankie? Dinner? Are we . . . ?"

"No, Papa. I mean, well, maybe. . . . I hadn't—"

Bella interrupts. "Yes, Papa, dinner. Merriem lives just down the road. I said we'd bring wine."

"You said *you'd* bring wine," I correct her.

"Right. So, we're expected at seven. I think you'll really like her, Papa. She's very friendly, isn't she, Frankie?"

"She's very nice," I agree.

"Well, there you are," Aunty Rosa says buoyantly. She surveys the cabin once more, talking almost to herself. "You know,

Frankie, this place could be quite cozy with a little care. Some throw cushions, good drapes." She looks at the floor. "Carpeting."

"Throw cushions," Vincenzo mutters under his breath, shaking his head.

Aunty Connie passes me her empty cup. "I think that's an overly optimistic assessment, *soru*. I am quite sure it is full of rats."

"Oh, no, Aunty," I say.

Aunty Connie gives me a withering glare. "At least Isabella is here with you. *Some* family. I wouldn't feel at all comfortable otherwise. Although . . ." She fixes her glare on Bella. "Francesca, poor girl, has been through enough without your . . . antics. You need to look after her. Can you do that?"

Bella blinks and looks at the ground. Even Vincenzo is staring at her.

"I don't need looking after," I protest, but no one pays me any notice.

"*Sì, Zia*," Bella promises softly.

"*Bonu*," Aunty Connie replies.

"Good!" Aunty Rosa celebrates with a quick clap of her hands, then gets to her feet. "That settles it then. Thank you for the coffee, Francesca, it wasn't dreadful. Giuseppe, will you drive us home before your dinner plans? I have an appointment at the salon."

"It was a long drive out here, you know." Aunty Connie gives me an accusatory look.

"I thought we might never get here," Aunty Rosa agrees.

My protest dies before it even leaves my mouth, replaced by an apology. "*Mi scusassi*."

Aunty Connie stands too, which is the cue for my father to join them. "We'll go back to town and Giuseppe will come back for this dinner with what's-her-name."

"Merriem," Bella says.

"Right. Miriam."

The aunties leave the cabin and Vincenzo gives me a kiss on the cheek. "Two words: hot tub," he whispers in my ear, then raises his eyebrows meaningfully. "Total party pad."

"Right. Thanks, Vinnie."

"Anytime," he replies, clicking his tongue.

Papa is the last to leave the cabin. He passes me the bag Aunty Rosa was carrying. "Rosa's biscotti are in there. Your favorites."

I take the bag; it's heavier than it looks. Aunty Rosa makes the best *nzuddi*: small, round almond cookies rolled in sugar, each studded with a roasted almond and flavored with cinnamon and orange.

Papa hesitates.

"Go, Papa. I'm okay here. I'll see you tonight."

He waits a little longer, the others now by the car, then lowers his voice. "I know about the Gardners not wanting you here."

I swallow. "You do?"

He nods. "Daniel Gardner called in. Poor boy, he's having a difficult time. I haven't told the aunties. They wouldn't understand it. Throwing out a daughter like that."

"Well, I'm not . . . I wasn't . . ." My throat tightens.

"It's not right," he says, shaking his head. Then he seems to gather himself and pulls me into an embrace. "I will be back soon, *duci*."

I nod. "I love you, Papa."

"I love you too, darling."

I stand in the cabin doorway, watching them all getting into the car.

Aunty Connie turns to Bella, who is leaning in the car window. "This Miriam . . . Is she Jewish?"

I see Bella restrain a smirk.

# Nzuddi

## "VINNIES"
### (ROASTED ALMOND COOKIES)

The name for these cookies comes from the nuns of Monastero di San Vicenzo in Catania who invented them. *Nzuddi* is derived from the diminutive for the name Vincenzo—*vincinzuddu* or *'nzuddu*—and thus is the English equivalent of "Vinnies." These are small and firm, not too sweet, cookies, perfect for serving with espresso.

*Makes 30 to 35 cookies*

7 ounces unsalted roasted almonds

1 ⅔ cups all-purpose flour

1 teaspoon ground cinnamon

1 cup superfine sugar

1 tablespoon finely grated orange zest

2 eggs

Juice of ½ lemon

2 teaspoons baking powder

TO DECORATE:

¾ cup superfine sugar

2 teaspoons ground cinnamon

30 to 35 unsalted roasted almonds (about 4 ounces)

## PREPARATION

Preheat the oven to 350°F. Line a large baking sheet with parchment paper.

In a food processor chop almonds until finely ground. Sift the flour and cinnamon into a large bowl, then add the almonds, sugar, and orange zest. Mix well before turning out onto a counter and making a well in the center. Break the eggs into the well, beat lightly with a fork, then add the lemon juice and baking powder. Continue mixing all the ingredients together with a fork until thick and slightly sticky.

To decorate, combine the superfine sugar and cinnamon in a flat-bottomed bowl. Roll a teaspoon of dough into a small ball, then roll in the cinnamon sugar. Place the balls on the prepared baking sheet. Press a whole roasted almond into each ball, pressing down lightly. Repeat with remaining dough (if you run out of sugar and cinnamon simply mix up some more).

Bake until the *nzuddi* are light golden brown, about 15 minutes.

Allow to cool completely before serving. They will keep in an airtight container for up to 2 weeks.

# Chapter Nine

· · · ·

In the afternoon, when Bella has left to buy wine for dinner, the mystery girl reappears. She's standing by the Adirondack chairs, holding a brown paper bag. Her lips are pressed together, as though she's bracing herself, but when she sees me she forces a smile.

"Hey," I say.

"Hi. Summer," she explains awkwardly.

"Summer Harrison. I remember."

She looks different today. She's still wearing the hat but her hair is different, fluffy, like she just brushed it.

She pauses before holding up the bag. "I brought you this."

I step over to her. The bag is heavier than it looks. I unroll the top and peer inside. Bread. Dark, round loaves, a sourdough freckled with something, maybe rosemary, a couple of sugared doughnuts.

"I'm going to Merriem's tonight," she says. "I thought I'd drop by and . . . I work at the . . . My brother owns the bakery. Flour-farm."

I glance at her. Her cheeks are pink. She tries that smile again.

"In Edison?" I ask. I remember lines at the place Alex called "the new bakery." We didn't usually stop in Edison on the rare occasions we came to the cabin together. Alex didn't like lines, and he was always in a rush to get here, to get to the ocean.

"Yeah. My brother and his wife, Ines, own it."

"It's supposed to be good," I say.

"It is. Rocky found his thing, his calling. Rocky's my brother." She pauses. "Actually Beacon's his name, but everyone calls him Rocky."

"Like Beacon Rock?"

"Yeah. Um, exactly like Beacon Rock. My mom . . . I think Rocky was . . ." Summer gives a funny frown. "Conceived there. Something like that."

We both smile.

"Not too many people know that," she confesses.

"If I meet him I'll just call him Rocky."

"Thanks."

We both look at the chairs but don't sit in them. Summer seems to be hesitating, for what reason I don't know.

"You didn't need to bring me anything," I say.

"No. I mean, I know . . . but . . ." She presses her hands into her jeans pockets. "I wanted to say . . . sorry, I guess, for the other day."

I think back to our meeting on the path. "Sorry for . . . ?"

"I was a bit strange."

"Oh. That's okay. I was too, probably. I've been strange a lot lately."

She gives a small, grateful smile. I add, "I kept thinking that I knew you."

She nods, but doesn't say anything.

"Do you want to sit down?" I offer.

"Thanks."

We both sit, but Summer's on the edge of her chair. A whistle comes out of the forest, interrupting us, and we both look towards it. Huia is skipping in front of her father, who raises his hand to us both.

Huia high-fives Summer. I glance between the two of them.

"School out?" I say.

"Yup!" Huia replies happily.

"Hey, Summer. You guys met?" Jack says.

I nod. "Does everyone know each other around here?"

"Yup," Huia answers for him.

Jack laughs and adds, "I know Rocky, Summer's brother, from paddle competitions. From before he went traveling and met Ines, that's his wife, in Portugal. I bought his old business when he decided to open the bakery. Rocky has always helped me out." He turns to Summer. "Merriem said you're coming to dinner tonight too?"

Summer nods.

Huia notices the bag on my knees. "Did you bring dough-nuts?" she asks Summer.

Summer nods her head at me. "For Frankie."

Huia turns quickly and gives me a longing expression.

"Huia!" Jack says, shaking his head.

"It's okay. There's a lot of food in here. I think I need assis-tance." I lift out a doughnut and break it in two, give one piece to Huia and one to Jack.

"Thank you," they reply in unison.

"So much for me starving in the forest, huh?" I murmur.

Huia shakes her head. "Nope, nope, nope." She's got sugar all around her mouth. Jack brushes it away with his thumb.

I lift out the other doughnut and split it in half like the first.

Summer shakes her head. "Oh, no, they're yours. I brought them for you."

"It's okay," I say, holding out the half. "I can share."

Summer stares at me and blinks. Her eyes are small and round and that odd blue-gray, like a winter sky. Her expression is strange. Sad. I remember Jack saying "surfing in Portugal" and a memory pops into my mind. A couple coming into the café Alex and I always went to; Alex introducing them to me. The guy, Travis, I'd met before, but not the girlfriend. Her hair was shorter then, and in braids.

"Summer . . ." I say.

She accepts the half doughnut from me. "Thank you."

"Summer and Travis."

She lifts her head quickly.

"I remember now. I do know you. We met . . ."

She nods. "At Marmalade. Yes."

"Sorry, I'd forgotten."

"It's okay," she says softly.

"Travis surfed with Alex."

"Yes." She seems to wince.

"Your hair was . . ." I gesture loosely with my fingers around my head.

"Yes. And . . ." She hesitates. "Me too."

"You . . . ?"

"I surfed. With Alex. Too."

She's still holding the doughnut. I feel Huia's dark eyes turn to me.

Jack wipes his daughter's face again and takes her hand. "Let's have a look for morels, bubba."

"But—"

"Just a quick look. I thought I saw a patch over there."

He leads her off towards the closest cedar. She lets go of his hand and skips over the gnarly roots.

Summer leans towards me. "I'm really sorry," she says, in that voice I've grown used to hearing. Pained, sympathetic, sad. I see her now, at the funeral. Long hair under a hat, eyes pink from crying.

"You were at the funeral."

She nods. "I should have said that I knew him . . . when I saw you the other day."

I glance in the direction of the sea. "He loved it out there," I mumble.

Summer looks that way too, as though we can see the water, though we can't. "He did," she says, her voice gentle.

I look at the doughnut in my hand. Split in half and broken, so it looks like a crescent moon. Like a C.


As the day slinks into evening I run a brush through my hair, while Bella and Papa talk outside the cabin. Papa is wearing brown pants, a pressed shirt, and leather shoes. The gold chain of the Saint Christopher medallion he always wears around his neck winks above the shirt's top button. Bella has uncovered a dress from somewhere, probably the trunk of her scuffed-up car, which I imagine contains a whole closet in a jumbled heap. The dress is long, the fabric covered with tiny butterflies in myriad colors. She has gold hoops in her ears and is wearing lip gloss. She's holding a bottle of prosecco. Papa carries a jute shopping bag with bottles of Italian red wine inside. From the window I watch them laughing together. It feels as though I'm watching a film.

Whenever Papa spoke to me of Bella I stopped listening. In the end he stopped telling me when she'd called and stopped begging for me to speak to her. I didn't care if the whole family thought I was stubborn. I preferred to pretend my sister had disappeared in a cloud of smoke. Like a magic trick.

I pull the brush through my hair in long, slow strokes. When we were small, after Mama died, Bella and I used to sit in front of the television and I would brush her hair and braid it. Her hair, wild and curly, was always full of knots. I would lay the palm of my hand against her scalp and brush gently so it didn't tug. The curls unraveled to fine fuzz, like candy floss, that stuck up around her head in a halo. She liked it best when I braided it into a kind of crown that looped at the front. I'd sit with the hairpins in my mouth, humming, while Bella sucked her thumb and Papa heated a frozen dinner one of the aunties had dropped off. After everything—the funeral, the unavoidable shadows Mama had left all over the house—it was a kind of peace. A relief.

I glance at my reflection in the warping window glass, use it to push earrings into my ears. Round, rose-gold studs, like minuscule buttons, that Zia Rosa gave me for my eighteenth birthday. I scowl at the dim reflection. It's ridiculous to be dressing up. It's ridiculous to be going out to dinner. There are dark circles under my eyes, and my cheeks hang as though I'm ten years older. I lick my pale lips. Trust Bella to have arranged a dinner date. She can't make it to a funeral but she can get herself invited to dinner within minutes of being in a place. Resentment pricks and scalds like heartburn.

I step out of the cabin, lock the door, and put the heavy key in my jeans pocket.

"*Bedda, cara mia*," Papa says. Beautiful.

Bella smiles at me. "Ready?"

I ignore her, walking past to take the shortcut through the forest. I breathe deeply to shore up my resolve. The sun is still in the sky, summer days not far away. The light is alive with dancing things—bugs, pine needles falling, a baby feather twirling to the ground. The forest is alive and verdant, packed with hopeful life-forms, growing and rising up. I fill my lungs and stride ahead of my sister and Papa, who is being careful with his clean shoes. Ahead, a bird startles and cries out as if cursing me. It's black and blue—another Steller's jay, or perhaps the same one, assessing my visitors and me.

Bella and Papa catch up when I reach the road. Heat bounces off the asphalt, warms my legs in my jeans. Bella is telling Papa about a friend who owns a gallery.

"She started it from scratch. She exhibits her own work alongside other artists in group shows that she names after the moon in season. Indigenous ways of naming the moon: mead moon, thunder moon, sturgeon moon . . ."

"They give the moon different names?" Papa asks.

"For the season. A way of telling time, I guess."

"Well, that's clever."

We pass a dented mailbox with a yellow flower painted on the side. The paint has peeled in the heat of many summers; the mail flag hangs askew. Jack was right: it is the ugliest mailbox on the street.

When we reach Merriem's, she steps into the doorway of the little green house, waving a dish towel. "Hey there! Come on in!"

Her hair is piled up on her head, and two big silver earrings swing from her lobes. Bella waves and grins. She turns into the house, beckoning us to follow.

We step up the path to her door and smell garlic, simmering butter, and freshly cut herbs coming from inside. A brown cat with green eyes slinks past us. He is large-boned, the size of a puppy, but quick.

Merriem's disembodied voice calls back to us. "That's Darwin. Hunk of a cat. Off hunting no doubt. Hopefully not a bird." She steps out of a room, presumably the kitchen, now holding a spoon. "I try to teach him not to hunt the birds, but . . . Come on out of the hallway. The dining room's just down the end there. Summer's laying some cutlery. We're still waiting on Jack and Huia. I'll abduct your wine in a minute."

Bella kisses Merriem's cheek and walks through to the back room. Papa follows, stealing a glance into the busy little kitchen, where Merriem seems to have five pots and pans working hard and in tidy order. There are dozens of copper pots and frying pans—some no bigger than a bread-and-butter plate—hanging from a rack on the ceiling.

Merriem wears neat cropped pants and a floaty cream blouse, with leather sandals on her feet. She stands by a wooden chopping board with a hillock of chopped dark green parsley on it. Beside her large range hood is a portrait of a nude woman holding a water jug. The paint—aqua and teal and cobalt—is thick, like butter, as though spread with a knife.

Merriem turns her head and gives me a soft smile. "How are you doing today?"

"Fine, thank you."

She nods, as though she knows better.

"I'll just . . ." I add, pointing towards the dining room.

"Make yourself at home, Frankie."

The back of the house, where Summer is setting the dining table, has floor-to-ceiling windows that look onto a brick court-yard. It is covered in terra-cotta pots filled with a mismatched collection of ferns and violets and succulents. There's a blush-pink climbing rose on a white wooden frame, and ivy growing up the opposite corner, as though they're racing to get to the middle, both sending out trembling, baby green tendrils. Beyond the courtyard there are a few maple trees, and, set farther back, stacked wooden boxes.

Papa and Bella are both at the table; Bella filling glasses with water from a green glass jug and introducing herself to Summer. It's a big, old, oval wooden table, with French bentwood chairs, and all the plates on it are pink. I take a seat next to Papa as Merriem ambles in, clapping her hands together.

"Right. Sorry about that, just had to get the risotto going. Well . . . anyway . . . wine?"

Bella passes her the bottle she's holding.

"Ooh, prosecco, wonderful."

"It's chilled," Bella says.

"Even better."

Papa stands and hands over his bag of wine. "I am Giuseppe, Francesca and Isabella's father. Thank you for having us."

"Giuseppe, *piacere*," Merriem says warmly, leaning over to accept a kiss on the cheek.

"*Parli italiano?*" Papa asks eagerly.

"*Parlo solo un po' d'italiano*," she apologizes. I only speak a little Italian. "I lived in Rome for a very short time. I should have learned a lot more. I know quite a few swear words." She lets loose one of her loud laughs, her earrings rattling.

Papa looks startled. "Ah, well," he says, smiling.

Summer catches my eye and she lifts her hand in a small wave.

"Merrrrrrieeeeem!" a voice calls down the hallway, followed by quick footfalls.

Huia bursts into the room. She is wearing a blue dress with a red ribbon tied around her wrist. There's a book in her hand, and she has blue sandals on, the first time I've seen her in shoes. Jack follows behind, carefully carrying a glass globe with a plant inside. His hair is brushed, his shirt ironed, with both sleeves rolled to the elbow.

Bella and Papa stand to shake his hand.

"Jack Whittaker," he says.

"Giuseppe . . . Joe Caputo."

"Bella"—she flashes a wide smile and glances at me—"Caputo." She adds, "I mean, I'm a Caputo too."

When it suits you, I want to say.

Jack turns to me. "Hi, Frankie."

"Hi, Jack."

"Summer."

"Jack."

After giving Merriem a firm hug, Huia comes to stand next to me.

"I saw another Steller's jay," I whisper to her. "Tonight. I think we scared him off."

She gives a big grin.

"Huia knows a lot about the birdlife here, don't you?" Merriem asks.

Huia nods and points at me. "I'm going to teach her."

"Frankie," Jack corrects her. He passes the glass globe to Merriem. "For you. Thanks for having us. Again. It's a Moon Valley friendship plant."

"You are a genius, Jack Whittaker," Merriem says, holding the glass ball up to the light coming through the windows from the yard. It reminds me of a Christmas ornament that Mama used to like: a glass ball with a dog in a striped hat riding a sleigh inside. The soil is layered in different colors—specks of pumice, sand, dark black soil—and it's like another world captured in a bubble.

"It's beautiful," Bella remarks.

"Jack is a botanical artist," Merriem declares.

Jack coughs. "I wouldn't go that far."

"No, he is. You should see his other work. He has these huge, incredible terrariums and bonsai gardens as if made for itty-bitty elves. He is very, *very* talented."

"Wow," says Bella.

"That's his *real* job," Huia whispers to me, leaning against my legs.

Jack glances at me, embarrassed. Merriem goes to the kitchen and quickly returns with a wooden tray piled high with thickly sliced bread and brightly patterned dishes of olive oil and dark vinegar.

The bread is vivid yellow. It crumbles in my mouth and tastes sweet, honeyed.

"Dandelions," Merriem says to me.

Papa is staring at his half-eaten piece. "I thought dandelion was a weed?"

"It is," Merriem replies with a grin. "Isn't it marvelous?"

"Yes, it's very nice," Papa says, still looking a little puzzled.

"Dad and I call it sunshine bread, eh, Dad?" Huia says.

Jack nods. "Rocky should sell it at Flourfarm," he suggests to Summer, who is sitting still and quiet, looking at me.

She snaps her head to him, cheeks flushing. "Yes," she says quickly, "he should. It's good, Merriem."

"Bless y'all," Merriem says, shaking her head and laughing. She pats Summer's shoulder and returns to the kitchen.

While Bella and Papa talk to Jack about his plants, Huia passes the book in her hand to me.

I touch the cover with my fingertips. *Native Birds of North America*, the title reads. "For me?"

"Only to borrow," she warns.

She watches as I flick through the pages, looking for birds I've already noticed but not known the names of. The song sparrow, a plain-looking thing that has a sweet, cheeky *chirp chirp*. The dark-eyed junco, which looks as if it's wearing a balaclava and sings a repeating phrase, over and over, in changing keys. I love to hear them trilling to one another as though rejoicing in the spring sunshine. Then I find the little bird that makes the most noise. The picture shows it facing right with a defiant tilt of its chin. Its breast is marked with brown spots and its back is olive brown. The book cannot show the little wing flicks it gives, like a nervous stage performer with a twitch.

Huia looks over my shoulder as I peer at the page. "Hermit thrush?"

I see that she's written "Singer!" in the margin in pencil, the letters round and dark.

I nod. "It's a noisy one, isn't it?"

"Yeah, one of my favorites."

I read the small description. "The females don't sing?"

She shrugs, then flicks through the pages to find one she likes. "A warbling vireo."

I read that it's uncommon in this region unless the summer is good.

"Thanks, Huia. I'll take good care of it."

She smiles, looks pleased. She sometimes seems so wise and clever, and other times as delighted as a very small child. I imagine her teachers must love her.

"Do you sometimes go to after-school care?" I ask.

"Yeah. Some days."

I glance at Bella. She used to help out at after-school care when she was a teenager. She's leaning in to talk to Jack, nodding with the tip of her thumb against her lips. She pours him a glass of prosecco. Summer has gone into the kitchen to help Merriem.

"Which one?" I ask.

"Jellybeans Montessori." Huia's smile has dissolved, she screws up her face.

"That good, huh?" Bella jokes, hearing her answer.

Huia glances down at her sandals, wriggles her toes. It reminds me how I used to hate when the *zias* pressed me for information about my day: How was geography? Did you have enough to eat? What did you do at recess?

"It's okay," Huia says. "We do poetry sometimes, I like that." She looks to her dad, who's now speaking to Papa about gardening. They're discussing fertilizer. She drops her voice. "All the other girls from school go to ballet class in Bow."

I nod slowly. "Bella and I learned ballet."

She gives me a sizing up kind of look. "Really?"

"Sure. Mrs. Talbot was our teacher."

"Did you like it?"

I ponder the question. Aunty Rosa convinced Papa to send Bella and me to ballet. Bella running around barefoot with Cousin Vinnie, and me with my face always behind a book, wasn't healthy, she declared. Ballet was supposed to save us from ourselves and turn us into ladies.

"It was okay," I say.

"Did you have to wear one of those skirts that stick out?"

"A tutu?"

"Yeah."

"No, we didn't get to that stage. We had pink leotards and white leggings, black shoes."

Huia presses her lips together thoughtfully. "They all have those black shoes."

I nod. Mrs. Talbot would send you home if you didn't have your black shoes. She was a force to reckon with. A caricature of a ballet teacher—hair scraped back into a bun, limbs lean and sinewy, face with a just-smelled-sour-milk expression.

"You want to take ballet classes?" I ask gently.

Huia shrugs.

"Do you like to dance?"

"I don't know."

"You don't know?"

"We don't dance very much at home."

Something in her face, her small frown, reminds me of Bella as a girl. We never danced much at home either. Papa said Mama was a beautiful dancer but her asthma stopped her from dancing often.

"What does your dad think?" I ask.

"He doesn't like the makeup and the dresses. He says it makes the girls look too grown-up, and that we've got plenty of time to be grown up, we should just be girls."

"Oh."

"He says he just wants me to enjoy being a kid."

That seems like a good explanation to me. "Well—"

Bella's voice comes to us from across the table. "Dancing's fun."

Huia and I look at her. I hadn't realized she was still listening.

"I did a night course in belly dance last year. It was very . . . freeing. Liberating. And I got to wear"—she drops her voice conspiratorially—"sequins."

Huia smiles but shifts a little closer to me.

"I bet you'd be a great dancer," Bella adds. "What does your mom say?"

Huia blinks. Her eyes are round and she looks to her dad, who glances away from his conversation with Papa to meet her gaze.

"What's that, bubba?" he asks, as though she's posed him a question.

"Ummm . . ." Huia mumbles.

"We were talking about after-school care," I reply quickly. "Huia says she likes the poetry."

"She writes great poetry," Jack says with a proud smile.

"Jellybeans has a good program. I mean . . . I hear that it does," I say politely, though clearly I have no idea.

"Bella used to work at after-school care," Papa says. "Did you know that one, Bella?"

Bella shakes her head. I stare at her pointedly.

"Frankie," she whispers apologetically. I look away.

Huia looks between us, then shuffles over to her father and climbs onto his knee. Papa and Jack resume their conversation, and Bella leans towards me.

I quickly stand, gesturing to the kitchen. "I'm going to help Merriem and Summer."

"Come on, Frankie," Bella pleads. I ignore her.

"Perhaps I can help too," she adds, trying optimism.

I lean towards her, drop my voice to a nasty hiss so Papa, Jack, and Huia won't hear me. "No, no, you stay here and keep saying stupid things."

She opens her mouth to protest but I am already turning, already gone.

# Chapter Ten

····

" Hey, honey," Merriem says sweetly, immediately passing me a spoon and getting me to stir the risotto. Summer is chopping more parsley. Merriem heads out the door, whistling and carrying wine.

"She's put you to work already," Summer says.

I slowly stir the creamy, fragrant rice so it doesn't stick. The smell reminds me of being in Aunty Rosa's kitchen. "Better than pretending everything is fine," I whisper, and am surprised I've said it out loud.

Summer is staring at me.

"I'm not really up for dinner parties," I apologize, then add, "yet." Though I'm not sure when I will be.

Summer looks at the kitchen door as if expecting someone to come through it. "You didn't want to come?"

"Not really. My sister arranged it."

"Does she often do that?"

"Arrange things for me?"

"Yeah." Summer has stopped chopping, the knife held over the parsley.

"Not really. She's been away for a long time. Living in Portland."

"Oh."

"She's not very good with this kind of thing. Grief, I guess. Our mom died . . . and then . . . puberty, I don't know. . . . Anyway, we're really different."

Summer nods, understanding. "Yes. You seem different."

I'm surprised. Most people want us to be similar, to be friends.

"Are you close to your brother?" I ask.

Summer tips her head. "Yes and no. He thinks he knows what's best for me."

"Does he arrange things for you?"

"Yes, he does."

"Do you do them?"

Summer shakes her head, then laughs as if in spite of herself. "Yes, I do." She shrugs. "He told me I had to come here—to Edison, I mean—so I came. Now I'm not sure if I'll go back to school."

"What are you studying?"

"Science. Marine biology. I'll never get a job in it. I just wanted to be in the sea so that's what I chose."

Alex felt that way too, I think, always wanting to be in the sea. Though he'd never have been brave enough to study something he couldn't get a job doing. His parents would consider that frivolous.

I turn back to the saucepan and stir. The risotto is close to being cooked. Summer chops the last few stalks of parsley.

Alex started surfing in high school, and became more and more enamored of it over the years. I thought it would go the other way, that he'd become less interested, but as soon as he moved out of his parents' place—as soon as we moved in together—he seemed to go surfing more and more often. I made jokes that once we were finally together properly, in our very own place, he wanted to be away from me. As though the ocean was his mistress. He kept his surfing friends separate from his regular friends, for the most part; both surfing and his surfing friends were a kind of secret, something just for him. I'd tried to understand it; I'd even tried to learn.

"He tried teaching me once," I tell Summer.

She rinses her hands and leans back against the counter. "To surf?"

I nod. "It was terrible."

"The first time is—"

"I know. I mean, that's what he said too."

I stir the risotto one more time, then turn off the gas element.

It had been an overcast day. We went out alone. Alex kept asking me if I was sure, as though he was hoping I might change my mind.

"I thought it was going to be easy," I say. "Get on the board, stand up . . ."

"Oh, well . . ." Summer's tone is empathetic, supportive.

"It's okay, I know. It takes practice."

Alex had said that too. "Babe, no one manages it the first time." Trying to be encouraging, but sounding annoyed. He was impatient, and I was stubborn and petulant.

"Try again," he'd urged, so I had. Again and again, growing more and more frustrated, getting clumsier.

"You're not concentrating. You're getting mad," he complained.

I argued that I wasn't, but of course I was. Mad as hell. I was also freezing cold and feeling stupid.

He tried to show me the basics, but he made it look too simple. Surfing was in his muscle memory, in his blood, in his thoughts. It was like his shadow, simply part of him. Watching his effortlessness made me even more angry, more belligerent.

We got out of the water and Alex showed me with the board on the sand. "Like this," crouching and holding, "to this," standing and balancing. I pushed at the sand with my foot, my arms crossed in front of me, my lips numb. "Are you even watching?" he'd asked, and sighed.

We got back into the water one more time, and the sea tugged me under and tossed me around beneath a wave, like a plaything, like it was laughing at me. I came up ready to go home, mouth full of salt, hair full of sand.

"It's not for everyone, right?" I say to Summer.

She gives me that sad, hopeful look that says it can be for everyone, should be for everyone. That surfing is the best thing in the world. Her strange, blue-gray eyes fix on me, like she wants to explain. I imagine her in the sea, like a fish, moving as though made for the water. She would know where to put her feet, how to balance, how to fall without hurting herself, without drowning. She's probably one of those girls who rides the waves as though she's dancing with the whole of the ocean; her and the water taking different roles, moving in different ways. The ocean leads and she simply responds.

Merriem comes into the kitchen. She pushes the risotto with

the spoon I've left resting on the edge of the pan. "All done. Good. Give me a hand, you two."

Merriem carries the enormous saucepan, a cloud of steam rising from it, into the dining room. "Spring risotto," she calls it. It's got snipped garlic scapes, tons of parsley, and just-wilted pea greens piled on top.

Summer carries a big glazed terra-cotta saucer full of tiny new potatoes with butter and freshly torn mint, and I bring the asparagus, which Merriem calls "speary-grass," served with simple seasoning.

Summer helps serve up, while Merriem tops up wineglasses. I take my seat.

Papa compliments Merriem on her risotto, while Huia gleefully pops a potato barely bigger than a coin into her mouth. Jack asks her to please use her cutlery, but Merriem reassures her that she likes using her fingers too.

I bring a spoonful of risotto to my mouth and blow. I glance at Bella who is quietly staring at her plate. Her expression reminds me of her as a young girl. I see her lying in her bed, curls pulled into uneven pigtails. Next to her bed, a window frames the neighbors' side wall and offers a peek into their kitchen. Sometimes, if Bella left the window open at night, she would wake in the morning smelling of the ginger and oil and onion they used in their evening stir-fries.

Once the food is cool enough, I eat as though I'm starving. The potatoes' skins squeak when I bite into them; the risotto tastes of soft, pungent scapes; the freshly cut asparagus is so crisp and sweet you could almost mistake it for fruit. Merriem smiles at me. We are all holding our stomachs by the time Merriem clears the table and brings out dessert, a bright pink and sticky rhubarb tart dotted with edible flowers. She doles out big scoops of homemade vanilla ice cream with a silver spoon she affectionately refers to as "the shovel," then adds a chunk of honeycomb to each of our bowls alongside wedges of the tart. Papa's eyes are wide. It's a feast worthy of Caputos. Merriem laughs at our expressions and implores us to leave what we can't eat, but of course it's so delicious we find corners and crevices in our bulging stomachs. Halfway through dessert I notice Jack adjusting the waistband of his pants, and when he catches my eye we smile at each other.

When dinner is finished, and Papa has helped Merriem serve espresso coffees, Jack pulls Huia's chair closer to his and wraps his arm around her. She lays her head against him and stifles a yawn.

Merriem glances at the book on the table. "Huia brought you some reading material?"

"Only to borrow," I say, using Huia's words. "She's teaching me about the forest."

"You didn't stay out here often? With . . ."

I shake my head, my gaze falling to the engagement ring on my finger. "A couple times, but not often. Alex did love it out here though. I mean, the cabin was special to him."

At the mention of Alex's name, Summer rises and starts clearing a few empty glasses. Her eyes look darker blue in this light, and I realize her pale eyelashes are coated with mascara.

"I got out some books for you to take too," Merriem says,

graciously changing the topic. She points to a little pile on a side table. "Rachel Carson's *Silent Spring*; Jackie Collins's *Lady Boss*." She winks. "A girl needs a little sizzle."

"Thank you." Aunty Rosa is a voracious Jackie Collins reader.

"I've got honey for you too," Merriem tells Bella, drawing her into the conversation.

"Are they your hives in the yard?" Bella asks.

I hadn't guessed the wooden boxes I'd seen earlier might be beehives.

"You are a beekeeper?" Papa asks.

"Sure am." Merriem grins. "And a potter. Mainly I'm a potter. But gardening and beekeeping come close runners-up. Hang on, I'll get your honey now." She goes to the kitchen and comes back with a container that she holds out to me. "See what you think of it."

I lift the lid and prepare to stick my finger in. "Just like this?"

She nods.

I press my finger into the container, puncturing the wax of the comb and coating it in honey. I pass the container to Papa, who does the same.

"Delicious," he murmurs, and passes it to Bella.

"Good?" Merriem asks.

"Good," we say in unison.

She laughs. "Okay, now I know for sure you're father and daughter."

Papa looks at me warmly and nods. I notice Bella sucking on her finger too, but she doesn't comment.

Papa asks earnestly, "You sell this honey?"

Merriem nods. "But I can give you some, it's no—"

"Oh, no, I couldn't accept it," Papa says. "Not after tonight's meal you have made for us. I will buy some."

"Okay," Merriem replies, smiling.

Jack clears his throat and I notice Huia's eyes blink open quickly. "Sorry, everyone," he says. "I think we're going to have to make our exit."

"No, Dad," Huia protests, her voice groggy.

"You're exhausted," he says with a laugh.

"I'm not," she says, yawning. The rest of us join in laughing. "Ohhhh," she grumbles.

"Thank you for the book," I say to her. "I'll do my homework."

"It was lovely to meet you," Jack says as Papa shakes his hand.

Jack points to his back. "Hop on, kid." She loops her arms around his neck.

Merriem gives him a kiss on the cheek. "See you soon."

He looks at me. "I'll swing by, see how you're doing . . . but there's no rush. . . ." He looks awkward again. We both know he's talking about the eviction notice from the Gardners.

"Thanks," I reply.

Summer comes out from the kitchen and I realize she's been in there for a while. As though she's been hiding.

"Are you going?" she asks. Jack nods. "I'll walk out with you. I'm tired," she says softly.

"You can stay here the night if you like," Merriem offers.

Summer shakes her head. "I'm looking after Rocky's boys tomorrow. I should go."

"Are you sure you're—"

"I'm fine. Just tired," Summer replies quickly. Then adds, "Thank you so much. Dinner was really lovely."

"Well, you pretty much made most of it," Merriem says, smiling.

"That's not true," Summer says. "Frankie did too."

"I stirred, that's all," I say bluntly, without thinking. Then regret it when Summer looks uncomfortable.

"It was really nice to meet you all," she tells Bella, Papa, and me. "You're a very nice family."

"Aw, that's a sweet thing to say." Bella reaches over to give her a hug, but Summer is awkward and it becomes clumsy and lopsided.

She turns and blinks at me.

"Good to see you again," I say. "Come by the cabin if you're over this way. Anytime."

Bella glances at me, surprised. I ignore her.

Summer looks between the two of us. "Oh. Okay. Thank you."

Jack smiles and tips his head. "Right. Say bye to everyone, Huia," he encourages.

"Bye to everyone," Huia chirps sleepily.

"We can see our own way out," Jack tells Merriem, who nods and doesn't stand. The three of them move slowly down the hallway.

Bella has her finger in the honey container again. "It's really yummy," she says.

It annoys me that she's still using her finger; I want to slap her hand away.

"How many containers would you like, Giuseppe?" Merriem asks. "I can sell it to you for five dollars a square if you like." She holds up her fingers to make an imaginary frame, to give him an indication of size.

"Two. No, three," he says. "I'll give some to Rosaria and Concetta. But I won't take them unless I pay full price."

"Full price is ten dollars. I'll give them to you for seven a pop because you're buying three. Deal?"

Papa nods happily. "I work at Mario's Cars and Repairs . . . the mechanics," he explains, sounding a little stiff. "I mean, if you ever need some work done. The prices are very good but we give discounts for friends and family. Of course."

Merriem laughs. "Mainly I ride a bicycle."

"Ah. The one with the basket, outside," he says, joining in her laughter.

I hadn't noticed a bicycle.

"Betty," Merriem says, lowering her voice as if she's telling us a secret. "After Elizabeth Cady Stanton."

"Ah," says Papa again, and nods as though he understands completely.

"Have you tried it with baked ricotta?" Bella asks, referring to the honey.

Papa nods enthusiastically. "That would be very tasty."

"Baked ricotta? No, I don't think I've ever eaten baked ricotta," Merriem says. "Is it good?"

"Very good. We'll have to bring you some, won't we, Papa?" Bella says.

Merriem beams. "I knew giving a discount would bring me blessings."

I glance between Papa and Bella and Merriem. It suddenly

feels too strange—to be here, without Alex, to have Bella at the table.

"I think we'd better get going too," I say. "It's been a lovely dinner, Merriem."

"You don't want another cup of coffee?" Merriem asks.

"Thank you but no, it's getting late. We should go." I stand from the table.

"Can't we help you with the dishes?" Bella asks.

"Oh, no. I find it kind of meditative. Darwin will keep me company. He'll be home from his roaming soon. He's a big brute of a cat but a little afraid of the dark, I think. Don't tell him I told you that."

Papa gives Merriem a kiss on each cheek, and we make our way down the hallway.

"Thank you," Bella says again. "The food was divine. We'll have to repay the favor."

"My pleasure, Bella. You all take care walking home. Do you want to take a flashlight?"

"We're fine," I say, eager to get back to the cabin.

I'm uncomfortable being with Bella, uncomfortable with her chirpiness. The conversation with Summer is weighing on me too, and my memory of that day at the beach when Alex tried to teach me to surf.

Merriem stands by the door and watches us go. Darwin slinks out of the yard and weaves around her legs. She picks him up and waves to us as we head down the road.

Bella sighs. "That was nice."

"She is a very good hostess," Papa agrees.

The solidity of the road softens to pine needles atop worn dirt as we turn into the forest. I walk on ahead and try to ignore the sound of Bella and Papa chatting. If I were to get in the car and leave now, I think, I would drive through Edison and back through North Seattle. Past the Gardners' house on the hill, see the hedge and the little gate, the white-trimmed windows if I look closely in the disappearing light. I would keep going past our old school, around the back of the main street, because you never know how the traffic will be and the backstreets are quicker anyhow. I'd pass the children's playgrounds and gas stations, and feel my heart thumping harder and faster in my chest. I'd pass a supermarket or fruit and vegetable store, and then, eventually, the neighborhoods that all look the same—garage, fence, mailbox, garage, fence, mailbox. Soon enough I would be back at our apartment. A cement-block building with only three floors and rows of little balconies. Square and solid and vanilla-colored. Our kitchen window the one with the crystal hanging in it, a birthday gift from a workmate. Instead, my feet tramp along the forest path that is becoming so familiar. I feel strange and tense and displaced. My heart pounds like I'm running.

Bella's voice knifes through my thoughts. "Frankie? Didn't you think that was nice?"

"I think Merriem is nice," I reply harshly.

"What's that supposed to—"

Papa interrupts. "Nonno was a beekeeper. Back in Sicily."

"He was?" Bella asks.

Papa nods. "*Sì,* he used to sell honey just like that, from his house. It was the best in the village."

If you believe Papa and the aunties, everything my family did was "the best in the village."

"And Huia, is that how you say it? She is a very sweet girl, isn't she?" Papa says.

"Very," Bella agrees. "Frankie?"

I turn and face my sister, glaring. "Stop doing that."

"Stop doing what?"

"Trying to pull me into the conversation. I just want to go home."

"Home?" Papa asks hopefully.

"The cabin, I mean. I just want to go to bed. I'm tired."

"I was just trying to—"

"I know what you're trying to do," I snap. "You're trying to have a normal little chat as though nothing's happened. Like the normal . . . *ridiculous* dinner, which you bullied me into, as though . . . as if . . . Alex . . . isn't . . ."

"Frankie, darling." Papa reaches for me.

"I'm fine!" I lie loudly, turning away.

Bella scrambles to catch up with me. "I'm sorry, Frankie. I know Alex is . . . it's awful . . . I just thought—"

"How many times do I need to ask you to leave me alone?"

"You need—"

"You don't know the first thing about what I *need*, Bella. What I need is for you to leave me alone."

"Frankie," Papa pleads.

I think of Papa and Bella at the dinner table, and outside the cabin window, laughing. As though the missing years have been forgotten, as though they didn't happen. As though Bella didn't cause us any trouble, any pain.

"You might be able to move on and act like she wasn't a total delinquent," I say. "You're a better person than me, Papa."

Papa cringes. "Oh, darling, I'm—"

"But I can't," I say firmly.

"Won't," Bella mumbles.

"Bella . . ." Papa pleads with her now.

"Right. Won't," I say. "Can't and won't."

Bella gives a little cough. Papa looks at her with alarm.

"Oh, *please*!" I say, rolling my eyes. "Don't go sad on me now."

She doesn't reply.

I walk ahead again, quickly. A thrush flies out in front of me, late for bed, rushing back to a nest. I turn, gravel crunching under the spin of my foot. "And while we're talking about it"—though we weren't—"what on earth made you ask about Huia's mom?"

Bella blinks. "I didn't know—"

"Didn't you see her face?"

Another cough.

"Is this about her mama? What happened?" Papa asks carefully.

"I don't know," I say, barely restraining myself from shouting. "I just know you don't go asking about a person's mother if there doesn't seem to be one around."

Papa frowns at me. Bella's head hangs.

"You . . . *you*," I point at her, "of all people should know that. Or have you become completely clueless?"

"Frankie." Papa's tone is warning now.

"I . . ." Bella starts, but doesn't finish.

I turn from them both and walk into the forest. There are

long, black shadows on either side of me. The ghosts of Alex and Mama. Or perhaps just the cedars and firs reaching towards the moon.

When I'm in bed, the quilt over my head, Papa raps softly on the door. He speaks through the crack between door and frame. "You know you can come home, *cara mia*? I mean, with me?"

I pull down the quilt. "Yes, Papa."

He opens the door then and stands in the frame, knowing not to come any closer. A squirrel, or what I assume to be a squirrel, scampers across the roof.

Papa looks up with concern. "How do you sleep here? With all the noises?"

"They can be comforting, I guess."

He cocks his head. "I know why you don't want to go home. I understand. You know that, don't you, darling?"

I remember sobbing coming from Mama and Papa's bedroom; Zia Connie shutting the door and turning me towards the kitchen, promising gelato from the freezer. Women in black everywhere, like a murder of crows. A slap across the hand for wearing Mama's comb in my hair, followed by remorseful kisses and embraces that were too tight. When we were in high school, Papa finally boxed up all her clothes, but their wedding photos were still on his dresser: black-and-white faces, young, full of life and hope.

At Alex's funeral he whispered to me, "It gets better." It was the only platitude I believed, because it came from him.

When I say nothing, Papa knows that my mind is made up. He sighs. "Well, at least I feel a little better knowing that Merriem is nearby. She will keep her eye out for you both." He doesn't mention Bella by name.

"Yes."

"Her honey is very good. It really is like Nonno's, you know. And yet from bees and flowers on different sides of the world."

The light is almost gone from the sky and sleep is starting to lean heavily against me.

"Papa?"

"Hmmm?"

"You should go before it gets too dark. The drive . . ."

"*Sì*. You are right."

"I'll be okay, Papa."

He clears his throat. "I know, darling. You always are. My strong girl. Stronger than the rest of us." He lightly drums his fingers on the door, thinking.

"Don't ask me to be nice to her," I warn.

"I wasn't going to." He sighs again. Turns to leave. "*T'amu bedduzza.*"

"I love you too, Papa."

# Spring Risotto

A spring vegetable lover's adaptation of a classic Italian dish

*Serves 4*

3 tablespoons butter

2 shallots, finely chopped

4 garlic cloves, thinly sliced

1 ½ cups risotto rice (such as Nano Vialone)

¼ cup dry white wine

3 ½ cups chicken stock

2 handfuls of spring vegetables (see Note), such as a combination of 8 stalks asparagus, cut into 4-inch lengths (first halved lengthwise if fat); 12 fresh, shelled and peeled fava beans; a handful of baby spinach leaves

2 tablespoons chopped fresh chives

Sea salt and freshly ground black pepper

3 ounces parmesan, finely grated

2 tablespoons crème fraîche

2 tablespoons fresh oregano leaves

## PREPARATION

In a saucepan, heat the butter over medium-high heat. Add the shallots and garlic and stir occasionally until tender, 5 to 7 minutes. Add the rice and stir to toast, 1 to 2 minutes. Add the wine and stir occasionally until the liquid is almost absorbed. Add the stock 1 cup at a time, stirring constantly until the stock is absorbed before adding more. Continue until all the stock is incorporated, the rice is al dente, and the risotto is creamy, 10 to 15 minutes.

Add the spring vegetables and cook until just tender. Stir in the chives. Season with salt and pepper. Stir in the crème fraîche and all but ½ cup of the parmesan. Stir until parmesan is just melted and remove from heat.

Serve garnished with fresh oregano leaves, the reserved parmesan (2 tablespoons per serving), and freshly ground black pepper.

*Note:* Substitute with any local and fresh spring vegetables available, such as zucchini, yellow squash, fiddleheads, leeks, and peas. Vegetables should be cut into similar sizes to ensure that they all cook in the same time.

## Chapter Eleven

· · · ·

In the morning, I stand at the window and wait for Bella to go for a walk before I make espresso. As soon as her curly head bobs into the distance, behind trees and bushes, I light the camp stove. I thought she would have gone home with Papa, at the very least for the comfort of a warm bed and breakfast. In her car, the front passenger seat is laid back as far as it will go but it still must be unpleasant to sleep on. She doesn't seem at all achy or inconvenienced as she strides off into the forest. I focus on the espresso pot. Even if I can't figure out why she's staying I'll be damned if I'm going to give her coffee. If she's as Caputo as she claims, the caffeine deprivation will surely drive her away. But, used to making an espresso for Alex, I make too much.

When a pickup truck pulls up and Jack gets out, I pour the excess into another cup and wrap a cardigan around my pajamas.

He glances at my pajama bottoms and shoes with untied laces.

"I made too much coffee. You want some?"

He nods. "Thanks."

I sit in one of the Adirondack chairs and he joins me, sitting in the other. We take quiet sips of the black coffee.

"I don't have any milk," I explain.

"I drink it black."

"Sugar?"

"Nah."

"That's handy. I think the ants have gotten into it."

Jack smiles. "Yeah, you've gotta watch them."

We both look out at the trees, the dozens of shades of green in juxtaposition. Alex studied biology in high school. He could identify the different plant species much better than I could. He once told me there'd been a scientist in almost every generation of Gardners—chemists and physicists mainly, but Alex preferred biology. Apparently biology was a lesser form of science, according to the Gardners.

"You faring okay out here?" Jack asks.

"Yes, I'm fine."

I should probably thank him for checking up on me, but I don't want to encourage more company. Although, if I'm honest, Jack's company isn't so bothersome. Bella's, on the other hand . . . I look towards her parked car and notice a plastic Virgin Mary on the dash.

"Dinner was nice," I say politely.

"Merriem's a great cook."

I recall the sleepy dark head against Jack's shoulder last night. "How was Huia this morning?"

"Bit tired. I just dropped her at school." He frowns. "She wasn't too keen. Complaining about having to go to Jellybeans this afternoon."

"She mentioned ballet classes last night."

"Did she?" He seems surprised. "Yeah, she wants to go. I just . . ." His voice drifts off.

We both sip our espresso.

"Bella and I did ballet classes," I say. "Our aunty made us go."

Jack looks at me. His skin is the same color as Cousin Vinnie's, though I'm convinced Vinnie uses a tanning bed. Jack's eyes are exactly the same as Huia's: as dark as a bird's, perfectly round, set in bright, clear whites.

"Our mother died when we were little," I explain, a little out of step with the conversation. I tend not to talk about Mama.

"Oh, I wondered . . ."

"She had bad asthma. She was ill quite a lot." I don't add that it's a miracle Bella and I don't have it, though it is. Aunty Connie says it's because of Mama's prayers.

"I'm sorry to hear that," Jack says.

"It happened a very long time ago."

"Still."

"Yes, still."

I have so few memories of Mama, and the ones I do have are warped and worn from recalling them, like old photos. Among them: her pitch-perfect but wispy singing, the way she frowned when she was peeling mushrooms, playing with our hair as she read us stories, ironing Papa's shirts with great puffs of heavy steam, laughing at Papa, holding his hand on the couch, and gossiping on the phone to her friends, to my aunty Lisa.

"We went once, to the dance school," Jack says. "It was an open day. They lent Huia a leotard and did her makeup. I mean, they did all the girls' makeup—I guess it was part of the promotion." He draws a breath. "I don't know. She just looked . . . so different, not like my Huia."

I remember the makeup we had to wear for dance recitals and how much I hated it. It was thick and greasy, like paint, like a disguise. Bella had loved it—the dressing up, the preening, the pretending. She and Aunty Rosa had giggled and oohed and ahhed in the mirror. Aunty Connie hadn't approved of the makeup; she'd whispered to Aunty Rosa that we looked like *buttane*, whores, and Aunty Rosa had slapped the top of her hand and hissed, "You can't say that, *soru*. Think of Marcella; they're her girls. She'd turn in her grave!"

"I hated that makeup," I say.

"Yeah? Huia liked it. I couldn't stand the stuff. She looked too grown-up. Like . . . well, a bit like her mother, I guess."

At the mention of Huia's mother, Jack frowns.

"Is she . . . ?" I ask softly.

He glances at me. "Dead? Oh, no." He gives a wry laugh. "No, she's not dead. Not that I know of at least." He balks. "I'm sorry, that's a dreadful thing to say. She lives in New Zealand. Or Australia. Last I heard she was on the Gold Coast."

"She isn't in contact with Huia?"

"Nah." Jack shakes his head and sniffs. He looks towards a puddle of sunlight on a grove of sword ferns, their shoots like green fingers reaching up out of the earth. "Maybe I should just let her go to dance classes," he murmurs.

"She's a great kid," I say after a moment's silence.

"She really is."

We both turn to watch a white car creeping along the driveway. Daniel Gardner, behind the wheel, raises his palm to us. Jack straightens and I wave back. He parks the car and steps out.

"Hi, Frankie."

Alex's voice in another body. It makes me shiver.

"Hi, Daniel."

He pushes his hands into his pockets. I notice his hair is growing out of its neat cut, it's getting a little ragged. He's wearing black jeans and a loose T-shirt.

"You must be Jack?" Daniel says.

Jack shakes his hand and glances at me.

"Daniel Gardner," I explain.

"Oh, of course," Jack says. "I should probably get going."

"Sorry, no, don't let me interrupt," Daniel says.

"No, you're all right. I'm . . . I've got . . . rounds to do." Jack nods to me. "I'll swing by another time. Thanks for the coffee."

"*Uncinnè problema*," I say, No problem, then start to explain, "I mean . . ." But he's already headed towards his truck.

Daniel remains standing. I gesture to the seat beside me.

"Isn't this . . . fraternizing with the enemy, or whatever they call it?" I tease gently, thinking of the eviction letter.

He gives me a pained look. "Mom . . . she's having a rough time."

I nod. As is Daniel, clearly, his face too pallid for his age.

"How are you?" I ask.

He shrugs. "I should have come back sooner. I was going to and then . . ."

He looks so terrible I reach out to pat the back of his hand. "Hey, it's good to see you now."

I think about how it must be at his house—the silence and

grief between him, his mom, and his dad. The Gardners don't process emotion like the Caputos. Tears are private. Stoic is practically part of the family motto. At least my aunties wailed with me at the news of Alex's death. At least Papa never hid his tears when Mama died or told us to buck up.

I change the subject. "When are you back at college?"

He frowns. "Soon. A few more weeks. I had an internship at a local law firm, just doing basic stuff, filing, admin."

"That sounds good."

"I quit."

"Oh."

"I wasn't . . . handling it very well." He clears his throat. "There's always summer, and I'm happy to have some time off, to be honest. Last semester was hard work."

"No one will think badly of you for taking a break."

He gives me a grateful look. "Thanks. I think I just need some time. Mom and Dad don't agree, of course, but . . ." He shrugs. Then he retrieves a black iPod from his pocket. "I brought you this. I didn't know if you had any music."

"No, I don't. Thanks, Daniel."

Daniel plays the guitar. Alex used to tease him about never seeing the sunlight, he spent so much time in his room practicing.

"It's mainly local stuff. It might not be your scene, but, well, I couldn't live without music, so . . ." He shrugs again.

"That's really kind of you."

"Oh, well, no . . ." Suddenly he looks guilty.

I look down at my sneakers. "Did your mom send you?" I ask in a whisper.

He doesn't reply.

"Daniel?"

"I think they might sell . . ." His voice is thin, unanchored.

"That can't be true."

My voice comes out harsher than I expected. Daniel looks alarmed.

"Alex loved this place!"

"I know," Daniel says sadly.

"Your mom never liked me."

"Oh, no, she just—"

"C'mon, Daniel."

I'd had this argument with Alex too, many times. "Mom likes you," he'd say, "she's just not good with women. She's used to being the only woman in the house; she has no daughters. She probably worries that you don't like her." I always let him win because I wanted him to be right. But it was bullshit. Bullshit. Bullshit.

Ahead of us are two Douglas firs, standing like twins. They remind me of Mr. and Mrs. Gardner posed at their front door, as though they're pillars holding the house up. Mrs. Gardner in a long skirt; Mr. Gardner in a Ralph Lauren shirt. Like the first time I met them. Indelibly pressed into my memory.


"It's a pleasure to finally meet you, Francesca," Mrs. Gardner said. "Alexander has told us all about you."

"Come on in," Mr. Gardner said, opening the door.

"Coats and bags go there." Mrs. Gardner gestured towards a replica antique hatstand near the front door.

As we walked to the sitting room, Alex squeezed my hand before letting go. Daniel was perched on the couch, wearing a pressed shirt like Alex, his hair brushed neat. He seemed to be trying to make himself as small as possible, barely speaking as we discussed the summer heat and Mr. Gardner's recent election to the board of the local Rotary club. I glanced over at Alex, wishing I was sitting on his lap and watching a movie, his arm wrapped around my waist.

"Frankie?" Alex urged.

"Sorry?"

Mrs. Gardner was blinking at me. "What do your parents do? Your father, I mean. . . . Alex told us about . . ." She stuttered to a halt, glancing at Mr. Gardner.

"He works at my uncle's shop," I said. "Mario's."

Mrs. Gardner looked to her husband.

"She means he's a mechanic. I know the place," said Mr. Gardner. He smiled and I returned the smile gratefully.

"Oh, right, a mechanic," Mrs. Gardner replied slowly.

"Drink?" Mr. Gardner asked, standing. "Gin and tonic?"

Mrs. Gardner nodded. "Thank you, dear."

"You kids?" He looked at Alex and me.

"We'll have Cokes," Alex answered for us both.

"Alex," Mrs. Gardner murmured.

"Please," he added.

The conversation turned to school and the subjects I enjoyed. I told them that I worked at the school library a few lunchtimes a week and that my favorite teacher was Ms. Gordon, who taught art history. Mrs. Gardner murmured something under her breath that only Alex and Mr. Gardner seemed to hear.

Mr. Gardner said firmly, "The public school is fine."

"Just," I heard her whisper, clearly disagreeing with her husband.

Alex shot me an apologetic look.

"Why don't I give Francesca the tour?" Mrs. Gardner said, standing, drink in hand. "You boys can get the barbecue going."

"Ah . . ." Alex stood too, but I gave him a little nod and said, "Sure. Thanks, Mrs. Gardner."

I smoothed down the skirt of my dress and picked up my glass. Mrs. Gardner led me out into the yard, pointing out the kitchen and guest bedroom and bathroom on the way. The yard was beautiful—soft lawn edged with rosebushes and rosemary. There was an outdoor setting of white wrought iron, as if we were in Paris or one of those Hamptons homes you see in television shows. Mrs. Gardner started telling me about the roses but I wasn't paying much attention. I was wondering whether my dress was too short and if I should have tied up my hair.

"Alex says your family is European?" Mrs. Gardner asked.

"Yes. Well, Italian."

"Italian." She seemed to consider it and then gave a tight smile. "Yes, you remind me of someone actually, but she was French. Which part of Italy?"

"Sicily."

"Ah."

I immediately wished I had said Calabria. Calabria sounded more glamorous than Sicily. Some mainland Italians called us Sicilians "*Terroni*." But only Mama was from Calabria and Papa's side, the Sicilian Caputos, easily overpowered Mama's family and their influence. I watched Mrs. Gardner's gaze drop to my shoes and then dart back up to my dark hair. She gave another of those smiles, the ones that didn't reach her eyes.

"We're very proud of Alex," she said.

I nodded, and felt a drip of condensation from my glass of Coke hit the top of my foot.

"He's a very smart boy."

"Yes."

Mrs. Gardner looked at her feet. "He's always made very sensible . . . choices."

I didn't say anything.

She lifted her head and smiled at me. "He's never been a child to worry about. A source of pride for Marshall and I. He thinks things through and makes the right choices. We expect he'll become a lawyer, like his father, or go to business school."

I didn't tell her he was talking about studying biology.

"It'll mean he'll have to go away to college, I'm afraid."

I nodded. Alex and I had talked about that. He didn't want to leave Washington State. I'd wanted it to be about missing me but something told me it was probably the ocean he couldn't part with.

Out of the corner of my eye I saw Alex and his father standing by the barbecue. His father was wearing a striped apron. Daniel was there too, carrying a plate of steaks.

Mrs. Gardner leaned towards me. "Never mind, Francesca. Enjoy being young. It's a fun time, isn't it? Not *real*, you know, but fun."

I stared at her, but she'd been diverted by Mr. Gardner calling for the tongs.

"I'd better help them out," she told me, already stepping away across the lawn. I watched her go, her mauve silk skirt moving around her calves.

Alex had waved to me, his smile sweet, his eyes concerned. I'd forced a smile to reassure him and he had winked at me before turning back to his father.

"Daniel?" It's Bella's voice, puffing a little, coming out from the trees.

"Bella? Bella Caputo?" Daniel stands up quickly.

Bella's cheeks are red and she's smiling. "Daniel Gardner."

Daniel blinks. "You look . . . different."

Bella laughs. "I've been for a run. Well, jog."

"No, I mean different like . . ."

He's still standing.

"Not sixteen?"

"The hair . . . and . . ."

"Oh, yeah, the hair. You look just the same." She has her hands on her hips, getting her breath back.

Daniel glances at her car, then tips his head at the cabin. "Are you staying here too?"

Bella looks at me and then back at him. "Yeah."

"I didn't know—" he starts.

"She's not really staying," I say.

"I am," she retorts.

"No, she's not. She's sleeping in her car."

"There's only one bed in there. You need another bed," Bella tells Daniel. Like it's a hotel.

Daniel looks at me, then to Bella, and back to me again.

"You don't need another bed," I say.

"Another bed would be good, I think. Also a hot tub." Bella laughs. "Vinnie was saying he thinks they should get a hot tub," she tells me like I don't already know.

"Vinnie's a *testa ri pipa*," I reply angrily. A lead head.

"Sure," she says, shrugging, "but he's right about the hot tub. It would be amazing." She looks up into the forest canopy.

"Why are you even *here*?" I hiss at her.

She stares at me.

Daniel says, "I thought you were back in Seattle with your dad."

"So did I," I say. "Nice surprise."

"Yeah," Daniel says, completely missing my sarcasm. "I got the group e-mail when you went to Rome, to the museum by the Spanish Steps," he adds, his voice rushed.

"Oh, yeah? That was a few years ago. Giorgio—"

"Chirico," he finishes. "I looked him up. I really like his stuff. Actually I bought a print—*The Red Tower*?"

Bella grins. "*Love Song* is my favorite of his."

"*Love Song*—yeah, that's great too. Do you like Dalí?"

Bella went to Italy with our cousin Giulia a few years back. Giulia's a travel agent and she won a trip for two with one of the airlines. I hadn't read my sister's group e-mails—I don't like group e-mails—and Bella always writes lazily with dozens of exclamation marks.

"I love Dalí," she replies. "I want to go to his museum."

"Where is it?"

"Catalonia, Spain. It's a trip—you should check it out online.

It has these enormous . . . egglike things dotted all around the top of the outside wall and it's pink and it looks like a castle. . . ." She laughs. "It's hard to explain."

"It sounds awesome," Daniel says, nodding.

Silence falls between the three of us. Daniel shifts his weight from one foot to the other.

Bella clears her throat. "Anyway, I'm not going to be traveling for a while. I'm using my vacation time now." She looks down at her feet. "I work at a senior citizens' home. I lived in, actually, for a while, but now I have my own apartment. It's tiny but it's all mine."

"You own it?" Daniel asks.

"Oh, no," she replies, laughing again. "But I used to live with a lot of others and now I'm happy to be by myself. Though my neighbor's cat thinks I'm her second mommy. She eats me out of canned fish."

"Who's there now?" I ask, then curse myself for being curious.

Bella beams at me. "A friend's house-sitting. Valentina. She just came back from a volunteer project in Sierra Leone so it worked out pretty well. Work gave me extended leave. I've chalked up a lot of vacation days." She turns back to Daniel. "Bet that's not where you thought I'd end up, in a seniors' home?"

*No,* I want to answer for him.

Daniel shakes his head. "It seemed like you just vanished."

*I wish,* I think, cruelly and unfairly.

Bella's smile fades fast. She turns to me as if she can read my thoughts. "Well, I didn't," she whispers. "Anyway," she says, turning back to Daniel. "What are you doing here? Have you come to check up on Frankie?" Her tone is strange now, a little prim.

"Yeah," he says.

They look at each other, as though I am not there or I am a child they are discussing, and I suddenly want to be out of my pajamas and in real clothes.

"Mom and Dad might sell." His voice is more convincing than before but it still has an inflection that makes the statement sound like a question.

"Is that so?" Bella says, folding her arms across her chest. "They're going to sell a heritage cabin that's been in the family for generations?"

Daniel's cheeks grow pink. "The land is quite valuable."

"Sure." Bella's voice is cynical.

I stare at my sister, whose gaze at Daniel is now cool and glassy.

"I didn't know you were here too," he mumbles again.

"I cannot believe your parents are trying to kick my sister out." I watch Daniel swallow.

"What kind of people—" Bella continues, but he cuts her off.

"Mom's having a really rough time."

"And Frankie isn't? You'd think your mom would be pleased— rapt—that she could offer Frankie a place to get away to think. To be away from it all."

I stare at Bella. *Away from everyone but you*, I want to say, both incredulous and speechless. None of the Caputo has been knocked out of her, I realize. She has always been more comfortable being upfront than I have, showing her cards.

Daniel's looking at me, apologetic. "I know . . . I'm sorry."

"It's okay," I say. "I mean, I can go . . ."

I can't say it. I picture the closet with Alex's clothes hanging in it;

the bed with one side empty. The toilet seat always down. A single espresso cup. I feel my stomach lurch and look, suddenly, to Bella.

She catches my glance and turns to Daniel. "Frankie isn't leaving. She's staying here. You can tell your parents that."

Daniel is looking at me but I don't meet his eyes.

"Frankie . . . ?"

Shit. He sounds so much like Alex I feel dizzy.

I see Alex's toothbrush in the cup next to mine. His towel on the hook on the back of the door. A surfing magazine next to the couch. That framed photo of us at the New Year's party where I'm laughing so hard my eyes are squeezed shut, and he's wearing one of those dumb headbands with glitter numbers on top and his mouth is so wide open I can practically see his molars. *Caro Dio.* I feel myself drooping towards the ground.

"Frankie?"

*Alex.*

"Leave her, *I'll* help her," I hear Bella say. Her voice is a murmur now as she talks to Daniel.

"I'm sorry," the Alex-voice says. I don't know if it's talking to Bella or to me. "I'm sorry."

"Shhh, shhh, shhh," says Bella, sounding like the sea.

# Chapter Twelve

. . . .

I'm not entirely averse to acts of rebellion. Not that you'd know it. I did well at school, got a good job—even if others thought the council was boring—and was about to marry a good man. A conventional life had always appealed to me. I wanted to marry my high school sweetheart, wanted a house with a picket fence, a son for Alex and a daughter for me, and wanted us to become snowbirds in our old age. I know the thought of that kind of life sends shivers up a lot of spines, but it suited me. It was safe. A cookie-cutter kind of life, perhaps, but to me it seemed so happy, sweet, and American. It was all I ever wanted.

But I did rebel sometimes, in my own way. Generally in ways no one else noticed. I stuffed our circulars into neighbors' mailboxes rather than take them to the trash. I walked around our apartment naked with the curtains open. Once, drunk at a house party, I peed in the corner of a coatroom because the toilet was occupied. I giggled all the way home and Alex couldn't work out what was so funny.

Whenever I did anything rebellious or "bad," I never got

caught. People always assumed it was someone else, or an innocent mistake. They never gave Bella the same benefit of the doubt. She got blamed for all sorts of things, whether she did them or not. Plucking the nasturtium flowers off their stalks and tossing the petals about the yard; pressing a fingertip into the blanket of fresh cake frosting. Bella was always assumed guilty.

And, for the most part, I was a good girl. Because I wanted to be. I didn't want to try drugs or stay out all night partying. I wanted to be wrapped in Alex's arms, watching the moonrise, talking about furniture and baby names. Now it feels as though I've been cast adrift from my life. As if the thick rope that kept me bound to it, to Alex, to my things, has been hacked through, the threads sawed and frayed and unraveling. Now I'm staying in a cabin that isn't mine, and where I'm not wanted, and which I can't seem to leave.

I'm vaguely aware of being put to bed, of something being slipped into my mouth, of the Alex-voice apologizing over and over. I want to ask him to stay but can't seem to manage the words. I'm tucked under covers and someone strokes my back. There's the sound of the ocean—*shhh, shhh, shhh*—above me and around me. I realize I am crying when I notice the pillowcase beneath me is wet.

The room grows quiet; the sound of the waves meeting the pebbled shore slowly subsides. My body lifts a little as a weight leaves the bed, and my breath falls into a slow and steady rhythm. It's one of those sweet days where the light is like water, like honey, liquid and slow. The dust motes sway and sparkle like phosphorescence. My eyelids feel as though they are weighted. The light in the room fades . . . returns . . . fades. . . .

Mrs. Gardner had been right about Alex deciding to go to business school. But he had stayed in Washington State to study rather than considering an Ivy League college, much to his mother's chagrin. I was sure she blamed me for that but she had no further to look than the ocean if she wanted to find the responsible party. Besides which, Alex wasn't that keen on change, much like Mrs. Gardner herself.

Alex studied accounting and before he started an internship in an accounting firm—organized by his father, who played golf with one of the partners—we took a road trip with his friends, Jason and Angela, to Cape Disappointment State Park. It had been a strangely hot summer that year, hotter than any I remember before or since. We didn't know, of course, that it would be one of our few vacations all together. That summer is perfect in every detail in my mind, as if captured on film. All four of us in the car, singing as loud as we could, and falling apart into laughter.

We rented one cabin for all four of us, to save money. The days were so long, even though we didn't wake up till practically noon, by which time the cabin was steaming hot. We were always up late into the night, drinking and talking and laughing, and a few times the camp caretaker had to come tell us to keep the noise down. We were too young to care about disturbing other people's sleep; we were wrapped up in our own little universe. It was *our* summer, the one we'd never forget. Eating whatever junk food we picked up at the gas station down the road, sunbathing till our skin tingled, pushing one another into the cold sea, roasting marshmallows, slugging beer straight out of the bottle, and dreaming about our lives to come.

There wasn't supposed to be phosphorescence at the beach. I'd never seen it before that night. I think it had something to do with rising salinity and an algae warning that everyone had ignored. Alex and I went down to the water in the pitch dark. There was something unusual about it, even from a distance: it was as though the dark water was reflecting the starry sky above. But the glow was moving, shivering. Alex took my hand but said nothing as we stood at the edge of the sand and stared at the glittering, shimmering water, the tiny sparkles moving with the gentle lap of the waves. We were the only people on the beach.

We kissed on the shore with our toes cooling in the wet sand, Alex's hands in my hair. Then we looked at each other and giggled, both thinking the same thing. He lifted my T-shirt off of me, and I did the same to him, then we wriggled out of our shorts.

He pulled me against him and kissed me again before flicking the bra strap off of my shoulder. "Race ya," he said, thumbs already hooked into the elastic of his boxer shorts.

"No fair!" I cried, but he was already in the water, stirring up fluorescent-crested waves.

I fumbled with my bra, and then almost tripped getting out of my underwear. Alex, watching me, roared with laughter. The image of him, as I waded in, is burned into my memory. Torso deep in black water, surrounded by glowing phosphorescence, lit from above by a full moon, he looked like a kind of sea god. More beautiful than Michelangelo's *David*, which I'd seen in Florence.

The water was cold on my bare skin. My nipples puckered and stood straight. When I reached Alex he pulled me to him and they grazed his chest. We kissed and laughed and splashed, watching the sparks of the phosphorescence that seemed to activate with our movement. We dragged our fingers through the water, swatted the tops of the ripples and kicked our feet. Then Alex gathered me into his arms and laid me horizontal against the surface of the water, as if ready to be baptized, moving me round and round in a slow circle. I remember the sound of the water in my ears, the dazzle of the phosphorescence, and, behind Alex, the luscious, buttermilk moon.

We could have rushed back to tell Jason and Angela about the phosphorescence, but instead we stayed there alone, as long as we could, in the water. Then we dashed up the sand to fetch our clothes, before stumbling, wet and naked, along the shoreline. We made love under a tree, where the beach became grass and we were tucked away from view. It was late by the time we dried ourselves off and wandered back to the cabin. By then Jason and Angela were fast asleep, curled into each other in a single bed like a pair of caterpillars.

I struggle through memories and thoughts as though wading through syrup. I open my eyes a little but they quickly fall shut again. There is a presence in the room and movement. Voices. Not Alex's.

"Shit. There's enough food here to sink a tanker."

"Battleship."

"Huh?"

"The saying is, 'enough food to sink a battleship.'"

"Huh?"

"Don't worry."

"This bread is actually good."

"It's from Flourfarm, a bakery in Edison. There's a girl who works there, Summer. She dropped it off."

"Is she cute?"

"I'm going to ignore that. She seems really nice. I think she knew Alex."

I screw my eyes shut even tighter, then try to open them. The voices are by the sink, putting things into the cupboards.

"Don't eat that, it's for Frankie."

Through a mouthful: "She's not gonna miss a few cookies. Seriously. She could live out here for a year with all this stuff."

"Well, she's not going to live out here for a year."

Laughter, muffled. "Yeah? Like you're an expert. You get a degree while you were in Portland?"

I hear Bella sniff. "No, but I've seen grief. A lot of it. Don't act like you have a clue. She's my sister."

"Sure."

The movements stop. I manage to open my eyes and see two figures by the cupboards. The light from the window makes them difficult to see.

"What's that supposed to mean?" Bella says.

"Nothing."

"Go on. What were you going to say?"

"Nothing."

"Didn't sound like nothing, Vinnie. Say it. Don't make comments like that and then not say it. I've been away too long? I don't act like a sister?"

Vinnie shrugs. I want to lift myself onto my elbows but I'm still too groggy.

"She didn't ask me to be a bridesmaid. She doesn't want me around. What was I supposed to do? Papa told me about Alex, and I was there."

"Hiding outside in your car."

"Yeah, hiding outside in my car. I'm no good with funerals, all right? But I was there."

The memory of the car outside the Gardners' house comes back to me. Peeling yellow paint, figure on the dash.

"You didn't have to run away," Vinnie says.

Bella sighs. "Really? You're going to start in on me about that again?"

Vinnie makes a clicking sound with his tongue. "Blood is thicker than water."

"Yeah, no kidding. You ever clean up blood, Vinnie? No? Well, I have. Don't act so smug. It was complicated and you know it."

Bella continues to put things away. Sleep is finally, slowly, leaving me. Vinnie watches Bella work, his arms crossed.

He glances down at a bicep and gives a little shrug. "Yeah, well, why is she so pissed at you? Is it something else? Something to do with her guy? The *merigan*—Alex."

I manage to prop myself up, blinking as fast as I can, as though it will help the sleepiness dissipate.

"You shouldn't call him that," Bella mutters.

"*Chiddu facia calari'u latti sulu a sintillu.*" He made the milk dry up.

"Where'd you pull that saying from? God, Vinnie, come on. He wasn't that boring."

"What was with those two anyway?"

"What do you mean?"

"Why didn't he come to things? Why didn't he, you know, touch and kiss her like a normal—"

"Please don't tell me you're putting yourself in the 'normal' category?"

"What do you mean?" Vinnie's voice is lilting, teasing.

"You suck the face off of a girl when you are given half a chance."

"I don't."

"You do. It's gross."

"I'm just sayin' it was a bit weird. . . . He didn't really seem to be into—"

"Stop!" That's my voice, louder than I imagined it would be. Both Vinnie and Bella spin around.

"Frankie—"

"Hey, you're awake."

"Get out of here!" I shout.

Vinnie steps towards me. "Mom and your dad, they sent me over with some food."

"I don't want *you* here either."

He manages to look a little hurt. "But—"

"Both of you. Out."

Bella sets down the tinfoil package she's holding and steps towards the bed. "Frankie . . ."

I shake my head. My whole body feels leaden. "What did you give me?" I press my hands against my temples. "I feel terrible."

"Just a little, um . . . diazepam to calm—"

"What?"

Vinnie laughs and shakes his head.

Bella looks at him doe-eyed. "She was practically catatonic. . . . You weren't here. . . . Daniel was upset too. I had a bottle in the car—"

"What *is* it?" I ask fiercely.

"Just Valium."

"Valium. Right."

Bella looks like she's about to cry. "Frankie, you were really upset. It really wasn't that much. A lot of the patients take it and I know how—"

"Just get out."

She nods and murmurs, "Okay."

Vinnie watches her leave, grinning. "I never thought about her getting drugs. I mean, with the seniors' home and that. When I hooked her up with that job I should have—"

"Vinnie?"

He turns to me. "Yeah?"

"Please go away."

"You didn't really mean . . . me too . . ."

"Yeah, I really did."

"Oh." He steps towards the door, before turning back, one hand on the doorframe. "I just wanted to ask you . . . about a few friends coming here. Not many. I mean . . . seriously, this pad could do with a . . . If you had a hot tub, man—"

"Vinnie." I point to the door.

"Right, right. Got it."

After I've washed and dressed, I slip on the black watch. Alex's watch. It's the first time I've worn it since the day it was given to me and it rolls around on my wrist, thick, black, and plastic. It's ugly; probably the reason Mrs. Gardner let me keep it. If he'd been wearing his wedding ring, if we'd been married, I wonder if she would have let me have that.

The truth is, I don't know what else they found or what they gave to his mother as evidence or consolation. I've never asked. Maybe they gave her the bag he took out surfing, the one that probably had his other watch in it, the gold one his mom and dad gave him when he turned twenty-one; the one he wore to work. It had a saying inscribed inside, something in Latin. A family motto. I can't remember it. I just know that Alex preferred the watch that now hangs down against my hand, threatening to fall off. He wore it surfing, and when he was surfing he felt free. "Out there," he'd tell me in whispers, in the dark of our room, his skin still smelling of wet suit rubber, "I'm nothing. Or everything. I don't know." And then he'd laugh because he was making no sense.

He always laughed more after surfing. His body was loose, his shoulders relaxed. He'd be tired, but somehow filled up from the inside. His hair thick with salt, dried crispy; the whites of his eyes pink; the skin on his hands tanned from the sunlight reflecting off the glassy surface of the water. And that was how he disappeared. Feeling like a fish, feeling like himself, like nothing and everything, caught in the lick of the ocean, a giant tongue that drew him in and swallowed him whole. It wanted him for itself.

I run my finger over the plastic joints of the watch strap, hardened from sun and water and wear to the consistency of bone, a knuckle or a shin. The big face of it stares at me; silver buttons I don't know how to use stud both sides. It's 4:09 p.m. I have slept most of the day.

*It*, what we had, wasn't weird. We weren't weird. I hate Vinnie for talking about Alex and me like that. I want the memory of Vinnie's dumb voice saying dumb things, as per usual, out of my head.

And Valium? Who has Valium in their car? I was almost starting to believe Bella's life was normal: a regular job, one she's kept for some time, a house, a neighbor's cat. Now I wonder if any of it is true. Perhaps she doesn't live in Portland at all. Perhaps she lives in her car and sells prescription drugs on the street. My mind skips through horrible imaginings. Homeless. Addict. Prostitute. I curse myself for that last one. I'm being nasty. But it's her fault that I am. If she would just leave me alone I might find some peace.

My ghosts might visit, wrap their misty arms about me, console and hide me. Bella's presence is driving them away and me into the bright light of reality like a rabbit scared out of its burrow. I hate her for it. I hate them both. I wish that water was thicker than blood so I could be done with the whole bloody lot of them. Except Papa, of course.

When I peek out of my window, it's not Bella but Huia I see, picking her way through the ferns with a basket. She's wearing a red cardigan, as though she's Little Red Riding Hood. I walk out of the cabin.

"Hey, Frankie." She skips over.

"What are you doing?"

"Foraging," she says delightedly. "Look."

She lifts her basket so I can see the contents. The bottom is covered in little green coils. They're strange and pretty, curled like commas. There are also some ferns, different from the ones around the cabin.

"Fiddleheads," she tells me. "And some licorice fern for Merriem. Merriem says the forest is full of treasures."

It sounds like something Merriem would say; I can even hear the way she'd say it. I imagine what the aunties would think of the ingredients in Huia's basket. They'd frown to start with, inadequately restrain their concern that the girl has to pull things out of the forest in order to eat. *Doesn't her father buy groceries? Where's her mother? She's much too thin for a growing girl.* Then they'd look again. *You could batter and fry them,* Aunty Connie would say, *like zucchini flowers.* They'd start arguing about which seasoning to use, which herbs, whether to fry or roast, serve with pasta or on bread.

"I'm looking for morels," Huia tells me in a whisper.

"What are they?"

She giggles. "Mushrooms. You don't know?"

I shake my head.

She assesses me. "Do you wanna come with me?"

"Oh, I—"

"It'll be fun," she urges.

"Well . . ." I glance around, checking for Bella, but can't see her. I suddenly realize her car is gone. My heart lifts. "Okay. I'll come."

"Yes! " Huia sings out and I can't help but smile.

As we walk, she tells me how yummy morels are, and how they grow in areas where there's been forest fire and how you have to keep your eyes peeled. She bulges out her eyes to demonstrate, making me laugh.

It turns out her eyes are much better trained for foraging than mine. To me, the forest is simply green and vast, but Huia knows exactly what she's looking for and points things out from a distance. But slowly I learn. I distinguish devil's club and stinging nettles and salmonberry. I spot the hummingbirds that dart and quiver around pink flowers. I spy a patch of fiddleheads and start plucking before Huia warns me to take only a few so the plant can keep growing for next season. I am the student.

The fiddleheads are aptly named, shaped just like the top of a violin, and soon Huia declares her basket "full enough" of them. We dawdle through the forest, aimlessly it seems to me, though she appears to know exactly where she is, pausing every now and then to watch birds and pick flowers. We sit on a log that's sprouting soft, hopeful ferns, a "nurse log," Huia calls it, and I show her how to make a crown of daisies. She gets me to make the slits in the stems with my nails and then weaves one for me too.

Soon, the light is starting to dim. Time has slipped away from us. Huia is several feet away from me, knee deep in jewel-green fronds.

"Perhaps we should call it a day." I gesture with her basket, now in my hands. "You've got a good haul."

"Yeah," she replies with a shy smile. She steps over to me and we both investigate our harvest. She tugs, gently, on the hem of my shirt. "Come to my house."

"Oh, no, I should be—"

"Pleeeeeease?"

"But your dad—"

"He'll be okay. He's working on a terrarium."

"I don't want to interrupt."

"He won't mind," Huia insists. "Honest."

I mull on the invitation, keen to avoid my sister who may be back at the cabin. "Are you sure?"

"Yes, yes, yes!"

She takes hold of my hand and skips so I almost drop the basket.

"Hey, whoa! Careful." But we're both giggling.


Huia grips my hand most of the way, dragging me along like an unwilling puppy, until we reach the driveway, which she half runs, half skips up to reach a small white weatherboard house pretty well enclosed by tall trees. There's a small concrete statue of a rabbit by the door and a pair of work boots with a girl's hair clip attached to the top of one. I find myself plucking it off as we walk past, and moving it between my fingers.

Huia smiles at me and pushes the door open wide. "Come on."

I step inside.

"Dad!" she calls, walking ahead of me towards the back of the house.

We pass through a short hallway with a row of wall hooks holding jackets and a bright yellow rain hat, and three doors leading off it. Then a kitchen and living room out the back, with an entire wall of sliding doors, much like Merriem's place. The homes were probably built at the same time, in the 1960s or '70s, as vacation houses. Huia slides open a door and strides out towards a newer, black studio building, beckoning me to come with her. She's still calling for her father.

A door opens at the side of the studio and Jack pokes his head out. "Hey, bub." He spots me trailing behind. He smiles. "Oh, hi, Frankie."

"Hi. I—"

"I told her she could come," Huia interrupts. "That you wouldn't mind."

"Of course I don't mind," Jack says.

Huia grabs hold of her father's hands, which are in dirty, thick gardening gloves, and climbs her feet up his legs like an acrobat.

Jack groans. "You're not as small as you once were, circus girl." He turns to me. "Do you want to come in for a look? I was just finishing up before putting on the kettle."

Huia leaps off her father and skips ahead of us. I step inside and glance around. The outside of the studio is stained black, but inside the timber is raw and exposed. It smells as though it could be cedar. There's light coming in from a huge rose window at one end and a large skylight in the roof, partially open.

Jack goes over to a crank on a wall and twists it to close the skylight. Flanking him are shelves upon shelves of glass containers: some tiny globes, like the one he gave Merriem; others almost a meter tall. Many of them house little ecosystems of tiny ferns, moss-covered stones, ground cover dotted with purple flowers shaped like stars. It's like bonsai gardening but with more elements. And more wild somehow—less manicured. The smell in the studio is heady, dark, and fecund: the rich, musty soil mixed with the sweet, strong fragrance of the resin in the timber.

I step around the large wooden table in the center of the studio; on top of it is a terrarium in progress—a tall glass vase half-filled with stones and plants and surrounded by a scattering of soil—to reach the shelving, where I stare at the rows of vases and their mini-worlds. In one I notice a tiny silver bird perched in a tree.

Jack follows my gaze as he unpeels his gloves from his hands. "For Huia," he whispers, then adds more loudly, "If she doesn't drive me crazy before I'm finished."

"Hey," Huia protests halfheartedly. She's dipping her hand into a bag full of pebbles.

"She still wants to go to ballet classes?" I whisper back, but Huia's humming and no longer listening.

Jack nods. "She's unlikely to give up on an idea once she's got hold of one."

We both watch her till she looks up and demands, "What?"

"Nothing." Jack laughs and turns back to me. "Tea? Or I can do coffee but I've only got instant."

"Tea is fine."

"Good. Huia and I made banana bread on the weekend. We can have that too. What's the time?"

I look down at Alex's watch, and Jack does too.

"Hell. Dinnertime," he says. "Where does time go?"

I shrug. The watch falls back down my wrist.

"It's this place," he says, "*Te ngahere*. The forest."

I stare at him. The word he uses almost sounds Italian. Huia skips over to us. "We found heaps of stuff, Dad. Enough for dinner and then some. Right, Frankie?"

I nod. "A *lot* of fiddleheads."

"Is that so? Well then, we've got a bounty. Lucky you're here, Frankie, or we'd turn into fiddlehead blimps."

"Daaaa-ad," Huia groans, splitting the word into two syllables.

"What?" he says.

"Nothing." She laughs, mimicking his reply from earlier, then tugs on one of his trouser pockets.

# Chapter Thirteen

. . . .

It's comfortable inside Jack's house. The kitchen is stripped, as though he's in the middle of a renovation. All the cupboards above waist height have been removed, with timber shelves replacing them, and it's clean if not finished. Huia shows her father the basket and they go through everything inside. Then Jack plucks two cups and saucers from a shelf—green cups with saucers covered in a floral print.

Huia is busy chatting about school. "And then Nora said she wasn't going to get a pink backpack anymore but that her favorite color's purple now because—"

"Fetch the banana bread, bub?"

Huia on one leg. "Because . . . purple . . . is . . . a . . . much . . . *cooler* . . . color."

Jack rolls his eyes at me. "Right."

Huia hops back with the bread. Jack cuts two thick slices and puts them into a toaster.

"Pink is for little kids."

"Butter?"

Huia hops to the fridge. The kettle finishes boiling and Jack drops tea bags into the cups.

Huia stops hopping and looks at me. "Hopping's hard work."

"Sure is." I try not to smile.

"So, Dad . . ."

"Yes, Huia."

"I was thinking . . ."

"I'm not getting you a new backpack."

"But I didn't even ask yet!"

"You having banana bread?"

She shakes her head, disarmed.

"How about you do some coloring then? After we've had some tea I'll get your dinner ready."

I lean over the kitchen counter. "I don't want to interrupt—"

Jack waves away my concern. "Nothing to interrupt. We're just going about our boring business, eh, Huia?"

She nods, then dashes off down the hallway. When she returns she's holding a very large notepad and a fistful of coloring pencils.

Jack plates up steaming-hot slices of banana bread with generous, melting swipes of butter, and nods towards the teacups. I pick them up and carry them over to the living room. There's an old lounge suite in faded and nubby corduroy with fat arms that have wooden rests for mugs or plates. I take the couch and Jack takes the armchair. Huia crouches on the ground and lays out her paper on a pine coffee table. I blow on my tea and we both watch her. She declares that she's going to draw birds for me, so I can learn. She expertly draws the outline of a wing, outstretched, and picks through her pencils to find the right shade of brown.

"Huia told me she's named after a bird," I say.

Jack nods. "That's right. A New Zealand native bird."

"But they're all dead," Huia says, lifting her head from her drawing.

Jack laughs. "They are extinct. But they were quite beautiful—a bluish black color with a metallic sheen . . . I mean, I never actually saw one. They had long tail feathers, tipped white—"

"And the female had a long, curved beak," Huia adds, curving her index finger.

"Yup," Jack says.

"And the boy bird had a short, stumpy one," she says with a degree of satisfaction.

"Well, I dunno about stumpy."

"Not as *interesting*."

"Fair enough, bub, not as interesting," Jack says. "Their feathers—well, the whole of them really—were very valuable. They were regarded as treasures. There's a painting of one of my—our—ancestors wearing a cloak with a line like this"—he drags his finger across his chest—"of huia feathers. They're really striking."

Huia stands as though she's remembered something and wanders towards the hallway.

"Sometimes she reminds me of my sister," I say, thinking out loud.

Jack tips his head. "Yeah?"

"Yeah. Maybe it's the hair. The dark curls."

But it's more than that. It's something to do with the way she dashes here and there, her thirst for life, to know more, to know everything. It makes me feel sad and strange. I'm reminded of Bella and me in the yard at our nonna's house, before she passed away. Bella used to pet the rabbits while I, like Huia, gathered food from the garden.

"We had fun today. Foraging. I haven't done that before."

"Huia loves it. I blame Merriem."

"I used to help my nonna in the yard, and Papa too, a long time ago, but not gathering out of the forest like that."

"What did your nonna grow?"

Green beans, Swiss chard, onions, garlic, cucumbers, peppers, eggplants, rapini, parsley, rosemary, oregano.

"Everything?" I answer with a smile.

Jack smiles back. "Sounds like my Nan. She had a veggie garden out the back of her place that fed all of us."

"You've got a big family?"

"Yeah, you could say that. Where I'm from we all kind of . . . muck in."

I nod. "That's what we do too."

"I never knew Nan to turn anyone away. If you were there, you got fed. She was never put out. She'd make it work, make it stretch. Even if there was only one bit of meat, she'd just add more veggies and more bread or eggs. I wish I'd learned more from her."

I know what Jack means. Everyone tells me that Mama was a good cook. I've learned some things from the aunties, but they make Sicilian food. Mama didn't even speak the same Italian as the Caputos. Sicilians and Calabresi are known for having some tension between them, but Papa thought Mama exotic because she was from Calabria, despite the fact that Calabria is just across the water from Sicily, and the two of them actually, technically, were American.

"My nonna used to keep rabbits," I say.

"In Seattle?"

I laugh out loud at Jack's surprised expression.

"Yup. In her backyard, till it was time for them to be eaten. Then the older cousins and my uncles would prepare them."

"You and Bella helped with that too?"

"Just me. I'd get Bella busy doing something else."

Jack smiles. "I'm the second youngest of my siblings. My sisters used to protect me like that too."

I shrug. "She was only little. Besides, she really loved those rabbits—she would have been upset." No one charged me with protecting her; I just knew it was my job. Till she made it too hard. I change the subject. "So you're from New Zealand?"

Jack nods.

"We left several years ago."

"What brought you here?"

Jack laughs a little and drops his head, and I spot those silver hairs in his crown I'd noticed the first time I met him. The rest of his hair is as black as ink and shiny. I find myself touching my own hair, hoping I remembered to brush it.

"What's so funny?" I ask.

"I won a green card. I dunno, it still seems kind of funny. I went to Hawaii for a paddling competition and heard how you could win a green card, and later, when I . . . needed a change, I put my name in the lottery."

Of course I've heard of the green card lottery. People asked us about it on family trips to Europe, even strangers, as though it couldn't be real. People couldn't believe a country like the United States had such an arbitrary system for granting citizenship. I thought it was wonderful. There were all the usual rigorous processes and then there was the lottery—a piece of good old-fashioned American spirit. Luck. Fate. Hope.

"And you won," I say.

"Yes."

"Well, that's something." The way it comes out makes it sound as though he somehow made it happen.

"It sure is. Pure luck," he reminds me. "I took it as a sign. I wouldn't be here without it, wouldn't be working for the Gardners and the others."

At the mention of the Gardners I feel my stomach form a fist. I take a breath. Jack looks like he wants to apologize but I glance down at the watch on my wrist, avoiding eye contact.

"What brought you here, specifically, I mean? Washington State? The work, Chuckanut, Edison?" I ask, my voice a little softer.

"Umm." He glances out the glass sliding doors. The trees stand like unapologetic eavesdroppers, their branches furred with leaves and needles, tops leaning in a little. "I guess it was more a running away from than a running to."

That I understand.

"I needed to be somewhere different, somewhere I could be a new person . . . you know? Without anyone calling me 'Jacky boy' and expecting the same shit from me. Sorry . . ." he adds, for swearing.

"It's okay."

"We didn't have firm plans. I knew Rocky, Summer's brother, from my paddling days. After I won the green card Rocky said he could get me some landscaping work, and I could bring Huia along to jobs. It was pretty reckless really. Especially with her being so young." He glances at me as though to check my reaction. "But that was a while ago. We're settled now."

"I wasn't—"

"No, I know. I just wanted you to know . . . in case . . . Well, a lot of people don't trust a father with a daughter. They think a girl should be with her mother. They think any child, boy or girl, should be with their mum. Some people think it's weird, unnatural."

Jack's brow is furrowed. I know what he means. People were always asking Bella and me, "Where's your mom?" as though Papa was invisible. And they always said "mom" when they meant "parent"—get your mom to sign the camp forms, get your mom to write your name on it, get your mom to drop you off. I remember Papa taking me for dinner one night to celebrate my first full-time job, and the way the waitress looked at us, first at him, then me, then back to him. At the end, when Papa was paying the bill, she gave me a strange smile, a sympathetic look, as if she wanted to say, "You can do better than that old dude, honey."

"I don't think it's weird," I say. "Papa raised us. He did a great job."

"Yes he did—do a great job. I want to make sure Huia has a good, stable life, just like your father did for you. I see how important that is. The beginning of her life wasn't very stable."

He doesn't explain any further, and I don't ask about Huia's mother. I'm not sure I can carry any more heartache. I prefer to think of Huia springing from the forest, like the sprite Merriem says she is; fresh and green as a shoot, barefoot and chattering to the birds in their own language.

I take a bite of the bread. It tastes of banana and cinnamon and walnuts, and the toasting has given it a crust. The center is soft and warm and cakey.

Huia returns to the living room with things to show me. A stamp from New Zealand peeled off a postcard from her grand-mother, Jack's mother. A book about foraging that she borrowed from the library, with big words she needs some help with. She sits next to me on the couch and we start to go through it. *Characteristics, encounter, compound, distinguish, tenacious.*

Jack stands and brushes crumbs from his shirt before heading into the kitchen. I hear the gas element clicking and igniting and then the sound of oil sizzling.

Huia leans against me. We flick through the illustrations to find the plants we gathered and others we saw.

The air smells like gently frying garlic and oil. It reminds me of home, and for a moment my breath catches in my throat. I have a vague and distant memory of Mama in the kitchen. She is out of sight but I can hear her singing and there's that same smell—oil and garlic in a pan—the way all good meals start. The beginning smell.

Huia begs my attention and we look back at the book. There are so many things we can't collect yet, things that summer and fall will bring. Berries, for instance. And I recognize some plants I saw on the path to the ocean, before Bella arrived, but didn't pay mind to. It strikes me that we only notice things when they're suddenly of use to us.

Huia finishes my slice of banana bread without asking, crumbs sticking to her pink lips. I have the urge to kiss the top of her head, her curls that smell like lemon-scented shampoo and fresh air, but don't. I notice that it's quite dark outside and wonder, idly, how I'll find my way home, though darkness no longer scares me.

Jack serves Huia a plate of fiddleheads and sausages, with a little puddle of tomato sauce on the side, then refills my cup with fresh tea. A phone rings in the hallway. He goes to answer it as Huia gobbles the fiddleheads and swings her legs and tells me how good they taste, talking with her mouth full.

"Right. Uh-huh." Jack glances back at me. I can hear the conversation from his side only. "Right. So . . . how many? . . . No, no, I think I can handle that, Bob."

I sit up straighter, consider standing.

"No, I don't think the Gardners need to . . ." He gives a forced laugh; his brow's furrowed. "Ha! Yes, well, you know how . . . Yes, Bob, okay, I'll be right there."

Jack hangs up the phone, and I stand. Huia looks between us and puts her fork down.

"The cabin?" I ask.

He nods.

"*Merda.*"


Huia slides in between Jack and me in the front of the pickup truck. Jack's spades and rakes and other tools rattle in the tray as we drive towards the cabin. When we arrive, we have to park quite far up the driveway because it's crowded with other parked cars. A black one with large, shiny hubcaps, a rusted Toyota, and Bella's buttercup-colored bomb—no surprises there. The music is loud, and there's lots of laughter and someone whooping.

"I'm so sorry," I mumble to Jack, but he doesn't hear me, striding on ahead of Huia and me.

I see the cabin, a dark shape behind an orange bonfire with flames like fingers that wave at us. I take hold of Huia's hand.

"Stay close to Frankie," Jack instructs her through the thumping of the music.

I peer into the dim light for someone I recognize but see only strangers. Two guys in the Adirondack chairs, drinking from long silver cans and laughing with their mouths wide open. Others are perched on cars, and there's a couple up against a tree, kissing as though their lives depend on it. I pull Huia closer to me. Jack's standing in the doorway of the cabin.

"Hey," one of the guys in the Adirondack chairs says. I ignore him. "Hey," he says again, "aren't you a Caputo too?"

Huia glances up at me, but I continue staring ahead. My chest tightens. *Bella.*

"Yeah, yeah," the guy says to his mate. "She's a Caputo, man. Look at her, would you?" He sucks airs through his teeth.

"You a friend of my sister's?" I ask bluntly.

"Who?"

I scowl. "You know who."

The guy in the other chair pipes up. "I know you—Francesca, right? My brother went to school with you. Ballard."

"That's great," I murmur. "Come on, Huia."

"Hey . . . hey! Weren't you with that guy, that hockey player? Yeah, Al or something?"

I freeze. "Alex. Gardner. This is his family's cabin," I say, lifting my chin and wishing Jack would come out. I squint into the dark, looking for him, but the brightness of the fire makes the rest of the forest even darker. I'd even take seeing Bella at this point. At least it'd be someone familiar to be furious with. I will the guys in the Adirondack chairs to disappear in a cloud of smoke.

"Oh, yeah, that guy. Shit. Didn't he die?"

Huia glances at me again, her eyes wide. My stomach tightens and my breath quickens.

"Oh, yeah, that guy . . . I saw it in the paper," the other one says.

"Yeah, man, it was in the news. He was really young, right? Like, your age?"

"Nah, more my brother's age. But young, yeah."

"And this is his cabin? That's spooky."

"Yeah, that's spooky, man."

I notice now that one of the guys is holding a cigarette, except it doesn't smell like a cigarette. I grip Huia's hand and she nestles into me.

"You're trespassing." My voice is taut.

"Nah," one of them says, passing the joint to his friend.

"Yes, you are. This cabin belongs to the Gardners. You need to leave."

The guy with the joint sucks on it and considers me. "Don't that mean it's yours then?"

"Yeah, don't you get it now?" the other guy says.

Jack reappears in the cabin doorway, but he's facing inside. Huia looks at him, but doesn't let go of my hand. It's my right hand, the one with Alex's big watch on it.

"I don't get anything," I say through gritted teeth. "I get *nothing*." I glare at them. "You have to go. The police are coming."

Both guys look at me, paying attention now.

"Frankie?" A voice behind me.

I turn to face Daniel; he's shoving car keys into his pocket.

"Daniel? What are you doing here?"

Both guys stand. Daniel blinks at them, but they're busy downing the last of their beer and extinguishing the joint, wrapping it in tinfoil.

"I heard—" Daniel begins.

"I'm sorry," I say. "I wasn't here, I didn't—"

He shakes his head. "It's not your fault."

"Jack's inside. This is Huia, his daughter."

Huia blinks at Daniel. He bends down to her level.

"Hey, Huia. It's a bit noisy, huh?"

She nods, then presses her face against my side.

Daniel shrugs and stands. "I'm not great with kids."

"No. It's just . . . this . . ." I nod towards the bonfire and then the cabin, the source of the noise. "It's frightening her."

"Yeah," Daniel says, frowning. "Frankie, I'm sorry, but I had to—"

Jack comes towards us. His face is grim. Bella follows him. My heart pounds, angrily, at the sight of her. I could burn holes in her with my glare.

"Hi, Daniel," she says calmly.

"Hey, Bella. Are you okay?"

I shake my head and interrupt. "'Hi, Daniel'?! What the hell?"

Bella stares at me. Huia surrenders her grip and moves to her father.

"What is this?" I bellow.

"I know," she sighs, her voice measured. "It's out of control."

"Out of control? It's a mess! There's a *fire*!" I point to the flames, rage clotting my throat.

Jack tries to say something, but I ignore him. "You could have burned down the entire forest, and the cabin!" I yell.

Bella blinks at me, her eyes round and glazed, silent.

"And you . . . Are you *stoned*?" I hiss.

She doesn't answer, just continues to stare.

"Um, excuse me, Jack?" Daniel steps towards Jack and the two of them, along with Huia, now next to her father's leg, move away from us. I hear Jack apologizing to Daniel, and then Daniel apologizing back. The whole time Jack's big hand is against the side of Huia's head, to make sure she's still with him and to protect her from the thumping music. The two guys in the chairs have vanished, and I can't see the kissing couple by the tree.

Bella moves closer to me. "No, I'm not stoned," she hisses, sounding incredulous.

"Well, you look stoned," I shout. "I told you to leave, but you didn't. Instead you drugged me up on Valium! And now I come back to *this*!"

"Frankie, stop. You don't—"

"No!"

"This isn't what you think. I didn't—"

"Frankie?" Daniel says, cutting across Bella.

But I squeeze my eyes shut and wave my hand across my face. "No!"

Behind my eyelids I see the dark, rectangular hole in the green earth. How did Alex fit in that hole? He was so much bigger than that.

I jerk my attention back to the present. "Bella brings trouble wherever she goes. I'm sick of it!"

"Frankie, no, it wasn't Bella's fault," Daniel says.

I glance at him. "Please don't fall for it, Daniel. *Any* of it."

Daniel glances at Bella, who is staring, sadly, back. "Bella's a hurricane," I say spitefully. "She leaves a wake of mess behind her. Always. A dusty, shitty pile of . . . broken . . . mess."

Bella is biting her lip, and in the light that flickers from the bonfire I see her cheeks are wet.

Jack steps forward. "Frankie, she's your sister," he says in a gentle voice.

"She's no sister!" I shout at her, my voice warped. Huia recoils, hides behind Jack. "She left! She just . . . *ran away* . . . because that's what she does."

"That is not true," Bella says firmly, though her lips are quivering.

"You can't say she's not your sister, you can't ever say that, Frankie," Daniel pleads.

"Can't I?" The voice coming out of my throat doesn't sound like my own.

I'm vaguely aware of new lights coming and going in bright waves. The sound of car tires.

"No, you can't, it's not fair!" Bella says. "You blame me for everything. You think you're so perfect?"

I shrug, like I don't care what she has to say.

"Yes, you do," she says hotly. "You think you're better than me—with your perfect apartment, your perfect life, everything in order. Always the 'good one.'"

"*Someone* had to be!"

"You like it that way!" Bella shouts. "You act like I'm a big thorn in your side, but without me, without the bad sister, you wouldn't look half as good. In fact, you'd look—"

"What? Huh? What?" I challenge.

"You'd look ordinary!" she says, pointing at me. "You'd look scared! Your life is just a bunch of habits you can't get out of. Which is the truth of it, isn't it? You're just scared!"

Her words feel like a punch in the stomach.

"Don't," Daniel begs, but Bella continues.

"You knew why I had to leave. *You knew.* You could have helped me. You should have helped me. You did nothing. I needed you!" Her voice cracks.

I ignore her sadness, the anger in me bubbling over like boiling water. "Are you going to tell them what *you* did?"

"What I did?" Her face is wet and confused.

"You talk about how I let you down. How you needed me and how awful I was. How about you?"

She frowns, unsure.

"With him? With my . . . I saw you, Bella! I saw you."

"What are you talking about?" She glances around, as if someone else might have the answer.

"At the barbecue! I saw you!"

Her hand goes to her mouth. I feel a wave of satisfaction, but it's followed instantly by nausea.

Bella shakes her head, her voice steady now. "This whole time, that's what it's been about? That stupid—"

"What?" Daniel says. "What is she talking about?"

The lights are so bright now—two blinding headlights. And red and blue lights, circling, hitting the trunks of the trees. We become black figures, dense as statues, glued in place like pieces in a diorama. The music is extinguished and the forest seems to reverberate with the sudden silence.

Vinnie stumbles out of the cabin. He sees me and points. "Hey, *cuscinu!*" He's got a huge grin on his face and a stain down the front of his shirt. I stare at him and then back to my sister, whose hand is now shielding her face, protecting her eyes from the glare of the lights.

"Nice flowers!" says Vinnie, pointing to my hair.

Reaching up, I feel the crown of daisies Huia made for me earlier, the flowers soft and wilted.

"Oh, who called the cops?" Vinnie slurs, his arm dropping. Then he falls down the steps and laughs into the soil.

# Banana Bread

Perfect for an afternoon snack; serve in slices
either plain or brushed with butter and grilled in the oven.

6 ounces walnuts
3 large ripe bananas
1¼ cups light brown sugar
3 eggs, lightly beaten
⅓ cup extra virgin olive oil
⅔ cup whole milk
¼ teaspoon salt
2¼ cups all-purpose flour
1½ teaspoons baking powder
1 teaspoon baking soda
1 teaspoon ground cinnamon

## PREPARATION

Preheat the oven to 350°F. Line a 9½ x 5-inch loaf pan with parchment paper.

Place the walnuts on a baking sheet and roast for 10 minutes. Remove, roughly chop, and set aside. (Leave the oven on.)

In a large bowl, mash the bananas. Beat in the brown sugar and eggs until combined. Slowly stir in the oil. Then stir in the milk, followed by the salt, stirring as you go. In a separate bowl, sift together the flour, baking powder, baking soda, and cinnamon. Add the flour mixture gradually to the banana-milk mixture. Stir until thoroughly combined. Stir in the walnuts.

Scrape the batter into the loaf pan and bake until a skewer or knife inserted in the center comes out clean, about 1 hour 10 minutes. Let cool in the pan for 10 minutes before turning out onto a wire rack to cool.

May be wrapped in foil and kept for up to 5 days or frozen for several weeks.

# Chapter Fourteen

· · · ·

There are two police officers, one tall and lanky, the other shorter and older, with his shirt threatening to jump out of the waistband of his pants. I hear Jack call him Bob.

Bella rushes to Vinnie, who's still sprawled on the ground, giggling.

"Sorry, guys," Jack tells the cops. "It's wrapping up. I just got here."

"We got a call after we spoke to you," the older cop says. "Mrs. Gardner. She was quite insistent."

Daniel turns to me. "I was trying to explain . . . about Mom . . . she heard about the party."

Bella has her arm around Vinnie and is trying to help him up, but he's much bigger than her and uncooperative. I see now that she's sober and capable, whispering urgently to Vinnie, trying to get him to his feet before the police are through speaking with Jack.

I turn my attention back to Daniel, my heart still beating fast. "It's her cabin. I mean, it's fair—that she should call the police," I mumble.

"It's not that bad," he says, embarrassed. "Bella said she'd sort it out with Vinnie."

With the music off, the party does seem smaller than it first appeared. As though the sound had taken up space. I glance around, looking again for the couple by the tree, but they too seem to have disappeared. Up the driveway, two cars slowly pull away. The taller policeman turns to watch them, asks his superior something.

Vinnie is finally on his feet. He grins at me and slurs, "Heyyyy, Frankie. You weren't here. Sorry. Party got a tiny bit"—he shows me an inch of space between his thumb and forefinger—"out of hand."

"This is *your* doing?" I say.

Bella is steadying Vinnie, her hand wedged into his armpit. She locks eyes with me.

"Awww, it's not so bad," Vinnie implores, his voice sliding.

"*Vaffanculo*, Vinnie," I hiss at him.

Daniel is with Jack now, both men speaking with the cops. I can hear them making a case for letting us deal with Vinnie. The three of us stare at one another.

Vinnie giggles. "Look at that, huh? A family reunion! Come on, you two. It's happy time!"

"No, it's not, dickhead," Bella says, shaking her head. She helps Vinnie to one of the chairs and he falls into it like a sack of flour. She turns to me, seems to steel herself. "I'm sorry. What I said was mean."

"I saw you," I say again. My voice is strange, some of the fight gone out of it.

"So you said. At the barbecue. The summer before I left, right?"

"You were kissing," I accuse.

Vinnie glances up at us, his mouth a slack, drunken O.

"No. We weren't," Bella says firmly. "Didn't you ever ask him about it? You spent all this time punishing me instead?"

I don't reply.

I never asked Alex about it. I didn't want to know what had happened, or why. I didn't want to know if he liked kissing my sister, if he thought she was pretty, if he wanted her more than he wanted me. I'd thought about it a lot, and then time had covered it over, made it smooth. And hard. Lately, I'd begun thinking about it again. Now we were going to be married. Should I ask him? What would I say? *I saw you once; it's been on my mind, not always but sometimes. I'm sure it wasn't your fault.* And then there were the questions behind the questions; the ones I didn't want to ask; the ones that might come spilling out after. *Do you really want to get married? Do you really love me?*

"You were kissing," I repeat, wanting, strangely, to be right about this. I see Bella's dark hair swinging as she leans in, her raspberry red lips. Evidence.

"*No*, Frankie." She sighs. "I tried . . . I'm not proud of that . . . but he said no. We didn't kiss. He wouldn't." She takes a deep breath. "I didn't know that you saw."

"Well, I was there and I did see," I say angrily, but somehow the picture seems less vivid now, less spiky. I'd expected Bella to be horrified, mortified, but she just looks pale and tired, as I imagine I look. I'm suddenly exhausted.

"I'm sorry, Frankie," she says again. "Nothing happened."

"I don't believe you," I whisper, but I'm unsure what I believe anymore.

The older policeman is at my elbow. "Good evening, miss. Bob Skinner. I understand you're staying here?"

He gestures towards the cabin, and I nod.

"It's . . . Well, Mrs. Barbara Gardner has contacted us and technically you're trespassing, I'm afraid to say."

I nod again and glance at Daniel.

"But . . ." The cop takes a deep breath that lifts his gut and makes his pants sag a little. He reaches to hoist them up, then scratches his neck. "I heard about your circumstances from young Mr. Gardner here, and Jack's a very helpful . . . presence on Chuckanut . . ."

I look between Daniel and Jack, who are saying nothing.

Bob continues. "As I understand it, you weren't the instigator here."

Vinnie snorts from the chair. Bella presses a hand against his shoulder to quiet him.

"Officer, there's someone coming to pick up my cousin very shortly," she says. "She should be here in just a few minutes."

In Bella's shadow the stain on Vinnie's shirt is less noticeable, and he's looking down into his lap, which is a mercy as the officers probably can't see his red, glazed eyes.

As if on cue, another car pulls into the driveway behind the cop car and dims its lights. We all watch as Giulia, Zio Mario's daughter, walks up the drive. Her hair is dyed blond and lifted off her neck in a long, sleek ponytail. She's wearing tight jeans tucked into coffee-colored boots. She spots Bella first, raises her eyebrows, then nods to Bob and his counterpart.

"Officers." Giulia holds out her hand. "Giulia Caputo."

The tall policeman shakes her hand first, then Bob. They're both silent.

"Right. *Mettiamo quest'idiota nella macchina,*" she says to my sister, speaking in that secret language between cousins. Let's get this idiot in the car. She flashes a smile at Bob. "Family, eh?"

Vinnie mumbles something as Bella takes one arm and Giulia takes the other.

"Ah, ma'am," Bob starts, but Giulia is busy telling Bella, in Italian peppered with a few Sicilian insults, what a fool Vinnie is, how she was on a date, and how much she wants to drop him on his fat head. The officers blink and listen to her voice, her tongue licking the Italian vowels. Her lips are glossy and her eyelashes are long and dark.

Daniel rushes to assist Bella, and soon enough Vinnie is bundled into Giulia's car.

"We'll look after him," Giulia says, lifting her eyes to Bob's. "Don't you worry. He's not going to get off easy. Right, Frankie?"

I agree with a nod. I'm thinking of killing him myself.

Giulia whispers to me to take care of myself, then adds, "*Statti bene.* Don't worry, I'll deal with this numbskull."

"Well," Bob says uselessly.

When we look around there's no longer much evidence of a party. A few cans, the bonfire to put out, although it's died down considerably, the music off, the cars and crowd slid away like snakes into the bushes.

Jack steps forward. "Before you go, Bob . . ."

"Well, I'm not sure we're finished here yet."

"Merriem and I were stuck on something the other day. I suddenly thought, Bob Skinner's our man."

"Merriem?"

"Uh-huh. About morels. You're a morels man, aren't you?"

"Morels? Ah, yes . . ."

Giulia's car pulls away, the taillights a pair of red eyes. Giulia's right: if the aunties find out that Vinnie's been causing me trouble, that the police came, he won't hear the end of it. A night in a cell would be preferable to the wrath of the aunties.

I notice that Huia's let go of her dad's hand and the taller policeman is now showing her the controls inside the police car. He'd switched off the siren lights but at her request he puts them on again. Bob Skinner glances at the car and the lights, then turns back to Jack and resumes their conversation about morels. They start discussing the areas of the forest that had some fire last summer. "Fire brings more morels," Bob explains, gesturing with thick fingers. Jack gives me the thumbs-up behind his back.

I walk inside the cabin. It smells of stale alcohol and the full ashtray on the table. The quilt on the bed is crumpled and there's a plastic bag half full of garbage by the counter. I wonder if Bella tried to tidy up before I got here.

I find a bucket under the sink and fill it with water. I go back outside and pour the water over the fire, watch the crimson embers sizzle and smoke. The night air seems full and heavy. The police car lights flash blue and red into the blackness, though they are less menacing now that they're just for show, for Huia. Jack and Bob are still deep in conversation about wild mushrooms. Something seems to lean against me. It makes me turn but there's no one there. Still, I feel a weight in the space beside me. I turn back to the fire and the weight seems to follow.

I hold my breath. *Please don't go.*

My chest feels like it's going to fracture.

*You didn't kiss her.*

*Of course not.*

But instead of making it all better, resolved, I still feel empty and confused.

I take myself off to bed. No one seems to notice. I get under the covers in my clothes.

I lay my hand against the sheet and will Alex to take it. Yearn for the weight of another hand, real or ghostly, to fill it. I lie in the dark and long for him in a way that reminds me of an earlier time.

It happened after a trip to Italy, and I vowed never to go again. It wasn't that I didn't love Italy. The romantic version—with your lover pressed against your side in the summer heat as you sip a pale lager or a glass of *Carricante* with the sun sinking—is gorgeous. My Italy wasn't that version. My Italy was full of relatives and long, hot drives in the car with Papa swearing at the map; afternoons spent with relatives speaking too fast and in too strong a dialect for me to keep up. My Italy was drifting off into daydreams about Alex. I missed him so much it was an endless ache. When I got back, I covered him in kisses and clung too tightly to him as though he might evaporate. He smiled down at me and, ever so slightly, leaned away. That tiny pulling away felt so huge, like a rip in the tide, a dragging away from the shore. *I don't want you so close*, it said. *I don't want you.*

I kept a smile on my face, spoke about my trip and the food and the weather. Alex asked polite questions, looked interested, grinned. But there was something in his eyes, a wandering, taking him away to someplace else.

"What have you been up to?" I asked.

He talked about helping his mom clear the yard, his part-time job at his dad's office, surfing. I saw that wandering again. My throat tightened. When he put his arm around me it felt different. It was a different arm, a different touch.

"Did you . . . meet someone?" I wanted to sound nonchalant, but couldn't.

"What?"

I cleared my throat, made a shrug. "Did you meet someone else?"

"No. No, of course not." He ruffled my hair. "Why would you think that?"

I wanted to say, because everything feels different. Your touch, the way you look at me. Everything. Instead I said, "I just really missed you."

He gave me a sideways hug. "Yeah, me too, Frankie."

It was warm, but not like before. Not like, I want to be next to you my whole life. Alex had wanted me since high school. He had wanted me before I knew it. His wanting me had made everything brighter. His wanting me made me feel like someone worth wanting. I wasn't sure what I would be without it; what would be left.

I told Papa I didn't want to go to Italy again. I told him I was too old for it. Alex became more affectionate again. He came back to me, just not quite the way it had been. Never as full of boundless love; like at Cape Disappointment, with the sparkling water running over our skin. Certainly no longer a sweet, teenage love. That's what happens, I told myself. People grow up. We can't be teenagers forever. It's a mature kind of love; we're becoming adults.

I believed that he hadn't met another woman. I believed he wouldn't lie to me about it. But perhaps he had met someone else. We had created a little him-and-me world; a world I loved to be in twenty-four hours a day. Without me around, without my arm in his, my head next to his on the pillow, without our dates, dinners, and plans, perhaps he had met someone. Perhaps he had met himself. An Alex Gardner outside of our little universe. And perhaps he missed him.

It was never anything to do with Bella. The two things were entirely unconnected. But I had linked them together in my mind. The panic, the fear of losing him, of not knowing what would be left without him. I had heaped the blame on her, in huge doses. Bella was right: I was scared. I had been scared of losing Alex and it had been easier to blame her. That made sense. She was unreliable. She wrecked things. She was trouble. It was far easier to hate Bella for a kiss that never really happened than to face the coolness, the space, between Alex and me. Hating Bella gave me something to do. Losing Alex just left me dumb and empty-handed.

A loss that had started long before the ocean took him for good.

# Chapter Fifteen

. . . .

When I wake in the morning, the cabin smells worse than the night before. My clothes stink of bonfire smoke and ash; my hair is dirty and greasy. In all the time I've been staying here I've not really missed a shower. Until now. Now I want a shower more than I want a coffee.

Outside, a bird is calling as though its heart will break if it doesn't get a response. Finally a mate replies and they twitter to each other across the roof of the cabin. I'd forgotten to draw the curtains and sunlight now pours in the window and across the floor. It's the heat that's making everything smell worse—the alcohol spilled on the floorboards, garbage still in its bag, cigarette ash and butts in the ashtray.

When I walk out the front door I see Bella's car, the only one left among tire marks. She's curled up on the driver's seat, her head resting on her hands. Next to her, on the passenger seat, is Daniel. He's flat on his back, with his mouth open. Alex used to fall asleep like that sometimes. On the couch, watching reruns of hockey games.

Next to their car, a butterfly makes a wobbly landing on a foamflower bush. Its antenna twitches wildly, as if struggling to discover where it is. When it opens its wings I take a sharp breath. Yellow with elegant black stripes. In the warmth of the morning sun it opens and closes its magnificent, vivid wings, perhaps drying itself out from the clenched fist of a cocoon. I remember something about butterflies only living a day and wonder if that's true. I resolve to find out what kind of butterfly it is and add it to my list. Steller's jay and now this butterfly. I can ask Huia or Merriem if they know. I can learn these things, the names of trees and birds and insects. That would impress Alex.

I imagine him smiling as we lie together on a blanket, staring up into the treetops, the golden light bathing us both. A perfect light that keeps him mine forever. I tell him the names of birds as they call out and he reaches for my hand. His fingers are cool and soft against mine.

I step over to Bella's car. People look younger when they're asleep. Bella's skin is smooth, her lips soft and parted. Daniel is so surrendered to the shape of the seat, his head tipped right back, hair messy, a small trail of drool by his lips, that he could be a boy. I knock on the windshield. The Virgin Mary on the dash gives a little wobble of her hips, like a hula dancer.

Bella stirs. I knock again and they both wake up. Daniel startles and gasps. Bella stretches and opens one eye. She rolls down the driver's window.

"Oh, hey, Frankie," Daniel says, blinking.

"Hey."

Bella doesn't say anything. She is waiting for me.

I clear my throat. "I'm going to make coffee." Then I turn back to the cabin.

"Is that an invitation?" she calls to my back.

I shrug and hear Daniel yawning.

Daniel leans against the bookshelf while Bella perches on the edge of the bed. They sip their espressos in silence. I stand at the sink and watch them, letting my own coffee slip down my throat. They both look weary and unkempt.

"How did your mom get the laundry done around here?" I ask Daniel.

He lifts his head. "Huh?"

"Clothes? Washed?"

"Oh." He smirks a little. "I don't think she ever stayed long enough to get a bunch of dirty clothes. She did them in the washing machine at home, I guess."

I notice Bella glance down at the dusty hem of her long dress. She is shoeless, a toe ring glinting.

"We stayed longer with Granddad," Daniel adds, rubbing his eyes. "I think we might have washed underwear in a stream, near the ocean perhaps. I have a vague memory of soap . . . and underwear."

Bella gives a wry laugh.

Daniel looks at her and smiles. "It was fun staying here with Granddad. He didn't worry about much. We got dirty, climbed trees, hunted things. I can't remember him really supervising us that often. I think his idea was that boys should be let loose to look after themselves. We ate whenever we wanted, roasted marshmallows for dinner, that kind of thing."

"Sounds good," Bella murmurs.

"S'mores with peanut butter?" I prompt, remembering Alex telling me about them.

"Yeah." Daniel smiles at me. "I'd forgotten about that. That's how Granddad had them, with peanut butter."

I glance out the window. Alex always spoke about this place in a kind of spellbound way. "Alex told me a bear got into the cabin one year?"

"Yeah, that's right. It made a mess getting in." Daniel shakes his head. "It took more than the peanut butter but that's all Granddad was upset about. He loved that stuff. We saw the bear just as it was leaving the cabin. It was huge."

"Alex was scared."

"He didn't seem scared. He told me bears don't like the taste of kids. Boys, especially. I believed that for years." He smiles sadly.

From the window I notice some cans we didn't pick up last night and the burnt patch of ground where the fire was. There's an empty plastic packet out there too. And the trash bag by my foot. I tap my fingers against my coffee cup, thinking, and hear Bella clearing her throat.

"Frankie used to do that too."

I turn back to her.

"She used to say things to make me feel better."

Daniel stares at Bella but her gaze is locked with mine.

"Especially after Mama died, right, Frankie? Remember how you kept me believing in *Babbo Natale*—Santa Claus?"

"You were little," I say simply, and remember that's what I said to Jack about Bella and the rabbits. She had been little—a slight thing, with sweet, loose curls and eyes so wide you felt like you could fall into them if you weren't careful. The least she could have, after everything, was *Babbo Natale*.

"Vinnie told me he wasn't real," she admits, "but I wanted you to think I still believed in him. Not just because of the presents."

I know what she means. I had liked us both pretending, together, that he was real. I drink the last of my espresso and hold Bella's gaze. We are silent for a few long moments.

"I just need to get something from the car," Daniel says.

Neither of us looks at him. He leaves, wordlessly, and Bella and I continue staring at each other.

"I'm still angry with you," I say.

"Nothing happened."

"You left."

"Yes. But that was complicated. There are things—"

"You think I'm boring. That my life is ordinary."

She purses her lips. Takes a deep breath. "I shouldn't have said that."

"Hell, Bella, you were acting up so much. Stealing stuff—Papa's car . . . Do you remember any of that?"

"Yes." She looks ashamed.

"I *had* to be good. You *made* me be the good one. I had no choice."

She lifts her chin, speaks quietly but clearly. "You were always good, Frankie. You got everything right. The grades, the guy. I couldn't be you. I wanted to be. Sometimes. But I didn't know how. I never got it right. Everyone said I was the naughty one. Even when I was little. Even the aunties."

I stare at her and feel thrown off course. *Especially* the aunties, she should say. I hadn't thought about that, how the family always made comparisons between us. How them saying those things might make her feel. I'd just thought it was the truth.

"It was better for me to go," she says. "Start over. I didn't think I'd be away so long. I thought we would . . ."

I wait for her to finish but she doesn't. I'm reminded of Jack, of him saying how people expect you to be the same, the way they've grown used to thinking of you.

I change the subject. "You were talking to Vinnie . . . about the funeral."

"Yeah."

"You were there?"

"I didn't come in."

"Why not?" My voice is more needy than I expected.

Bella lifts her gaze, noticing my tone. "I hate funerals. And I didn't know if you wanted me there."

I nod. Had I wanted her there? Probably not.

She continues to stare at me, as though reading my mind. And suddenly guilt takes over from anger, and it rattles me. Like the world is splitting into pieces and trying to put itself back together in a different way. I look at the floor, and am relieved when Daniel comes back into the cabin, clearing his throat. He's holding a small stereo.

"I got some music—to play while we tidy this place up."

He stands next to Bella, as though they're on the same team. She gives him a grateful smile. Not even one of her flirtatious ones.

"Okay . . ." I say, pushing the floor with my toe. "So you're not leaving then?"

Bella assesses me, her eyes round like Huia's. She shakes her head.

"I don't need looking after," I warn her.

She shrugs. Not agreeing but not willing to argue.

"Right." I turn to put my coffee cup in the sink, so my back is towards her. I don't want to look at her child-eyes. "Well, I don't want bears. Someone has to get rid of the trash."

Neither Daniel nor Bella responds.

"And we need more food. Clothes. And laundry powder. I'm sure Merriem will let us use her washing machine."

"Or Jack?" Bella adds helpfully.

"I don't think it's fair to ask Jack," I say quickly.

"Why?"

"He's busy . . . with Huia. And he works for . . . I mean . . ." I glance at Daniel.

"I'll clear the trash," he says. "I know where there's a public bin."

"You don't have to."

"No. I mean, yes, I do."

I pause. "Thank you."

He clears his throat. "I want to ask you something."

"Me?"

"Um, both of you."

"What is it?"

He glances at Bella before turning to me. "I want to stay too. Can I?"


Daniel is outside, erecting two small tents and camp stretchers he pulled out from under the bed, all covered in a thick gray snow of dust. I stuff laundry into a plastic bag, Bella watching me.

"I didn't know there were tents," I confess.

"Daniel said they were his father's. They're not in bad shape considering they're older than him."

I hold up the bag. "You got anything you want to add?"

She's surprised. "Yeah, are you—"

"Put it in then."

She heads outside to her car while I continue gathering dirty clothes. It is comforting to be doing something so mundane. And to take control, as though this is exactly what Daniel and Bella have been waiting for. When Bella returns she's wearing a clean T-shirt and blue shorts, with her dress and some other clothing balled up in her arms.

"Are you sure?" she says.

"No point just doing my own."

She drops her dirty clothes into the mouth of the bag. Underwear that's silky but worn, bright cotton panties with a daisy print, a chambray shirt with orange felt hearts sewn on the elbows, a long skirt. I knot the handles of the bag together and step out into the sunshine.

Daniel already has one tent erected, in a space between flowering trillium. He looks at me and smiles. It may be the most authentic smile I've seen on him in some time.

"I'll just get this other one up and then I might go for a swim," he says. "Wanna come?"

Bella nods. "Yeah."

My stomach turns. I haven't been down the path to the ocean since the day Bella arrived. I hold up the laundry bag as an excuse.

"Maybe later?" Daniel asks, but I don't reply.

"We'll drop off the trash after the swim," Bella says to me.

"Thanks."

"Do you want me to come with you to Merriem's?"

"No. I'm okay."

Bella walks over to Daniel, who's now putting together an ancient-looking camp stretcher. The thin silver poles are speckled with rust and he's having to work hard to press the pieces together. Bella picks up two bits and assembles them, frowning with determination.

As I drive away, I glance back at the scene; the two tents and the cabin in a cozy huddle. It looks as though a mom and dad and a couple of kids, or maybe some college friends, are getting away for a spring break. The sunshine will change the color of their skin just a shade or two, and the salt in the air will thicken their hair. They'll swim and fish and think all day about what they're going to eat for dinner and did someone remember the graham crackers? All it needs is a crackling campfire and a few sparkling fireflies, laughter hanging in the air.

I glance at the laundry bag beside me as I drive along the road, past the mailbox with the flower painted on its side, then past Merriem's little green house. I'm thankful that she isn't in the yard as I turn my focus to the road ahead. The curve of it, a dark snake nudging into the forest and away, away, away.

# Chapter Sixteen

. . . .

I lower the window and let the cool air whip at my face. Trees stream by as a collective: a smear of green and a blur of branches. In places they thin out and the sunlight floods in. I think of all the seeds hidden in the soil, splitting and reaching up to the light.

I'm not running away, I tell myself, not really. I will go back to do the washing. I'll go back by lunch or maybe dinner. I just need to move. To be part of something moving. To have that feeling of the ground pressing up and rolling away beneath me. To see different pieces of sky, and rush past different pieces of dirt.

I will go back. I just feel . . .

I can't even finish the thought.

It's not long before the scenery starts to look the same. My thoughts turn to the film reel playing in my head. The wedding that never happened comes to me in waves, like a jumbled edit of home videos. Tiny slices, close-ups, laughter, faces tipped up to listen to speeches, smiles above the rims of wineglasses. There's Alex at the altar, his grandfather's stained-glass window making patterns on his suit with colored light. As I walk to meet him, I see he is holding back tears. Cut to the kiss. A perfect kiss that turns the world into a beautiful chasm, which I fall into willingly. A heady, heavenly kiss. Cut to the reception: clinking glasses with Bella, sitting at the head table, leaning my cheek against Alex's shoulder. Cut to Mama drying the corners of her eyes, though she was never going to be there. Cut to a dance floor. Another divine kiss and a cheer that circles us. Me throwing my head back with laughter. Pushing a knife into a perfect cake with three tiers and snow-white sugar flowers.

The car slips along the road as if it's on tracks. A truck passes me hauling two big trailers full of tree trunks, stripped of branches, bark peeling like sunburnt skin. The driver sits so high up he seems barely to notice me. The car pulls towards the middle of the road a little as the truck flies past. I wonder how long I can drive before I run out of petrol. I wonder if I'll end up heading towards Oregon, as Bella did, or straight to the Canadian border. I think about the car lifting from the road and becoming airborne. Unencumbered, surrendering gravity, floating.

Once, on a trip to Italy, we flew from Sicily to Rome in a small plane, small enough that the hostess let us see inside the cockpit. Papa came with us, Bella gripping the leg of his pants, both of us with our hair in braids. The pilot patted our heads. He had a coffee beside him, with a cookie on the saucer, and he smelled like Nonno's cigarettes. Bella hid herself behind Papa and sucked on her thumb, an old habit that Aunty Connie was trying to break. But I was transfixed. The cockpit was a marvel of buttons and levers and flashing lights. The pilot showed us which buttons did what, his set of headphones, and the gold wings on the band of his hat. The endless sky beyond, laid out in limitless possibility, was the most brilliant blue. A proper blue, light and bright, not like the ocean or the sky in Washington. In our seats we were just in a plane; here in the cockpit, we became a bird.

The hostess offered us candy. I took one but put it into my pocket. This was no time for eating candy. My heart was dancing in my chest.

When Papa led us back to our seats I kept glancing over my shoulder, wishing I could remain in that cockpit. I could still see the sky, streaked with clouds that looked like steamed milk. But the pilot waved and the curtain, with its severe pleats and squares of Velcro, was fastened shut once more.

Back in our seats, I looked at Papa. His face was thin and tired, the face he'd grown over the past year. He looked like a different man from the one who had kissed my mother full on the lips every morning, and brought her Italian chocolates studded with roasted hazelnuts every Friday. "Look after your papa," Aunty Rosa had reminded me before we went on the trip. "He loves you girls, you know. Take care of him."

I did love him and wanted to take care of him. He was my papa and I'd carry the world if he asked me to. I already planned to have a good, safe life and keep him company forever. But seeing that big, blue sky made me feel like my insides had been rearranged. The idea of going anywhere in the world, of running away. Of flying. It made me feel thrilled and a bit sick all at once. Like driving on an open road when no one knows where you are.

I wanted to go to Europe for our honeymoon. I'd collected travel brochures from my cousin Giulia, the travel agent. Alex wasn't keen. We were in bed one night and he'd slipped his hand into my hair, rolled a strand around his finger. I could smell the hand soap from our bathroom on his broad fingers. Lavender.

"I've been thinking about France," I said.

"In general?" he teased.

"After the wedding."

"What's wrong with Hawaii?"

"Nothing is wrong with Hawaii." There was a great deal on flights and a five-star resort in Oahu. It was all-inclusive: room, food, cocktails by the pool. The photos showed huge beds covered in crisp, white linen, and palm trees curving in from the shore. "I just thought . . ."

"It's a really good deal," Alex reminded me.

"I know."

But I've never been to France, I wanted to say. I kept finding myself staring at flight prices to Paris at the travel agency where Giulia worked. Mama and Papa had been to Paris once, on their way back from Italy, before she had me and Bella. Mama kept a tiny Eiffel Tower statuette on her dresser, right under the mirror where she put on her earrings or checked her hair. I imagined crowded cafés and buttery croissants, the earnest quiet of the Louvre, the gray rooftops and slow-moving Seine. Plus, I wanted to show Alex Italy. Perhaps that was the real truth of it. Italy was right next door.

"You don't want to go to Hawaii?" Alex asked.

"It's not that. I just thought France could be something different. We could see Paris."

He frowned. "I don't know that I'm a Paris kind of person, babe."

"But you've never been to Europe."

"Yeah, it just doesn't . . . appeal. There's everything you could ever want right here in the States. Cities, country, deserts, mountains, sea."

"Sure, but—"

He lifted my chin with a finger, looked into my eyes. "My Italian girl." His voice was sweet. "You need to go, don't you?"

My heart lifted. "Are you sure?"

"Of course. We're getting married, not shackled. You should go."

*You* should go.

"Your dad will be going back again soon, right? Or your aunties? When did they last go back? It feels like last year. Was it last year?"

I said nothing.

"Frankie?"

"Three years ago. They went three years ago."

"There you go. They're due, right?"

I nodded.

He pulled me in tighter, kissing my hair. "One last trip before we have kids. You should do it."

"Yeah," I said in a small voice, as he reached over to turn out the light.


When I spot a small truck stop, I pull over and get out of the car. I fill up with petrol and then head inside. The shop smells like linoleum and dust and petrol and fried food. There's a warmer with hot dogs and burgers in foil bags like presents. The attendant looks at me warily. He's chewing gum.

I point to the coffee machine behind him.

"Milk or sugar?"

"Neither."

"Huh," he grunts as I hand over coins retrieved from the glove box.

There's a tiny counter by the window, which I sit at, the steam from my coffee warming my face. It smells dreadful. Burnt and acrid. Taupe-colored bubbles cluster on its surface.

The attendant grunts again and I turn to see him flipping the pages of a tabloid magazine. The cover story, I notice, is about an actress who has lost her baby weight. There's another headline about a celebrity who's getting thin for her wedding, and yet another who's checked into rehab and wears dark glasses almost as big as her petite face. The attendant doesn't seem to notice my staring.

It's so quiet in here, despite a ceiling fan, covered in grease and old dust, which clicks on every rotation. It feels peaceful. I wonder, for a moment, if I could stay here forever. Like one of those cardboard cutouts they have of celebrities or NASCAR drivers advertising something or other. Car oil, chocolate bars, pop. I could stay till I get shuffled into a corner by the toiletry products that rarely get purchased—tampons and deodorants. Stay till my cardboard becomes thin and nibbled at by moths, my colors fading. No one would notice.

A bell on the door jingles and a trucker steps inside, his feet heavy. He's exhaling noisily, almost puffing, and has to lift his whole stomach to pull up his pants. He nods to the attendant. "Bruce."

"Big John." The attendant slips his magazine underneath the counter as Big John helps himself to a packet burger. "Okay out there?"

"Good, yeah. Quiet. No rain."

I glance out the window and see Big John's big truck, like the one that passed me on the road. Filled up with logs, all the same size and shape.

"White?" Bruce asks.

"That's right. And some sugars. None of them diet ones, eh?"

I stare down at my coffee. The bubbles have burst and now there's just a strange light brown ring around the outer edge. Big John takes a stool at the other end of the counter, though it's so small there's only a couple of feet between us. He glances at me before unwrapping his burger. The smell of it fills the air. Meat and grease mainly, something sweet, the sauce perhaps. It looks like someone sat on it. The lettuce hangs dejectedly out the sides, darkened from the heat of the warmer.

"Not from round here," he says.

I lift my gaze from burger to devourer. Shake my head. I wrap my fingers around my coffee cup, more for a sense of purpose than an intention to drink it.

"What brings you?"

When I blink at him, he answers for me. "Getting out of town?"

"Yeah."

Big John chews his burger slowly. He's in no rush to get back to his truck. Some sauce falls to his chin and he reaches for a napkin. I notice that Bruce is back to reading his magazine. He's towards the middle of it now, where he's surely learning the secret to slim thighs. It probably doesn't involve truck stop burgers.

"No one's from round here is what I notice. Well, maybe Bruce," Big John says.

Bruce hears his name and lifts his head. Big John waves his palm to reassure him we don't need anything. Bruce's head drops back to his glossy pages.

"I think he might be from Oregon," he says.

Big John looks as though he might ask Bruce where he's from, then decides against it and continues with his burger. It's spilling sauce all over the place and he mops up the drops with a surprising amount of care and attention.

"I'm Canadian," he says.

"I met some New Zealanders," I reply, surprising myself. I hadn't intended on saying anything.

Big John smiles at me. "Really? Well, that is something."

"My fiancé didn't want to travel. We were saving for a house. A wedding, then a house. That was the plan."

I look quickly at my coffee, pick at the seam of the cup with my fingernail. Warmth blooms over my cheeks. I can no longer be the cardboard cutout.

"I'm Italian. Italian-American," I mumble. "Someone told me once that if you dig from Italy straight through to the other side of the world you come out in New Zealand."

Big John's jaw pauses on his mouthful. He swallows. "Is that true?"

"No, it's not. As it turns out."

He chuckles. He's moved the foil bag so it catches the last

drips of sauce. He presses his finger into one of the puddles and brings it to his mouth. "People do talk some shit."

I nod.

"How long you going to be gone?" he asks before stuffing the last of the burger into his big mouth. It seems to vanish within his stubbled cheeks. There's not a crumb or drop of sauce on his face. He starts to clean his hands carefully, one finger at a time.

"Pardon me?" I say.

Big John swallows. The silence goes on for longer than socially normal. I wait.

"Till you're back. To your regular life, I mean."

"Oh, I . . ." The first thought I have is that he's asking about the cabin. With Daniel and Bella playing vacation out front, and laundry to be done and trash to clear. Meals to think about. Huia to forage with. Merriem. Jack.

"Don't mean to pry," he apologizes in a soft voice. He smiles and stands.

"No, it's okay." But I still can't seem to answer him. *My regular life.*

After pouring three sugar packets into his coffee, Big John presses a takeaway lid on top and picks up the cup. He touches the rim of his cap like an old-fashioned gentleman. Though his cap is no gentleman's—it's pink, tomato red once maybe, and the fabric is worn, fraying at the peak. "I'll leave you to your coffee." Then, turning his head a little, "Bruce."

"Big John."

I want to say "Big John" too, but I don't actually know him. Instead I nod good-bye.

"Have a good break, miss."

"Yes. Thanks."

I look down at my own coffee again as Big John leaves and the bell on the door jingles. A gust of air skates in and the place is fragranced, for a very short instant, with the scent of cut timber. Then it is gone, along with Big John.

I stand, leaving the full coffee cup, and head back to my car.

# Chapter Seventeen

· · · ·

There are three days of peace.

The forest wakes a little earlier each day. The sun stretches thin fingers down through the trees; the birds sing or chirp or cry or squawk. I watch the dust spinning in stripes of light. There are the same smells: coffee, the loamy soil, salt in the towels, burning wood, marshmallows starting to fizz and caramel.

Daniel and Bella swim every day, their skin drying salt-dusted and smelling like Alex after a surf.

I make espresso each morning, dark and strong. Daniel drives to wherever it is he takes the garbage. Bella has begun to sketch each afternoon, in a large notepad with a piece of charcoal.

I do the laundry at Merriem's house. She has a machine but I wash by hand in the deep laundry sink instead. There's something nice about having my arms plunged into warm water and making things clean. I wash Daniel's socks, a T-shirt that looks like one of Alex's old ones, Bella's underwear and tank tops. I realize that we're the same size, though we probably always were. I wash the contents of Merriem's laundry basket too: a long, mint-green satin slip; socks with bright spots; a faded paisley head scarf.

I seem to end up at Merriem's in the afternoons regardless of whether there is laundry to do or not, as though there is a magnetic pull to the green cottage, with its yard full of bees making honey, and I'm not the only one drawn to its homely charms. Huia visits after Jellybeans and before Jack hurries over to see where she is. We eat slices of date loaf with butter and drink hot tea while she asks Merriem about foraging and me about dancing and Italy and my favorite color and whether I would choose wings if I had to choose between them or a prehensile tail. I have to ask her what prehensile means. Huia points out birds that visit Merriem's yard for its spring treasures and tells me their names, where they're from, and how common they are. She is a skipping, pint-sized, bird encyclopedia. Jack fixes washers or changes lightbulbs while we talk, then tells Huia it's time to go home, which she negotiates over for at least another forty minutes.

There is a rhythm.

On the third night, I go to bed early while Bella and Daniel stay up tending the fire. As I close my eyes I hear a guitar. The music makes everything else go quiet. The strings picked over so tenderly, notes plucked out so beautifully they seem to tell a story. Of tears. Of loss. Like one of those Portuguese folk songs, where the singer wails and it cracks your heart like an egg.

The tempo picks up, the guitar talking fast, begging. And then slows again, slowly, slowly, like falling. One note. Then another. Putting one foot in front of the other. Slow and steady.

My heart beats against my palm, which is resting on my chest. The music is inside me. Pulling at me from the inside.

Then, in a sudden, hopeful way, it's over.

Bella whistles. "Encore, Daniel!"

But there is no more. Just the one beautiful song. Sweet, sad, and too short.

At Merriem's, on the fourth day, I hang out a few pieces of laundry on a wooden frame in front of the big living room windows. Merriem spreads honeycomb on slices of rosemary toast. Honey she collected from her hives, bread she baked. The smell is piney and sweet and comforting, like the forest.

Merriem gestures for me to sit and passes me a piece of toast, the heat still rising from it. "How are you doing?" she asks.

She's wearing a blue dress and a long cardigan that reaches down to her knees. Chestnut-colored wool, with a thick, loose weave. One of her earrings is a moon and the other is a sun. They remind me of similar terra-cotta versions that hang on Aunty Rosa's outdoor wall.

"Okay," I reply, retrieving dripped honey from the plate with the tip of my index finger. "Is it all right I'm here so often? I enjoy doing the laundry. I never thought I'd say that."

"Of course it's all right. It's nice to have the company. And sometimes doing laundry is just the ticket." She nods at the wooden frame. "It reminds me of hanging cloth diapers."

I frown. "You have children?"

She smiles, shakes her head. "I lived on a kibbutz. It was part of my work. Hundreds of cloth diapers, day after day after day, clothesline after clothesline. Like party pennants. I hated it at first. It seemed so dull. I think I had a different idea of what kibbutz life would be like."

"A kibbutz . . . in Israel?" I ask.

She nods.

I imagine Merriem in a kibbutz, transplanting her face on to the images I've seen of women with head scarves in faded colors, the sun high and hot in the sky.

"Ezra," Merriem explains, without my asking. "He was diabolically handsome. I was there for almost a year."

"Maybe I wouldn't like laundry as much if I had hundreds of diapers to deal with."

She shrugs. "You'd be surprised. I enjoyed washing diapers in the end. It was meditative. Simple. Ezra and I fought a lot. In the end I enjoyed the diapers more than him probably." She chews her toast noisily, then laughs. "Diapers don't talk back."

I glance at the washing on the frame. It's not just clothes I've been cleaning. The cabin is also tidy and scrubbed. I have swept it out, ancient gray cobwebs and all, then mopped the floors by hand with an old cloth. I've even polished the window with vinegar and newspaper, and cleaned the bookshelf, one dusty book at a time. I've finished *The Swiss Family Robinson* and read Huia's guide to birdlife from cover to cover.

"And the women," Merriem adds, "on the kibbutz, they were something." She sprinkles bee pollen onto the honey on her toast. "They'd been through so much and they worked so hard, yet they were cheerful. It left a big impression on me. Plus, they helped one another. They helped me. I'd never had that before." She passes me the bee pollen. "Women haven't always been so kind to me. I didn't have sisters growing up."

I nod, although I'm not sure how kind Bella and I have been

to each other. Not very; not at all. I still avoid talking to her if I can help it, so she spends her time talking to Daniel or swimming or taking her yoga mat down to the ocean.

"Bella's lucky to have an older sister," Merriem says. "Especially one that washes her underpants," she adds with a laugh.

"Oh," I say, glancing in the direction of the laundry frame, "I was doing my own."

Merriem just smiles and I return to eating my toast.

"Ezra died a few years ago," she says after a pause. "I heard about it through a friend."

"I'm sorry."

"It's okay. Cancer, of course. He had a family, kids and a wife. I think he was happy." She shrugs. "Still . . ."

My tongue feels thick in my mouth. I clear my throat. "Still . . . it hurts."

"Exactly. The country songs aren't wrong. It hurts. The Buddhists aren't wrong either. Life is suffering."

"Life is suffering," I repeat. My voice seems to have shrunk. I stare at her and ask, "Always?" I sound like a child.

Merriem shakes her head. She reaches over and takes my hand. "Not always."

I swallow. I can barely whisper, "When is it not?"

Merriem gives a small sigh. "Oh, darling. Just when it's not. When it's a good day in between the hard ones." She squeezes my fingertips. "When the sun shines and the bees make honey. When you're with people who love you. When you find treasures—like morels and fiddleheads and huckleberries. When there's toast." She lowers her voice like it's a secret. "When you're doing the laundry."

I nod, feeling tears welling. "There's no more laundry left to do."

"There's *always* more laundry. People make their clothes dirty every day."

"Well, thank God for that," I say ruefully.

"Truly," Merriem says. "You gotta start simple, honey."

Her eyes are wide, imploring me. I think of what Jack said about finding myself under her wing. I place my other hand on top of hers. Her skin is thin and soft and warm.

She shakes her head again. "You young girls, you have too much to carry. You . . . Summer . . . It doesn't seem fair."

I frown. I'd almost forgotten Summer. Meeting her in the forest. Her kindness in Merriem's kitchen.

"She lost someone too," Merriem says. "Someone she loved. An accident, she said."

Her face is full of compassion.

I drop her hand and stand up so fast the tops of my legs smack the table. I run back to the cabin, gulping down big, misshapen mouthfuls of fresh air.


As I reverse out of the driveway, gravel skitters under the tires. Bella stands in the door of the cabin, calls out, but I'm already halfway gone. I see her face is drawn and worried. I watch her lips make the two shapes of my name.

I drive too fast towards Edison. If I'm caught speeding I hope it's Bob Skinner's partner. I'll shamelessly scribble Cousin Giulia's phone number on his hand and speed off again before he has time to think.

*Edison, Edison, Edison.* My heart, pounding, seems to drum the word.

When I reach the town, both sides of the street are packed with cars. There are baskets full of spring flowers hanging under the eaves of Flourfarm, and tourists coming out with brown paper bags. Everyone is smiling. The throng is orderly, like bees returning to the hive. Tourists in T-shirts and puffer vests, hiking sandals. Smelling like sunscreen. A guy in an orange T-shirt and tan shorts glances at me and I realize I am panting. Adrenaline pumping through me like I'm about to run. Like I'm about to fight.

Despite the crowd I find Summer easily. She's wearing a black T-shirt with FLOURFARM printed across the front and her hair is in a ponytail. She's by a kids' play area in the corner, passing a stick of chalk to a boy holding a plastic yellow digger. When she sees me she smiles, but it fades fast.

I thought of things to say to her in the car. Things that might come out as a shout. Things that I now realize will turn into a cry, a sob. I find myself saying nothing and staring at her. She looks pretty with her hair up, and she's wearing mascara again today, her eyelashes long and pretty when she blinks at me. My gaze goes over her body, down her jeans to her dirty sneakers, over her breasts, back up to her face. I'm breathing hard through my nose, like there's just not enough oxygen in the air.

"Frankie." She steps over to me. "Are you okay?"

Her cheeks flush pink and I watch fear, or something like it, wash over her face. She knows. And she knows who I am.

She's known this whole time and I've been the fool.

I wrestle with the tone of my voice before it leaves my throat. I'm proud when it comes out even and not too rushed. "Who. Else. Knows?"

I see the swallow in her throat. Her cheeks turn a darker shade of red. She glances over to the counter and a tall guy, hair the same color as hers, same pale freckles, is looking over at us. Her brother. There's a huge line by the counter.

"All right, Sum?" His voice is drawling but protective.

"Can I use the office?" she calls back. She's still staring at me, her eyes wide.

"Sure thing."

"The kids . . ." she adds.

"I can see 'em from here," he says.

Summer points to a hallway and says gently to me, "Back there."

She walks ahead of me, her shoulders slumped, and I can hear her breathing deliberately, carefully, like me. In and out. In and out. Doing her best to stay contained. In control.

I hate myself for not completely hating her.

I hate that it feels like the pieces of the puzzle are coming together.


"Frankie—"

I cut her off. "You loved him?"

She nods.

I look around the office. It's a mess. There's a desk covered in papers, shelves above it with ring-binder folders, a swivel chair with the seat set low, and a café chair with a broken back.

I take the café chair while Summer sits on the swivel chair. By the desk there are a couple of sacks of flour, and the concrete floor is dusty and floury. I grip the edge of the seat, feel it press painfully into my palm and fingers, hear Summer clear her throat.

"Yes. But . . . it wasn't . . ."

"Did you sleep with him?"

"No," she says quickly.

"Did you kiss him?"

"Once."

She says it softly, more wistful than guilty. My head snaps up.

"I'm sorry," she adds, sounding genuine.

"How did I . . ." I say angrily. How did I not notice? How did I not *see*?

"Frankie . . ."

I raise my hand without looking at her. If I look at her now I will cry and I don't want to. Yet. *Shit.*

"When?"

"When . . . The kiss?"

"When all of it." I am scared, and desperate to know.

"We kissed a couple months ago. How long have I loved him? Probably a while." She draws in breath. It's ragged. "God. I'm sorry, Frankie."

"Who else knows?"

"No one." Then, "Actually, my brother. He only knows bits of it. He knows I needed to get out of Seattle. I thought I was getting away . . . from it . . ."

"Me too," I say bitterly.

"I told Merriem, I guess," she adds. "Sort of but not really. Before I knew you were here. Is she the one who told you?"

I nod. "She didn't mean to. She didn't know."

"No."

We are looking at each other now. I don't remember looking up. Her cheeks are less pink. Her eyes are red though. She wipes tears from her cheek with the side of her thumb.

"I feel stupid," I say coldly, shaking my head.

"I was going to tell you straightaway. Not when we met in the forest but the next time. Or at least I was thinking about it. But then Jack and Huia were there. And then . . . I dunno. I didn't expect to . . ." She looks pained. "I didn't want you to be such a nice person. You being nice, being nice to me, made it worse."

I rub my temple with one hand. "Did *he* love *you?*"

Summer doesn't reply. I can hear the muffled sounds of chatter from the café. It feels like a long time before she answers.

"I hope so. I know I'm not supposed to say that."

I glare at her, my voice rising. "No, you're not." I stand but don't leave the room. I point at her. "We were getting married. You knew that, right?"

She nods meekly. "Sometimes you don't get to choose—"

"Yes, you do," I say sharply.

She puts her head in her hands. "Frankie, please. Please sit down."

"You *do* get to choose. You get to decide what you get messed up in. You can walk away. You can make decisions."

I'm still on my feet. Now pacing.

"I know. Look, I know. Please, sit—"

"You play a part. No one has a gun at your head."

My voice is loud; it seems to bounce back off the walls.

"You *knew* he was getting married," I accuse.

"Yes . . . I mean, yes, I did. After I . . . started . . ."

"After what?" I demand.

"Please sit down?"

"No."

"Please, Frankie?"

"No!"

She stares up at me. I want to call Alex. I want to hear him tell it. I want to know what happened from him. But I can't. My heart is thumping. My chest aches.

Summer lowers her voice. "After I started falling in love with him. He proposed to you after I fell in love with him. I tried to stop. I really tried to stop loving him."

"You were dating Travis."

"We broke up years ago. Travis was . . . Travis is . . ."

I remember him more clearly now that she's talking about him. Laughter that shoved itself into a room. Grubby, green "lucky" sweater. Gold signet ring. A joker. A bully.

"I remember him."

Summer nods, as if she sees the recollection in my mind. "Alex . . ." Hearing her say his name makes me wince. Summer's voice softens. "Alex was kind to me after Travis dumped me. I'd met all the guys by then. We surfed together. It was good for me. Surfing has always been good for me. Especially when my mom started seeing someone new, when we moved . . . again. There aren't many girls that surf. It was better for me to go out with the guys than on my own. Safer. Alex watched out for me. I could trust him not to leave me out in the deep, to tell me where the rips were. Not like Travis. Travis didn't care if I was . . ."

Her voice trails off and I know she's thinking of Alex, under the water. Floating. Lifeless. A shape, a silhouette, in black. Arms and legs spread out. Like an X.

She starts crying again, but clears her throat and pushes on, her voice crushed. "I fell in love with him. I knew he had a girlfriend. I knew he'd had a girlfriend since high school. I had met you, briefly, that one time, but I tried to forget it. Whenever anyone said your name I tried not to hear it. I tried to pretend you didn't exist."

She reaches over to the desk, to a box of tissues. She pulls one out and presses it to her eyes. Mascara comes away like an ink stain. There's a mess of black on her face.

"But I did exist. I *do* exist." I'm trying not to cry now.

Summer nods sadly. "I know. It was stupid. Trying to wish you away. It was easier when you weren't . . ." She gestures, feebly, towards me. "Real," she finishes, sounding tired.

I blink at her and sit down slowly. "When did you kiss?"

She meets my eyes, questioning.

"You owe me."

"Okay." She takes a deep breath. "I told him . . . Alex . . . that I liked him. I couldn't say that I loved him, though I did—it was too much. It happened after a surf one Saturday. One of the guys had us over to his place when the weather turned bad. We started drinking beers. More people turned up. Someone put on music. Someone had a guitar. Then we were all spread out in different rooms, big enough to call it a party after a while."

"He didn't call me," I murmur. Though the truth is, he usually didn't. Surfing and the people who came with it were his world. I'd imagined him in places like that, sitting around having a beer, maybe two, after a surf, telling jokes, listening to music, talking about the waves. I'd never imagined another woman at the table, cold bottle in her hand, watching Alex's face. Watching him speak, watching him laugh.

"Then?" I press.

"We got a bit drunk. Drunk enough for me to finally tell him how I felt. Almost how I felt."

"Did he tell you about me?"

She nods. "Yes. He said he had a girlfriend. He said you'd been together for a long time."

I take another deep breath. "How did you end up kissing?"

She hesitates. "We were drunk . . ."

I shake my head.

"I asked him if he loved you."

My heart races. "And?"

"He said, of course."

Part of me soars when I hear this, but another part remains weighted. I know there is more. I pause, not inhaling. Summer looks conflicted, then she stares at the floor, clears her throat again.

"I asked him if he was *in love* with you."

"And?" My voice is a whisper.

"And . . . we ended up kissing. I kissed him. It was my fault."

"He never answered you?"

Suddenly my chest is burning. Like indigestion, but worse, from deeper inside.

Summer shakes her head.

*Damn you, Alex.* I want to scream. And run.

Summer continues, the truth like a bad tooth, loosened now, ready to come out. "After the party he avoided me for a couple of months. Then he told me he'd gotten engaged. All the guys were in the water already and he held me back on the beach for a minute and told me. He was . . . weird about it."

My hand goes to my mouth. I know the weird she's talking about. The Gardner stiff upper lip. The doing-the-right-thing voice. The convincing tone that has a crack in it. *Vaffanculo.* Alex had liked her. He might have proposed to me but he'd liked her. Or more. He just didn't know what to do about it.

I stand up again.

"I'm so sorry, Frankie." Her voice sounds far away.

Alex made the problem go away by promising himself to me. Ticking the box, casting a vote. But what was that? *What was that?* How long would it have lasted? My hand, across my mouth, is shaking.

Summer is crying. "I'm so sorry. I shouldn't have kissed him. He loved you, I'm sure he did. I don't know what we had, but it wasn't like you and . . . him."

I'm staring at her.

"He did love you," she says again.

I feel myself nodding. Willing it to be true. Yes, he did. He did love me.

Truth and past tense.

"Frankie?"

"I have to go," I say in a limp voice that isn't quite mine. Like a voice out of a dream. Or underwater.

"Please . . . ?"

"I have to go."


Sunlight bears in on me as I drive. But in my mind it's raining. Like that day, which feels long ago.

Rain lashed at the windows, the sky a warning gray. West Coast weather, a storm on its way.

Alex came in wet. His hair stuck to his head, his pants dripping on the floor, making puddles. He lifted his gaze to find me, fingers curled around a mug, legs folded underneath me on the couch.

"Hey." His eyes shone. He kicked off his shoes, shrugged out of his jacket, and took a step towards me.

"Pants," I said, pointing. They were soaked from the bottoms up.

He raised one eyebrow, lasciviously.

"They're wet," I explained.

"Uh-huh." He peeled them off and left them in a heap on the floor by the front door, moving to me. He wore green boxer shorts, the ones I bought him for his last birthday. His hands were freezing, his hair still dripping, even his lips were blue-rimmed. He leaned into me, slipped his fingers into my pants.

"Hey!" But I was laughing, trying to keep a grip on my mug.

"Good waves," he whispered into my ear, his lips leaving a chill against my warm skin.

"Yeah?"

He pressed a kiss into my shoulder. "Hmmm-mmmm." He pushed my hair away from my neck, left a trail of cold kisses along my collarbone.

"You're freezing."

He nodded and took the mug from my hands, placed it on the floor. Then he came so close I could see that even his eyelashes were wet, and his breath smelled like fruit and yeast, like he'd had a beer with the guys before coming home. And then closer. Hot fries, wet suit, board wax. His lips reached mine. His mouth was on mine. Warm mouth, cold lips. A kiss like in high school. Long and slow.

He pulled away for a moment to lift my shirt over my head.

I smiled. "I missed you."

"Come here," he murmured into my ear, the tip of his nose icy, sliding me down onto the rug.

I turn the steering wheel, take the corner too fast, but right myself on the straight. Blink hard.

Who was he thinking about? Me or her?

# Chapter Eighteen

· · · ·

When I skid into Jack's driveway, he's stepping out of his front door. He's got work boots on and he's holding his keys and wallet.

"Hey." His expression goes from happy surprise to concern. "Are you okay?"

I shake my head.

"Is Huia here?"

"No. Are you . . . What's . . . ?"

I shake my head again. My mind is wandering dark hallways. I hear music from another room. People laughing. See Alex and Summer against a wall.

"Do you want to come inside?" Jack asks.

"No."

"A cup of tea?"

"I don't want a cup of tea."

My breath is fast and shallow. Jack is blinking, waiting.

*I want my fiancé back.*

*I want my life back.*

*I want things to be the way they were.*

*I want to not know what I know.*

Jack reaches out. "Come inside, Frankie, you look . . . tired."

"No." I lean away from him, then stare at his hand. Travel the length of his arm, up to his face. "Do you like me, Jack?"

He doesn't reply.

I stare at his face and the pieces it's made up of. Dark eyes, full lips, skin the color of caramel. So different from Alex.

"I want to know if you like me," I demand.

"What do you mean?"

"You know what I mean."

He shifts his weight. "Yes."

"Yes, you like me?"

"Frankie, this is . . . I don't know if you . . ."

He's awkward. More awkward than I've ever seen him. It makes him look younger, more his real age.

"Why do you like me?"

He's frowning now. "Shit, Frankie, I dunno."

"If you like me, then tell me why," I insist.

He glances up to the sky, then back at me. Then down at his feet.

"You can't tell me why." I turn back to the car. My heart is hammering in my chest.

"Frankie!" Jack calls, but I don't turn around.

"Fuck you!" I yell, but it's not really for Jack. It's for Alex. Alex and Summer. I'm mad that I waited so long for Alex to ask me to marry him. I'm mad that I didn't realize. I'm mad that I pretended it was perfect. I'm mad at secrets as big as houses. Rage burns in my chest, in my throat. I'm even mad at this place, at the trees and the air and the everything. *Fuck you. Fuck all of you.*

I feel a broad, warm hand against my arm, the fingers curling around. "Frankie, hang on."

"Let go of me!" I growl. I turn just a little, to see Jack's face, pleading.

"What's going on? You've got to give me a minute." His voice is deep and gentle.

"No! I'm not waiting! I waited long enough!" I almost scream.

*He* wasn't sure. He made me wait. He loved *her*. I was an obligation.

My heart is pounding so fast it feels as though it's going to leap right out of me.

"Frankie . . ."

"If you like me, you like me, okay?"

"Okay."

"And if you can't say why, then you don't!"

"Frankie, I like you."

I tear my arm out of his grip. "Sure you do. But not as much as someone else. As the *next* someone!"

As the girl with the sand-colored eyelashes who wants to be in the ocean with you, who hasn't put up with all your faults for years and years, hasn't had to pretend there are no faults. That it's all just right. I feel myself starting to cry.

"Frankie . . ."

The words are lost now. My throat makes a tight fist around them. I lean against the car door. It's reassuringly cold.

Jack speaks softly. "I like you just because I like you, Frankie. I guess I think that I shouldn't like you right now, because of what you've been through. Because it's not fair on you. Because you have enough going on."

Tears are spilling down my face. Jack steps closer warily. I lean right onto the car, my forehead against the top of the roof. *Please*, I want to beg, but can't decide if I want him closer or farther away.

"Hey," he murmurs, "I like you because you're tough. Strong. But kind too. Broken, a bit, I guess, but not all the way."

Now I want to tell him to stop, but I'm crying so hard it's difficult to draw breath.

"You're beautiful. Of course," he adds, his voice a kind of honey, "you have to know that already." I feel his hand come to rest gently against the top of my arm. I want to slap it away and also roll into it, roll into him.

"And good. You seem like a good, decent, honest person. You're good to your dad. And mad with your sister but you put up with her anyway. 'Cause you love her and you reckon blood is thicker than water. You try to do the right thing. Maybe that sounds stupid, but it's something. It's something to me anyway."

I want to turn to look at him, but my face remains against the car, and the tears keep pouring out of me. I can barely draw breath quick enough to keep up.

"Frankie?" Jack says. "Is that what you wanted? I haven't done this for a long time . . . I'm not good at explaining."

His thumb is moving against my skin but he hasn't stepped any closer.

I shake my head. "It's . . . not . . . that," I manage to say between sobs.

But I can't explain what it is. What I've learned, and how it has nothing to do with him. Though I tipped all my anger onto him, though I've made demands of him. I've been unfair. So unfair. Tangled in grief and rage and guilt.

Jack's tone shifts. It's somehow firmer but still gentle. "Please come inside, Frankie."

I shake my head, rolling it side to side against the metal. I feel his palm slide down my arm to take my hand in his.

"You need to sit down."

"I should go."

"I'll make you some tea."

"I need to go."

"Enough going," he says decisively. "You're staying."

He pulls me just enough to lift my head from the car, then wraps his arm around me and guides me towards the house. My face is a mess of tears and snot, no doubt creased and pink, crumpled.

I drop my head. "He loved her."

"Who?"

"Alex. My . . . He loved Summer."

"Oh." Jack pauses. "I'm sorry, Frankie." His voice is warm against my hair.

I feel stupid. And tired.

"Me too," I mumble.

"Come on," he says carefully. "I've got to pick up Huia. I'll make you some tea and then leave you to rest. You'll have the place to yourself. Okay?"

He helps me up the steps. I feel my resistance slipping away—a shadow dissolving in soft twilight. My body is weak and shaky. I place one foot in front of the other, but Jack is practically lifting me into the house.

"Okay," I say, my voice wispy.

When I wake, I'm lying on Jack's couch and there's a full cup of cold tea on the table in front of me. A blanket falls away as I sit up. It's made of different-colored crocheted squares—lemon, apricot, fuchsia—bordered with black wool and it smells of lavender and cedar. I push my fingers through the holes.

Huia's laughter erupts somewhere in the distance; I turn my head to find the sound. Jack's voice is there too, deep and muffled. They must be outside.

Behind the cup of tea, in a brown cup with a matching saucer, is a small terrarium, round like a globe, with a circular hole cut in the side. The base is filled with dark soil, topped with velvety, bottle-green moss. There are plants, ferns perhaps, resembling tiny pines, reaching up to the top of the glass, and nestled among them, at the end of a path made from a dusting of sand and sprinkling of minuscule pebbles, is a tiny wooden building. It's been made by hand, the walls matchsticks stacked upon one another, windows no larger than a penny, a Tinker Bell–sized door. I reach in through the opening in the terrarium and touch the roof of it with the tip of my finger. It's the cabin. I sit back on the couch, the blanket dropping to my feet, staring at the little glass globe as though it's a dream.

There is still light in the sky. I stand and touch the outline of my car keys through the fabric of my pocket. I tear a piece of paper from an exercise book I find on the dining table and write a note with one of Huia's colored pencils. A purple one.

*Thank you.*

I pour the cold tea down the sink and leave the note on the kitchen counter.

That night I lie awake and ignore Bella knocking gently on the door. I hear her and Daniel outside, worrying about me, deciding what to do, and then there is silence as they go back to their tents. Daniel doesn't play the guitar that night and I am glad of it.

I stare up at the ceiling, the wooden beams, the fine gray web in the corner where a spider has made her home. I cannot sleep and I don't even try. Instead, I take myself back to the days before Alex was gone. Those days that were so ordinary, but have become so sharp, so bright, in their recalling. I have picked through them before, over and over, looking for clues. Signs that he was going to die. Signs I should have noticed. The ticking of a death-watch beetle. Stepping on cracks. Unlucky numbers. Black cats.

The weekend before, before everything changed, we went to brunch at our favorite café. It was the place I'd met Summer, who I'd then forgotten. Alex ordered the same thing he always ordered—the Big Breakfast without spinach, and an espresso. I asked for granola. We sat at the table by the window, watching people put their heads up close to read the menu taped to the outside of the glass. Watching families walk by with strollers, and teenagers in groups, and elderly couples with small, slow dogs.

"I met her here," I tell him. He continues reading his paper, of course. He's in the past and I'm here. The Seahawks haven't lost yet. He's reading about the upcoming game, and where he is there's a chance they might win.

"Summer," I say bitterly. "She came in with Travis and I met her. I forgot about it. Then I saw her again and we figured it out."

Alex turns a page.

"She's here. We're both here. Isn't that something? Like a bad joke."

He has a cap on—it's not quite, properly, spring—and a knitted sweater. He looks like a Gap commercial. His food will come in a minute and he'll smile at the waitress.

I lean in. "How long did you like her? How long were you thinking about her? Huh? Were you thinking about her when we were kissing? Are you thinking about her now?"

Alex is motionless. I want to reach over the table and strike him across the face. Watch the shock register. Watch the pink shape of my hand bloom on his cheek.

"I waited for you," I hiss. "People thought I was crazy. Thought that if you really loved me you would have asked years ago. *I waited*. Putting up with your mom, the disappearing on weekends. I put up with you."

Alex lifts his head and glances out the window. There's a woman looking at the menu, assessing and deciding. Her young son is holding her hand. The boy looks at me. His hair is sticking up like he just got out of bed, his cheeks as red as apples.

"I thought," I start and then draw breath. "That time when you tried to teach me to surf . . . I thought that if I learned how, maybe you'd ask me then . . . if I could be that girl. But I couldn't do it. I wasn't that girl." I shake my head slowly. "Why did you ask me, Alex? Why, after all that time? To keep me here? To keep from feeling guilty?"

Alex tips his head back down to the paper.

My voice rises. "You can't propose to someone because you feel obligated. It's not enough."

I think of the argument about the vows. Forever promises. About Alex agreeing to say whatever I wanted.

"What was going to happen after the wedding?" I shout. "Were you just going to keep on pretending it was all fine? That you didn't feel . . . trapped?"

The waitress comes over, carrying the Big Breakfast. Her name is Alice and she wears her dark hair in a braid that falls down over her chest, the tail curling around one breast. She places Alex's meal in front of him and he shifts his paper and grins at her. "Thank you, Alice."

"Fuck. You," I say to him.

Back then, in that moment, I'd wished for my food to come too. I'd been worried about fitting into the wedding dress, but Alex's breakfast smelled greasy and salty and good. He punctured a sausage with his fork, and I saw the juices spilling out and steam rising up. I was ravenous, wanted him to offer me some. His gaze was firmly focused on the plate in front of him. Sausages, eggs, buttered toast, grilled tomatoes.

"When did we stop talking?" I ask, but I already know the answer. A long time ago. Perhaps as far back as that trip to Italy. We talked less and less over the years. Because we knew each other so well, I'd told myself. Because there were fewer stories to tell. Because we were part of each other's stories now, him in mine, me in his; there was no reason to tell them. Because there were no new stories. Because it was comfortable.

Alex looked up from his plate, his cheek full of food. "You all right, babe?"

"Yes," I'd said. Stomach protesting otherwise. I'd looked at him, silently wanting him to share. Not asking. Wanting him to just know.

Now, in the cabin, sleepless and clear-eyed, I answer truthfully. "No."

In the morning, Bella comes into the cabin and I make her an espresso without saying a word. I have barely slept. My head hurts.

Bella waits until I'm sitting with a cup steaming in front of me, then says, apologetically, "Papa and the aunties are coming. For lunch."

"Seriously?"

"It's Sunday," she says. She blows on her cup, the *crema* moving under her breath. "Where did you go yesterday?"

"Edison."

"Edison?"

"Flourfarm."

"To get bread?"

It's such an innocent question I want to laugh. Or cry. Probably cry.

"To see Summer."

"Oh. Okay." Bella brightens for a moment, then frowns. "Why?"

I swallow a mouthful of coffee and don't answer her.

"Frankie?"

She tries again, in Caputo-speak. "*Soru?*"

"She loved Alex."

"What?"

"Summer loved Alex. She kissed him. They kissed."

Bella blinks at me.

"How did you . . . ?"

"Merriem said something. About Summer losing someone in an accident. I worked it out."

I don't add that it made perfect sense. That it made everything suddenly clearer and brighter, casting blacker shadows.

"Holy Mother," Bella says. "God, Frankie, that's awful."

"Yes."

"How do you . . . feel?"

"Not great."

"No. No, not great. Of course." She's nodding, her face a little pale.

"Angry. Sad," I add. "I can't figure out which. Both, I guess. Confused."

"Of course." She shakes her head. "I'm so sorry."

When I look at her she seems made of round things. Round eyes, round mouth, dark hair framing a round face. Like a child. I curse myself for the way I've been with her. The blame I've laid on her. *Blood is thicker than water . . .* Jack's the second person to say that recently. Guilt floods over me.

"I blamed you for kissing him. For trying to take him. And all that time . . ."

I can't finish. Bella looks like she might cry too.

"Oh," she whispers.

"I blamed you," I add, shaking my head at the ridiculousness of it. How obtuse I have been. "For everything."

She blinks at me and shakes her head in reply. But we both know it's true.

"I'm sorry," I say finally.

I go over to her and wrap my arms around her for the first time in a very long time. It's awkward for a few moments and then I feel her weight fall, gently, against me. She's still shaking her head and crying a little. I can feel the relief, tangible, moving through both of us.

"I just thought," I hear myself say in a hollow kind of voice, "that if I had what Mama and Papa had . . . If I could just hang on to him . . . it would all be . . . but nothing is . . ."

Bella lifts her head and nods at me. Tears slipping down her cheeks.

# Chapter Nineteen

. . . .

*La domenica è sempre domenica*—Sunday is always Sunday. Whether you like it or not. And Sunday is family day. There's no written rule but there may as well be. I know that it won't just be Papa and the aunties coming to the cabin, but a mixed bunch of Calabresi and Sicilians; whoever is hungry, whoever wants to gossip.

When I don't see my family, on a Sunday, the cousins ask questions later.

"You weren't at Mass."

"Where were you for baby Ella's christening?"

"How are you, stranger?"

A stranger, though I've seen them all just the week before. It's stifling.

Alex often went surfing on a Sunday and the timing wasn't coincidental. Before we were engaged it was easier because no one asked about him. Though we'd been a couple for a long time, and he came with me to other family functions, there was a silent understanding that we weren't yet betrothed and were, therefore, living in sin. The consensus seemed to be: don't mention it. But as soon as we were engaged, Alex became a Caputo, whether it suited him or not. Suddenly everyone wanted to see him on a Sunday too. I reeled off reasons till they became excuses.

"He's surfing."

"He's doing some work at home."

"He's with his family."

The last explanation was countered with, "Invite them too!" I could barely imagine Mrs. Gardner and my family together at our wedding, let alone sharing a casual Sunday lunch. I continued making excuses to my family while begging Alex to come along.

He just laughed. "They're your family. They want to see you."

He didn't get it. And I couldn't explain that without him I was a fraction, not a whole. No longer good enough by myself. My family wanted to see him and hug him and know all about him. They wanted to ask about his work and slap his shoulders and make him eat more than he was comfortable eating. He was one of us now. They wanted to be in his life like they were in mine—pushing in, interfering, loving, scolding, soothing.

I'm buttoning a clean shirt when Papa's car pulls up. From the window I watch him shake Daniel's hand, then bring him into a manly kind of embrace, brief but firm. Daniel stands with his arms at his sides so Papa makes like cannoli pastry, curling around him. He doesn't seem to notice Daniel's face blush pink.

Papa kisses Bella and they go to his car to remove things from the trunk. Folding chairs, cases of Italian sodas, boxes of food in foil. Daniel rushes to help. Bella starts setting up a picnic area in front of the cabin. I step outside with spare rolls of toilet paper for the outhouse.

"*Buongiorno, cara mia,*" Papa says, like Mama used to say in her Calabrese accent.

"Hello, Papa."

He comes over to give kisses on each cheek. I close my eyes. Papa's love is palpable.

"You look well, darling."

"Thanks, Papa. How are you?"

He smiles. "Good, *duci.* Work is very busy. I miss you, of course, but I know Bella is here so that gives me some peace."

Bella is unfolding chairs and placing them together in a huddle.

Papa clears his throat. "I was wondering if Merriem might be free for lunch."

I study him. "Bella said she invited her. I think she's bringing bread."

I haven't yet planned how I will handle seeing Merriem. How I will explain rushing out of her house. How things have changed. How tangled and clear it has all become.

"She needn't do that, we'll have plenty," he says, then adds quickly, "I wanted to ask her about her vegetable garden. Do you remember the garden we used to have in the yard?"

I nod. Mama and Papa had grown their own eggplants, zucchini, tomatoes, and herbs. Then Mama died and everything went to seed. One year Bella cleared it and planted wildflower seeds; it must have been just before she became a teenager. Before hormones propelled her into drinking and dark makeup and hair that hid her face. She was an energetic and curious kid, Bella. She collected snail shells and grew sprouts on her windowsill, kept jars full of fallen feathers. The wildflowers had bloomed that summer, lanky and thin stemmed, a dozen vibrant colors.

"I thought, maybe, I should replant it," Papa says. His gaze seems to be a million miles away. "It has been a long time. . . . Anyway, Merriem was talking about crop rotation. She says it helps, a little, instead of so much pesticide. And it makes the soil more healthy. Maybe I should learn about that."

"Merriem will help you," I say.

"I've already bought some seedlings," Papa admits.

"That's good, Papa," I say, lightly patting his back, and feel him straighten, appreciatively, under my touch.

Bella holds up a box. "Want these out, Papa?"

"*Sì,* Isabella. Actually, wait. Vincenzo is bringing a table."

"Vinnie?" I ask.

"Yes. He is bringing a long table," Papa says. "Apparently a good friend of his owns a very successful party-hire company."

"Of *course* he does," Bella says, rolling her eyes.

I find myself laughing. Bella glances at me, surprised, and joins in.

Papa looks baffled. "It is quite handy. He supplies trestle tables, marquees . . ."

I pat his back again. "Yes, very handy, you're right, Papa."

Bella smiles and shakes her head while looking through the contents of the box.

Caputos amble down the driveway carrying food, as if it's a common occurrence to lunch in the middle of a forest. There are plates of *arancini*, jars of pickled zucchini and eggplants, a platter of provolone and *galbanino* cheese in big, thin circles. Vinnie arrives in a pickup truck with a couple of tabletops and frames in the tray and flat-pack chairs that spring open easily. The chairs are white, probably rented out for weddings. Vinnie avoids my eyes while he works. He mumbles something to Bella, who slaps him across the back of his head. Daniel notices and glances at me with alarm, but Vinnie and Bella are soon laughing. I'm not so quick to forgive.

The aunties take the sturdiest chairs, the ones that Papa brought, at one end of a table. They direct the others to bring this or that, set out plates, tell everyone where to sit. They are still wearing their clothes for Mass. Rosa is in good pants with a knitted, mint-colored twinset, and Connie is wearing a linen dress and pumps, with pearls.

Uncle Mario talks with Papa and Uncle Roberto, Rosa's husband, all three of them standing off to one side, probably to avoid being ordered about. Mario's wife, Lisa, is herding her three sons, all in their teens and twenties, like they're toddlers. Cousin Giulia lifts her eyes from her phone and gives me a wink. She's wearing those tight jeans again and a light pink fluffy top that makes her breasts look like Sno Balls. Cousin Cristina, Vinnie's sister, has baby Joseph on her lap and looks tired. Her husband is chasing their other two, Emma and Marco, around the trees. Mama's ancient cousin Teresina, a widow, sits straight-backed and po-faced next to her fiancé, Cosimo, both of them in their seventies.

Aunty Connie calls for me to sit next to her and Aunty Rosa. Rosa pats my leg. "We missed you at Mass this morning,

Francesca. Father Gianni gave a very good sermon on forgiveness, didn't he, sister?"

"He did," Aunty Connie agrees.

"Cristina was there with the children. Marco is going to be an altar boy."

"He'll do a fine job at it. A well-behaved child," Aunty Connie adds.

I nod, and don't mention that Cristina gives Marco Milk Duds as a reward for keeping quiet during church. The kid is a menace by the afternoon but the aunties don't see it. The arrangement keeps almost everyone happy.

For a brief moment I consider telling them what I have learned. "Alex had an affair." But I don't. I probably never will. Is it an affair if they only kissed? Is loving someone else worse than sleeping with someone else? What are the rules? How upset am I allowed to be? With a dead man.

"Gabriella Favano had a beautiful jacket on this morning, didn't she, sister?"

"She did."

"Lilac. A kind of linen."

"Mauve."

"Yes, perhaps mauve."

It seems as though life is going on exactly the same, as though nothing ever changes. I watch Vinnie and Daniel at the other end of the table. Vinnie has rolled up his pants to show Daniel the scar on his leg where he broke it as a kid, the place where the bone had come out through the skin. Daniel is nodding but he's also glancing around the table at all the people, most of them talking loudly, some—Papa and Uncle Mario, for instance—in Italian. He seems a bit bewildered. I remember him looking the same way at our engagement party.

"How are you, my girl?" Aunty Rosa asks, carefully watching my face.

I shrug and smile. "I'm okay, Aunty."

"She's having some time out," Aunty Connie says sharply.

"I was just—"

"She's been through a lot," Aunty Connie adds, chin lifted.

"Bella's here with me," I reassure them. "And Daniel."

They both look over at Bella and Daniel, who are both peering at Vinnie's leg while he gesticulates wildly, Bella then rolling her eyes.

"He's Alexander's brother, isn't he?" Aunty Rosa asks.

I nod.

"Quite a handsome young man," she says approvingly. "He's taking some time out too?"

I nod again. Daniel is smiling at something Bella's saying, staring at her face, watching her lips move.

"That's good," Aunty Rosa replies, satisfied.

Aunty Connie straightens in her chair, smooths her dress, and nods too.

As the food is passed around, crusty bread getting stuffed with salami and roasted peppers and pickled eggplant, oil and vinegar dripping down fingers, paper napkins being dispensed, I see Merriem stepping towards the gathering. She's wearing one of her long dresses with a cardigan, and sandals with a silver anklet. Her red hair is piled on top of her head, the white strands catching the light.

Papa springs to his feet and the aunties put down their forks in almost perfect synchronization.

"Merriem," Papa says, beaming.

She accepts a kiss on the cheek with a wide smile. "Giuseppe. Great to see you again. Hope you've been enjoying the honeycomb."

"Oh, yes. Yes, it's delicious."

Bella brings over a chair and Papa makes room between him and the aunties. Uncle Mario introduces himself and pumps Merriem's hand. She laughs in that booming way of hers.

"Hi, Frankie," she says to me, her face cautious, testing.

"Hi, Merriem."

She doesn't ask if I'm okay, as though she already knows I don't want to be asked.

Papa gestures to Connie and Rosa. "These are my sisters."

Merriem reaches out her hand. She has a silver ring on every finger.

Aunty Connie blinks and shakes her hand. "Concetta."

"A real pleasure to meet you."

"And my other sister, Rosaria, Rosa," Papa says.

"Hello."

Aunty Rosa clears her throat. "You live nearby?"

"Very near. I'm just down the road."

"You've been here long?"

"Quite a few years now," Merriem says, and adds her standard explanation. "I followed a man . . . you know . . ."

"Oh. Well." Aunty Rosa looks to her sister. Aunty Connie is unmoved.

"Merriem grows vegetables," I say.

"She keeps bees too, just like Nonno," Papa adds.

"Yes, you said that," Aunty Connie replies.

"It's very nice here . . . with the trees. . . . Very . . . rustic," Aunty Rosa says to Merriem.

Merriem gives another full laugh. "Rustic, yes. Well, we like it. Darwin and me, I mean."

Aunty Rosa looks dismayed.

"Her cat, Zia. Darwin is a cat," I explain.

I catch Bella staring at me from the other end of the table. She smiles knowingly. I suddenly have a memory of hiding vegetables I didn't want to eat in my pockets at Aunty Connie's house. Surely that was Bella, not me. But when I search my memory, I realize they were my pockets, my fingers tucking the cooked vegetables, broccoli from the orecchiette perhaps, right down into the seams. Bella saw me do it and smiled, just like she is now. I return the smile.

Merriem settles into her seat and I watch as Vinnie passes her the bag of fresh bread rolls. Papa touches her elbow and begins asking her about the garden and her system of crop rotation.

The smells of the forest—the damp dark of the soil, the bleeding sap of the trees, the lemony cedar smell—all vanish in the company of the Sicilian food: the pungent garlic in Zio Mario's salami, the vinegar pickling the vegetables, olives bobbing in brine, roasted peppers, the ubiquitous, sunshine-colored olive oil. It's a kind of colonization. The forest is one of ours now.

After the rolls there is salad, and after the salad there is fruit. Cristina's older children become unruly so Vinnie and Bella walk them down to the water. Daniel stays with Cristina and baby

Joe. Cristina talks on and on, and jiggles baby Joe till he falls asleep, and then continues jiggling out of habit so his fat cheeks bounce up and down, his bottom lip hanging open and glistening with drool. Giulia takes her leave; she has a friend to meet, to the consternation of her brothers, who protest that they should be able to leave too. Uncle Mario clips Cousin Luca, the one who wants to join the army, across the ear and tells him for the hundredth time that Nonno took his children away from Sicily because of military service and here he is, the *imbecille,* wanting to join voluntarily. Merriem talks to Zio Roberto, the aunties speak to one another, Sicilian and Italian and English filling the spaces between the trees, silencing the birds.

When the salad and fruit are finished, Papa and I go into the cabin to make espresso. Aunty Rosa calls out to bring the sweets too. We find them in a box placed by the counter: almond-paste cookies, *brutti e buoni,* even *lingua di suocera,* mother-in-law's tongue. I put an almond-paste cookie in my mouth, let the sweet dough melt on my tongue. It's flavored with orange and cinnamon. Aunty Rosa is a great baker; no one makes treats like she does.

Papa smiles at my satisfied face as he fiddles with the espresso maker. "Rosa wanted to make your wedding cake. She did ours, you know."

"Aunty Rosa made your wedding cake?"

He nods. I think of a photo on their dresser: Mama and Papa and their cake; Mama holding the knife, Papa with his hand on the small of her back. They are both looking at the crowd beyond the photographer, grinning. Love and food: the Italian equation for bliss.

"What was it like?" I ask.

"Ahhh. It was . . . *bedda*." He sighs and smiles, and his gaze drifts off.

I wonder which part of their wedding he is remembering. The tables full of food, the kiss in the church, or Uncle Mario forgetting the rings and having to rush back to get them before the ceremony started. Perhaps his mama, Nonna, arguing with the waiter about the bad coffee. The sky being blue and perfect, even though it was April and the weather could go either way. I'd grown up on these wedding stories, little details ever so slightly changed in each recounting. The priest becoming more drunk, Mario more bumbling, the coffee more and more undrinkable. I felt as though I'd been there, amid the color of it, the music of it. The swish of bright polyester dresses, the tinkling of ice in glasses, the roly-poly singsong sounds of Italian and sharp bursts of American laughter.

I imagine Mama and Papa set apart, in a bubble of their own *vero amore*, whispering into each other's necks. Mama has a veil that she doesn't take off because it makes her feel like a bride, and Papa keeps his palm against her all night, thinking, *she is my wife.* They can't stop smiling.

Aunties and uncles come to kiss their cheeks and grab at their faces, saying, "*Tanti Auguri!*" Their American friends try out the new words they have learned, like *cassata* and *gelu di muluni*.

These stories were how I fell in love with a wedding. The idea of a wedding, the daydream. Crisp, pure, and white as a snowdrift. Elegant and flawless.

Papa nudges me. "Are you sad, *cara mia*?"

I nod. "*Sì*. I am sad."

But what I want to say is "disappointed." "Papa, I am so disappointed." One day I will tell him the whole of it. One day, but not today.

"I'm sorry, Francesca," he says, as though it is his fault, and stares at me, troubled, till I force a smile and look out the window.

He finally gets the espresso machine working, then hunts for extra cups.

I see Bella and Vinnie come back with the children, who are wet from the pants up. Merriem is laughing—I can hear her from inside.

I watch a charcoal-colored car, clean and shining as a seal on the rocks, glide down the driveway.

Mrs. Gardner squints from the front passenger seat.

# Lingua di Suocera

. . . . . . . . . . . . . . . . . . . . . . . . . . . . . . . . . .

## MOTHER-IN-LAW'S TONGUES,
### (MARMALADE-FILLED PASTRIES)

A traditional Sicilian sweet-and-sour treat for serving with espresso

*Makes about 24 pastries*

¾ cup semolina flour
1 cup all-purpose flour
½ cup granulated sugar
¼ teaspoon salt
7 tablespoons butter cut
    into pieces
2 egg yolks

2 to 3 tablespoons cold
    water
About 1 cup marmalade
    (any citrus fruit of
    your choosing)
Powdered sugar, for
    dusting

## PREPARATION

In a food processor, process the semolina for about 5 minutes, until fine and silky. Add the all-purpose flour, granulated sugar, and salt and pulse to mix. Add the butter and process until crumbly. Add the egg yolks, one at a time, pulsing to mix. With the processor running, add just enough water so the dough comes away from the sides of the bowl. Do not add too much water or the dough will be difficult to work.

Turn the dough out onto a floured surface and form a disk. Wrap in plastic wrap and refrigerate for at least 30 minutes.

Preheat the oven to 375°F. Line a baking sheet with parchment paper.

On a floured surface, roll the dough out to no more than ¼ inch thick. With a 3½ x 2-inch fluted oval cookie cutter, cut out ovals of dough. If you do not have a cutter you can make your own template and cut around with a knife or a fluted pasta cutting wheel. Gather and re-roll scraps and cut another 3 or 4 ovals.

Place about 2 teaspoons marmalade in a line in the center of each oval. Fold together the sides of each oval until they almost touch and pinch the ends (leaving the center agape). Place about 1 inch apart on the baking sheet.

Bake until golden, 15 to 20 minutes. Transfer to racks to cool. While still warm, dust with powdered sugar. Store in an airtight container.

# Chapter Twenty

. . . .

Papa walks down the steps behind me, carrying a tray loaded with as many cups as we could find.

Mrs. Gardner's pale blue eyes, morning-sky blue, are roving back and forth, taking in the scene. Her face is drawn and her clothes hang from her more loosely than usual. Mr. Gardner stands apart from his wife. He's holding the car keys as though they're a talisman.

"Giuseppe," Mrs. Gardner says.

"Mrs. Gardner. May I offer you an espresso?"

She purses her lips. She is wearing tan pants, a silk blouse, and a string of pearls. I watch Aunty Connie roll her own pearls between her fingertips.

"Barbara, Marshall," Merriem says, cheerfully, but only Mr. Gardner gives her a little nod. He catches my eye and gives me a tired smile before glancing at his feet.

Mrs. Gardner shakes her head at Papa, speaks in a clipped voice. "No. No, thank you."

Papa places the tray on the table and finds an empty seat, which he offers her. She refuses again. The Caputo chatter seems to have been silenced. Even the wet children are looking at the strange woman who hasn't been introduced. I open my mouth to do so when she cuts me off.

"My husband and I"—she turns her head to include him in the statement—"have come to inform you *personally* that you are trespassing."

Teresina looks at me, alarmed, and Bella comes to stand by my side. Aunty Rosa whispers to Teresina.

Mrs. Gardner continues. "We have sent several messages via our groundskeeper"—she emphasizes Jack's title—"giving you notice of the fact, but you seem to have ignored them."

Papa looks to Mr. Gardner, but he's staring past us all at the cabin.

"Barbara," Papa says, his voice low, "Francesca is staying for only a short time. It has been difficult."

"It has been difficult for us *all*," Mrs. Gardner says, "but that does not excuse taking advantage . . . breaking the law, in fact."

She eyeballs me and my stomach drops. I suddenly feel tiny.

"Hey, lady, you don't know what you're talking about." I glance over at Vinnie who's shaking his head. "Frankie? Breaking the law?"

Mr. Gardner steps forward and touches Mrs. Gardner's shoulder. "Darling, perhaps—"

She shrugs him off. "No. It's the principle of the thing. Look at them all—making themselves at home."

"We are here to support our niece!" Aunty Connie pipes up.

"Surely you can allow your own daughter-in-law, your *famiglia*, some time here?" Aunty Rosa hisses, incredulous. "It isn't being used. It needs some upkeep, to be honest."

Mrs. Gardner glares at her and I know what she's thinking: *She is not my daughter-in-law.*

Mr. Gardner whispers his wife's name again, pleading. Aunty Connie agrees loudly with Aunty Rosa. There's whispering all around: Teresina to her fiancé, who is nodding; Cristina murmuring to the baby, who's woken up; Roberto pressing the other two children to his legs, covering their ears; Vinnie frowning and muttering, lifting his chin; Mario's boys seeming suddenly taller and angrier.

My heart pounds as I feel the heat of Mrs. Gardner's gaze upon me. I meet it.

"It's not your cabin," she says to me, her voice low and steely. I notice the blusher on her cheeks, applied a little too heavily.

"I know," I reply.

"You won't get it. It'll go to Daniel."

Daniel moves towards us, but Mrs. Gardner doesn't notice him. She's leaning towards me, lifting her finger to my face.

"Mom," Daniel says.

"You're not a Gardner," she hisses at me. "You never will be."

"Mom!"

"Barbara," Mr. Gardner says.

"She won't have it!" she shouts wildly.

Mario's boys and Vinnie are all standing now. The trees seem to bear down. I feel sick. I look at Daniel, who stares at me and then at his mom. Mr. Gardner is trying to pull Mrs. Gardner away, and also trying to catch Daniel's attention, but Mrs. Gardner is loud.

"Let me go!"

"Come on, darling."

"Let me go right now!"

"I think it's best if we—"

She struggles out of Mr. Gardner's grip and cries, "Little . . . *whore!*"

I reel back, my fingers against my cheek, though she hasn't touched me.

"That's enough!" That's Bella and her body is right up against mine now, moving to stand in front of me. Papa has grabbed hold of my hand. Vinnie is close too, his biceps twitching, his jaw square.

"She let him go surfing that day!" Mrs. Gardner bellows.

"I couldn't stop him. . . . He loved the sea," I mumble uselessly, pleading with her.

"You think you know everything about your son? You think he was flawless?" Bella shouts at her.

I reach out to stop her. "No, Bella, don't."

Mrs. Gardner is writhing in her husband's arms, her silk shirt twisting. I can see her bra, the loose skin of her stomach as she struggles. When she yells spit comes out of her mouth. "She seduced him!"

"How dare you!" Bella screams.

"She did nothing of the sort!" Aunty Connie retorts, her voice shrill.

Bella is pointing, threatening. "Stay away from my sister! She's been through enough."

"Mom, please. Stop. Please?" Daniel is begging his mom, but

reaching out for Bella. I watch him take hold of her hand. Their fingers lace together easily, out of instinct.

Mrs. Gardner sees it too. "See? See! They are just like that other . . . French bitch! Get away from my boys! *Whores!*"

The Caputo men crowd in, tall and dark and silent as the trees. Mr. Gardner glances at them, eyes wide. Mrs. Gardner struggles in his arms, shaking her head from side to side. She spots something beyond the end of the table and lunges in that direction.

"Jack!" she calls. "Arrest her!"

I look up to see Jack jogging out of the forest with long strides. The men wheel around, confronting the new arrival. Jack glances at Mrs. Gardner and then to me, his eyes round. He's still looking at me when Luca, Mario's son, buries his fist into his stomach. There's the strangest sound, like someone punching a pillow rather than a person, and Jack folds down to the ground. "Jack!" I cry out.

And then Daniel is lurching towards Luca to pull him off Jack, and Luca's brothers are tearing at Daniel, and Vinnie's among it all too, and the table crashes on its side and the dark espresso splashes up Mrs. Gardner's tan trouser legs.

The cabin is mine.

It tumbles out in a chain of whispers. Mr. Gardner to Daniel, after his wife is finally in the car. Daniel buckles her into the seat as though she's the child; he's the only one she'll let touch her.

Vinnie overhears, and tells Bella.

The cabin was Alex's, it turns out, left to him by his grand-father, Hank Gardner, because Alex was his favorite. And Alex left everything to me. He made a will a few months ago, when he renewed a bunch of insurances, something I didn't know. So many things I haven't known.

The cabin key, in my jeans pocket, suddenly feels heavier.

"We'll contest it!" Mrs. Gardner wails from the car, her voice full of grief, her face and clothes crumpled.

The huddle around me starts to disperse. Zio Mario puts his family in the car; the boys with wild, happy eyes, his wife crying and reprimanding at the same time. Cristina has already left, her kids munching on big boxes of Milk Duds, nonplussed. Zia Connie and Zia Rosa wash dishes with Bella in the cabin, gossiping and admonishing too, no doubt, while Papa and Uncle Roberto stack chairs into Vinnie's pickup.

Jack offers to help clean up. Thanks to my cousins he has an eye that's going to go black and an angry red scratch across his collarbone.

I shake my head. "No, it's okay, thank you."

Together we look out at the mess. The table has been righted but the ground is still covered in broken crockery and food and discarded cutlery.

"Are you sure?"

I nod. "There are lots of hands."

Jack clears his throat. "I was coming to warn you. Mrs. Gardner called. She sounded . . . well, how she was."

"There was nothing you could do," I say.

"I've never seen her like that."

"She hates me."

Jack pauses, but doesn't disagree with me. "What will happen now? Will you stay?"

I tip my head, considering.

"Sorry, you don't have to answer that."

"It's okay. It's just that I don't know."

He nods, looks down at his feet. He's wearing black Havaianas; I'm surprised he ran as fast as he did in them.

"I'm sorry," he says again.

"It's not your fault."

He winces and clears his throat again. "No, I mean about the other day. I should never have said what I said."

I shake my head. "No, I asked. I was—"

"You were upset. I shouldn't have—"

"Jack. Stop. Please. I was unfair and I should be the one saying sorry. Please stop saying sorry?"

"Okay."

I think of myself screaming at him, leaning against the car, being helped into his house. A whirling, wailing, confused tornado of grief. Not unlike Mrs. Gardner. I squeeze my eyes shut.

"Maybe we should agree to pretend it never happened," I say.

Jack doesn't reply.

I open my eyes to find him staring at me, bruised and expectant.

"Frankie, if you ever want . . . a friend . . . or something. To talk or have a coffee . . ."

He looks away.

"Coffee?" I ask.

He nods, still not looking at me. "Coffee. Tea. Cake. A piece of bread . . . a walk. Pretty much anything."

"Anything," I repeat, dumbly, feeling oddly light-headed.

"Yeah. I know I shouldn't be saying this, but I don't want you to just disappear, if that's what you're going to do, without saying . . ."

"Okay," I mumble.

He looks down at his legs, brushes dirt from them, coughs. I can't stop staring at him.

"I should get back to Huia," he says. "Merriem said she'd get her painting eggs."

"It's not Easter," I say.

"I don't think it matters. They made Christmas cookies a few weeks ago."

I suddenly have a vision of Merriem and Huia peering into an oven full of baking cookies. The kitchen is warm and smells of cinnamon and brown sugar and there's a bowl of runny red icing on the counter with a wooden spoon in it that's already been licked. Huia's face is scrunched up because she's impatient, and Merriem has her arm around her. My tongue ties; I can't remember what I was going to say. I stare at Jack as my eyes start to fill with tears.

"Frankie? Are you all right?" His voice is thick with concern.

"Yes," I say, taking a quick breath. "Yes, fine, sorry. You should go. Huia will be getting worried."

"I can stay and help."

"No." It comes out too blunt and I regret it. "It's fine. Truly, I'm fine," I lie.

But when Jack does leave, retreating down the winding path through the trees that takes him out of sight, I realize my hands are shaking. The memory of Mrs. Gardner twisting out of her shirt, her eyes bulging and ferocious; learning that the cabin was Alex's all along and now it's mine; the image of Merriem and Huia together without me; and the thought of not being here with them and close to Jack—they all leave me trembling.

# Chapter Twenty-one

. . . .

I sense someone beside me and turn to see Daniel. He takes hold of my quivering hand and squeezes it. His presence is so much like Alex's it makes my whole body uncoil from the inside.

"I have to go," Daniel tells me. "I think Mom needs me right now."

I notice that he's changed into a clean shirt. I stand by while he pushes some clothes into a bag, his guitar beside him. I pass him a sweater he has dropped.

"Alex never told me about the cabin," I say.

Daniel nods. "I don't think he ever thought about it actually belonging to him. Granddad died a long time ago."

"Alex was his favorite."

"Yeah, he was."

"Your mom and dad thought it would go back to the family."

Daniel shrugs. "You were his family too, Frankie."

Tears threaten again. I feel as though I've stolen something. "I don't need it. It should be yours."

He shakes his head. "It was Alex's. It was his decision for you

to have it. I know you'll take care of it, choose what to do. . . .
It'll be right."

"I'm so sorry."

"It's not your fault. None of this is your fault. It will be okay.
In the end." His voice is weary and resigned. "I don't want a
cabin, Frankie. I want my brother. That's all I care about."

"I know," I whisper.

The idea of the cabin being legally mine is too strange to deal
with, and I know that Mrs. Gardner is serious about contest-
ing the will. I can't imagine it will be mine after the Gardners
are through throwing money and lawyers and rage into the fight
for it. Daniel is right. Beyond the strangeness is the fact that it
doesn't really matter. We both wish it was still Alex's and that Alex
was still alive.

I know I won't tell Daniel about Summer. Someone else
might, one day, perhaps, but I won't.

"No wonder your mom was angry," I say.

"She's really hurting."

"She never liked me, Daniel."

"No." He clears his throat. "I never understood it before.
Then today she mentioned the French . . . woman."

I think of standing on the lawn with her that long-ago day
when I had first met his parents. The cold glass in my hand and
the way she had asked where my family was from.

"She once said I reminded her of someone."

Daniel nods and looks uncomfortable.

"Her father had an affair. She was French. She might have

been a nanny. I'm not sure of all the details, but I know it broke Mom's family apart. It changed the way people thought of them all. I'm so sorry, Frankie, I never knew you reminded her of that woman."

"I never had a chance," I mumble.

Daniel continues, almost to himself, "I think she was messed up from what happened. She gets these ideas in her head about the way things need to be. They don't always make sense. Half the time I can't guess what the rules are, but when they're not the way they should be she can get pretty mad. It's been like that since we were little. Everything has to be a certain way."

I nod. That just about sums up my idea of Mrs. Gardner—everything has to be a certain way. The house, the yard, and, most of all, her boys. Especially her Alex.

"It makes life bearable, I guess," Daniel adds. "Safe. She can cope when she's in control. When things are exactly the way she likes them."

"I was never what she planned for Alex, was I?"

Daniel shakes his head. "But *nothing* is how she planned, Frankie. Or hoped. Just about everything is a mess and she doesn't know what to do about it. Alex's . . . death"—the word makes him take a breath—"she can't do anything about it and that makes her crazy."

I place my hand on his shoulder and he half smiles. I notice the violet half moons under his tired eyes. Looking down at his half-packed bag reminds me that he's the only son left. He will have to make everything better for his mom all on his own.

"I'm sorry," I say again.

"It's a mess—but, Frankie, it's not your fault. It's not about the cabin. It's just Mom and how she is. And right now she's in a lot of pain."

I nod. That I understand. For the first time in years I feel some empathy for Mrs. Gardner, knowing that her pain must ache and burn just like mine does. I always imagined that she was angry with me for somehow stealing her son away from her, and that she would make me pay for it. When she saw me, she saw a threat, a thief. When she saw me, she saw the French woman who had broken everything, robbed her of her happy family and changed her entire world. But now her son truly has been stolen. From both of us.

The two of us left so very empty-handed.


Daniel whispers a good-bye to Bella and we wave as his car disappears. Aunty Rosa kisses me on each cheek before she too gets into her car. Uncle Roberto gives a little nod from behind the steering wheel.

"Now," Aunty Rosa says, leaning out of the window, "you ignore the things that . . . woman said. It's not true. You're a good girl, Francesca. *Brava Carusa.*"

"Thank you, Zia."

She nods. "We'll see you at Mass next week."

I look over to Bella, who is now standing at the window of Vinnie's pickup truck. She pats the window frame twice. Vinnie gives me a quick glance as he turns over the engine; his bottom lip is swollen from the fight. I glare at him. *You are not forgiven.*

The pickup truck trails the car up the driveway. Bella and I watch them go.

Papa clears his throat behind us. We both turn to him. There's still some light in the sky but it's becoming violet. Papa has put on a thick, cream woolen sweater with wooden toggles at the neck, which he's had for years. There are patches on the elbows. He has a bottle of homemade rosolio and a couple of glasses.

"Zia Connie need some more help in there?" Bella asks.

"She's just packing up the last of her dishes, then I'll drive her home," Papa replies.

Bella nods and goes inside, and Papa gestures towards the two Adirondack chairs. We sit and he smiles at me.

"Did Mama make you that sweater?"

He glances down at it. "*Sì*. You didn't know?"

I shake my head.

"She made it when she was pregnant with you."

He passes me a glass. The citrus and herb smell is sweet and strong.

"Thank you."

Papa sips from his glass. "She was tired of making all those little shoes—what do you call them?"

"Booties?"

He smiles. "Yes, booties. And hats. She made so many that you got too big before you could wear them all. She was so excited."

The aunties have told me what a miracle it was for Mama to get pregnant with one baby, let alone two. I think Aunty Connie fancied she'd played a part with her constant prayers. Perhaps she did, although prayers couldn't save Mama in the end.

"It's getting cool," Papa says, glancing around.

"Hmmm."

"I didn't think you would stay out here so long."

"It's not been that long."

"I thought you would move in with me."

I don't reply. I'm now even less sure where I will live.

Papa sips more of his rosolio and sighs. "I should be with trees more often. So much forest in Washington. I never noticed. You know?"

"Yes, I know."

"Merriem says there are many hiking trails. Some near our neighborhood."

I glance down at Papa's leather shoes, his neatly pressed pants. I can't imagine him hiking, although if anyone could convince him it would be Merriem. My gaze lifts back up to his sweater. The knitting is thick and complicated. It's a timeless style; he could probably keep wearing it till the wool gave out completely. I'm surprised the color has held, hasn't grayed over time, but then that's Papa's care. He would wash it with Mama in mind, making sure to look after it just so. Perhaps even thinking of Mama while his hands are in the water; remembering her rounded, pregnant shape curled over the knitting needles, lit by the glow of the television, her dark hair falling down her slight back.

"Do you still miss her? Mama. After all this time?"

Papa looks at me. He hesitates. "*Sì*. I miss her still."

"I've been trying to do the right thing, Papa," I whisper.

"I know. Of course you have."

"I don't remember Mama much." There is guilt in my voice.

"You were so small, Francesca. You're not supposed to re-member." He tips his head to look up at the darkening sky. "She knows you love her."

I wonder what she would think of me now. I take another sip and watch Papa roll his glass in his hands.

"People talk about closure," I say.

He frowns. "What is this?"

"When you get over something, I guess. When it doesn't hurt so much."

"I don't understand."

"Did you have a time when it . . ." I can't think how to put it.

"Went away?" he asks.

I nod slowly.

Papa shuffles closer to me and puts an arm around my back. I can feel the thickness of the wool of his sweater, smell the slight damp in it from the chill air. Like Hudson's Bay blankets and winter coats. "Life becomes better. Things become better. But it remains. It always remains. I never had this closure." He gives me a kind look. "I'm sorry, *cara mia*. I would never wish this for you. It will get better. But, probably, it will never go away."

I nod. I know as much, within myself, but hearing him say it makes it real. Alex is gone. He will always be gone. Mama is gone. She will always be gone. Perhaps Alex and Mama are in the same place. Looking down on me.

"Darling?"

I look into Papa's face.

"You don't have to come back home. You don't have to do anything. But don't stay here too long." He reaches into his pocket and unfolds an envelope. "Giulia asked me to give you this."

"What is it?"

"A letter. From your travel insurance."

I take it but don't open it.

"Giulia explained to them what happened. They've given you a refund. A voucher. You can use it for other travel."

"Other travel?" I repeat.

Papa nods. "Life will be better, *duci*. But you have to . . . live it. You see?"

He squeezes me against him.

"Yes, Papa. I see."

Wishing that I did.

As Papa and Aunty Connie are leaving, it starts to rain for the first time since I arrived at the cabin. The rain smells different in the forest. In town, it smells warm, of steaming concrete, wet clothes, and wet hair. Here, I realize, you can almost smell it before it falls, as if the ground is opening itself up in anticipation. It's warm and mushroomy—loamy. And then the rain slowly patters down through layers of leaves and branches and whatever else lives far above our heads. Mosses, lichens, parasitic plants, microcosms nestled in protected crevices where branches reach out from trunks like arms.

Bella and I are struck dumb for a moment, then we run into

the cabin. Inside we lie, rain-splashed and a bit breathless, on top of the bed, listening to the drops.

When we were small and it rained, we would take a big golf umbrella outside and sit underneath it together. We had to curl up tight to both fit, with as many toys as we could manage, too. A couple of dolls, a teddy bear, doll furniture. We could play under there a very long time. Why it was different to play under an umbrella in the rain as opposed to being inside by a window, for instance, I don't know. Luckily for us it rained a lot in Seattle so we had plenty of opportunities to dash outside with Papa's big green-and-red-striped umbrella and make up stories and games, worlds, and dynasties. And when Mama died, it felt like there were just the two of us against the world. We were as close as twins for a while. Papa was grieving, and the aunties were busy looking after the practical things—Aunty Rosa making meals; Aunty Connie giving us our baths. The hushed voices, careful footsteps. *Those poor girls.*

Before Mama died, the house was always full of activity. When she wasn't sick, Mama was busier than a bee. She always had something to do and something to clean. In the summer, she made simple sauce and preserved lemons. In winter, she darned anything that needed mending and made lavender drawer pillows to keep insects at bay. Fall was for directing Papa to rake the leaves, and freezing meals for the winter. In spring, she harvested zucchini and kept the yard from going completely wild. In between the seasonal chores were the weekly chores for the family and the church. In between the weekly chores were the daily chores—meals, vacuuming, dusting, wiping things down, chatting to friends on the phone, making espresso and more espresso and yet more espresso. Without Mama, our house was strangely, horribly silent and calm. It was better to be outside in a world of our own making, the sound of the rain ping-ping-pinging off our makeshift shelter.

On the cabin's bed, I lie closest to the wall with Bella laid out on my left. The rain drums the roof. Bella is staring up into the beams, where graying cobwebs stretch out like hammocks in corners and crevices.

"I saw you talking to Vinnie. He could barely look at me all day," I say.

Bella sniggers. "Coward. He was supposed to apologize to you. Although that was before . . ."

I shake my head. "What a mess. Jack's properly hurt, you know. Trust Vinnie to be in among it all."

"It wasn't just him. Luca was the worst. Vinnie was trying to break it up."

I think of Vinnie's lip, puffy and sore looking, his guilty sideways look. It's true he didn't start the fight, but he always seems to be in the thick of things, always manages to find trouble. Then, whatever he's done, he gets away with it. The family treats him like he's a sweet and bumbling toddler.

"Why do you always defend him?"

Bella pauses. "We're a team, I guess."

"A team? He's becoming a thug. First the party, then today."

She shrugs. "We're the bad ones, you know? Besides, he's not actually bad. Not really."

"You sound like Aunty Rosa."

"*Mammina!*" she says, mimicking Vinnie, then laughs. "I'm not quite that blind. He's pretty naughty, I'll give you that, but he was trying to protect you today, in his own stupid way. If you needed him, Frankie, he'd be there for you."

"I'm not sure about that."

"No, he would be. He was there for me."

I turn to look at her properly. "He helped you get the job in Portland."

"He knew someone, a friend of a friend. . . . It's a long story. But yeah, he helped me. I'm not sure what I would have done otherwise."

I remember, again, the night she left. How she sat on the end of my bed, how I wanted her to leave. How, when she had left, it had felt like a weight off of me. A burden lifted.

Bella rolls onto her side. Her face is close to mine; I can see the faint, sepia freckles across the tops of her cheeks. "You know why I left, don't you?"

I nod. I saw it, in the bathroom. The packet torn open, the foil ragged, the severe little expiry date punched in the side. I didn't have the courage to look at it straight on, just sort of slid my eyes towards it, past the cup from the kitchen, right over to the far side of the sink. Two blue lines.

I was cowardly. Being mad at Bella covered it up, made it simpler. But fear was underneath. I didn't know how to help. Didn't want to help.

"What . . ." I start, then stop.

"Happened?" she finishes. "Well, you can guess. There's no baby, right? Or kid . . . He or she would be a kid by now. I found somewhere to get it done. Vinnie helped me with that too—I needed money. He told Aunty Rosa a story about a school outing. I don't know how he explained never going on the outing, but it was at the time Aunty Rosa was on that diet, remember?"

I frown. "The grapefruit one?"

"Yeah. Made her hungry all the time and . . . forgetful.

"Vinnie never asked for the money back," Bella adds.

Blood is thicker than water. Family helps family. Vinnie's no exception. Bella could be right about him.

"Did it hurt?" My voice is small and I feel myself almost wincing though the pain had not been my own.

She nods. Her eyes are round and glassy.

"Who . . . ?"

She looks away, back up at the cobwebs on the ceiling. "There was a party. It was . . . I was . . ." She takes a deep breath. "I'm not sure who, Frankie. It wasn't a good time for me."

I watch her eyes fill with tears. My chest aches.

"I was so . . . ashamed. I couldn't come back. I had to go."

Guilt courses through me. I should have helped and I didn't. Bella had been so young. So lost. She had needed a mama and ours was gone.

"And that thing . . . I mean, what you saw, with Alex . . ." Tears fall down her cheeks. "It was nothing, Frankie. Nothing happened. Alex just seemed so cool. My big sister's boyfriend. Blond and cool, so different from the rest of us. I guess I just wanted what you had for a moment. You seemed to have it all figured out. Like you knew the formula, you know? You and Alex . . . it seemed so normal. So safe and good."

I reach out and pull her towards me. I am crying too. I shake my head.

"I don't have it all figured out," I say, tears choking my voice. "I never have. There is no formula. I was wrong."

Bella reaches her arms around me, her face wet against my shoulder. "I'm so sorry, Frankie."

Her embrace is tight as the tears pour out of me and onto her. Into her hair, my cheek pressed against her head. *Soru.* Blood and bone the same as mine. The only one who knew how it felt, *exactly* how I felt, when Mama was gone. The one I have let down and pushed away. The one I have needed all along.

It feels as though my heart is drowning.

"Oh, *soru* . . ." Bella whispers sadly.

"I got it wrong," I sob. "I got it *all* wrong."

There are no words to make it better and Bella doesn't offer any. Instead she holds me tight while we both cry and the sky tips out rain onto the cabin roof.

We lie together till we both stop crying, and then for a while after that because it is the most normal thing in the world. Bella dries her eyes on her top. We study the spider crawling her web and the black, leggy dots that are her offspring. In all my cleaning I haven't had the heart to clear that web, the mother and her tiny babies. There are at least a dozen of them.

Eventually I get up and gather leftovers, making sandwiches for our dinner while Bella finds paper plates and napkins. We sit inside to eat and talk. I tell her about reading *The Swiss Family*

*Robinson* and she remembers we watched the movie together as kids. We talk about Merriem's cat, Darwin, about Bella's neighbor's cat in Portland, who is called Poe and who likes to sleep in Bella's potted plants. She tells me about her neighborhood, her favorite coffee shop, the patient who encourages her to sketch and paint, the one who tried to touch her breast, her boss, a guy she dated for a couple of months.

I tell her about my work, about Mrs. Fratelli, about baby Joe's christening when Giulia wore a minidress so short Aunty Connie ordered her home and she came back wearing a tube top. I tell her about a night in a hotel I won a couple of years ago, and the famous actress who was at the table across from us at breakfast the next day, eating pancakes.

When our dinner is finished, Bella pulls something from her bag and shakes it out. A faded navy blue shirt, the sleeve almost amputated. Then comes Mama's old tapestry purse, purple roses cross-stitched on the sides.

"What are you doing?"

She holds up the shirt. "Daniel's."

She retrieves a needle and blue thread from the tapestry bag, threads it through, and makes a knot.

"I didn't know you could sew."

"I spend a lot of time around old people." She lays her hands on either side of the tear, as if sizing it up.

"Do you like him?" I ask carefully.

She frowns, then shrugs.

"He likes you."

"I don't know."

"He looks at you as though the sun rises out of your eyes."

"No, he doesn't."

"He does. Do you think you might like him?"

She clears her throat and hesitates. "Maybe."

"You're allowed to. Like him."

She meets my gaze. "Yeah? Well, we'll see. I'm not very good at this kind of thing."

I remember Jack saying the exact same thing. Jack of the forest. Jack who wants coffee or tea or pretty much anything.

"Not very good at it? You're a shameless flirt."

She blinks. "Oh, well sure. That's a completely different thing."

"You mean *this* could be a completely different thing?" I ask pointedly.

"*Maybe*, I said." Then she tuts, as if it's impossible. "Sun rises out of my eyes . . ."

But it's true and I think she knows it. Bella can get guys eating out of her hand; that's not uncommon, but it's different with Daniel. She's different. Shyer, for starters, like she cares what he thinks.

Thinking of Daniel brings Alex's face into my mind. Across from me at brunch. Lit up with the glow of the television. Lying against a pillow.

"I think we'd stopped seeing each other," I whisper.

Bella glances up from her stitches. Her needle hovers over the place where it will next dive and pierce.

"Sometimes it was like he was a stranger."

She lays the shirt down in her lap.

"I'd been looking at that face for . . . I don't know . . . years?"

"A decade?" she offers.

"Yeah. I think I'd been looking *through* him for so long. You know what I mean?"

She nods.

"I'd gotten so used to seeing him. So used to seeing what I expected to see. I'd stopped . . . *really* seeing him." I take a breath. "He seemed cool at family things because he didn't like them, Bella. He didn't want to be there. He didn't get it."

"It's a big family. We can be pretty overwhelming."

I nod, but that's not the whole of it. Not really. Alex didn't understand what it means to be Italian *and* American. That both are important. That it's important to me, and that my family will always be there, bright and loud and getting in the way.

"He didn't want to go anywhere. I wanted to go to Europe. And he could never stand up for me, with his mom." I feel like I'm betraying him by confessing all of this. "Now I find out he might have loved someone else. That he kissed someone else . . ."

Bella was right about my life. Alex and I had been together for so long it was habit. Loving each other was habit. Now he's gone, everything is gone. The wedding, the morning coffee, the habits, and the ties. I'm free-falling. Through the vast, blue sky.

"Hey," Bella says softly.

"I'm not sure if he even really loved me."

"Hey," she says again, and leans towards me.

"I mean in an adult way. When we were teenagers, sure. But after? Sometimes it felt like we were just going through the motions."

"He loved you." Her voice is firm.

"He loved the Seahawks. And hockey. He loved the ocean. . . . Those were his favorite things."

"Frankie, I am sure he loved you."

"And her? Summer?"

She looks pained. "I don't know."

"He loved this place. He loved it here."

"Yes. And he gave it to you." She stares at me, love and loyalty in her eyes. "He gave you his favorite things, Frankie. This place. The water just there."

*I tesori.* The treasures.

"Do you see?"

"Yes," I reply, my voice thin as thread.

The coroner's report—Barbara Gardner had insisted on an autopsy—revealed a blow to the head, which they said was consistent with striking rock, probably on the ocean floor. It was hard to say if Alex drowned first or hit his head first, though the contact was likely to have caused only concussion, not to be the cause of death. I prefer to think he struck his head first. That the water curled around him like a lover and drew him down, and perhaps he was even laughing at the time. Laughing because he should know better than to get caught in a rip, imagining telling the others about it later. I prefer to think that he went down easily, almost willingly, the face of his watch glinting, his body in its wet suit as slick and dark as an orca's skin. That he struck his head before he could realize he was going to die, that he wasn't going to be telling anyone about it later. Before he felt the betrayal of the sea, the one he had loved best of all.

Bella turns her eyes back to the cloth. I watch the needle take its downward dive into the fabric. Straight through and back up again. Like a bird catching fish in a calm sea. Down and up. Down and up. She is making sutures in Daniel's shirt. Tiny, perfect sutures, making it all right again.

# Rosolio alle Erbe

HERB CORDIAL (LIQUEUR)

A sweet after-dinner liqueur that was originally
made using rose petals but is now made with a variety of
ingredients and flavors, including lemons, berries, and oranges.
Rosolio improves as it ages, so drink after storing for
approximately two to nine months.

*Makes about 3 quarts*

25 fresh lemon verbena leaves
20 fresh bay leaves
4 fresh mint leaves
3 whole cloves
A 1-inch piece cinnamon stick

1 large strip of lemon zest
1 liter vodka
5½ cups sugar
5 cups water

## PREPARATION

Put the herbs, spices, and lemon zest in a jar. Add vodka and
cover tightly. Let stand in a cool, dark place for 2 weeks.

In a large saucepan, combine the sugar and water in a large
saucepan and bring it to a boil, stirring until the sugar is completely dissolved. Remove from the heat and let cool.

Strain the vodka through a fine-mesh sieve or cheesecloth into
a bowl (discard the solids). Add the vodka to the cooled syrup in
a clean glass bottle or large jar with lid. Cover tightly, place in a
cool and dark place and let stand for 8 days.

Strain the cordial through a coffee filter to remove any green
deposit that may have risen to the surface, and pour into bottles.
Cork tightly.

Store in a cool, dark place and serve after 2 to 9 months of storing.

# Chapter Twenty-two

· · · ·

Merriem brings us breakfast: cinnamon rolls stuffed full of nuts and brown sugar and smelling of still-warm butter. She's got Huia with her; she'll drop her off at school while Jack's doing some landscaping work on another property. We sit in the wan morning light, all four of us on the two Adirondack chairs, in seats and on arms, as the ground is still damp from yesterday's rain.

"Yesterday was a bit of a ride," Merriem says, smiling. "Are Sunday lunches always like that?"

"Not always quite that bad," I reply wryly.

"You Caputos are full of surprises. You rushing off the other day . . ."

I haven't yet told Merriem about going to see Summer. I look at Huia, her chin covered in icing and sugar, and Bella, still dressed in her clothes from yesterday, and decide not to. I take another bite of my cinnamon roll as Merriem continues, ticking things off with her fingers, ". . . a good ol'-fashioned rumble, new love . . ."

I glance again at Bella, who doesn't meet my eyes.

". . . parties, the police being called. Things haven't been so exciting round here for a long time." She laughs.

Huia finishes her roll, brushes her fingers against her top, and dashes off to scale a tree. We all watch her.

Merriem leans towards me. "What's the plan now, honey?"

I shrug.

Merriem then turns to Bella, who says carefully, "I think I'm going to move back to Seattle."

I turn to her quickly.

"If that's okay." She's staring at me.

"Okay with me?" I ask.

"I don't want to be in anyone's way."

"You wouldn't be in anyone's way," Merriem says cheerfully.

But Bella is still looking at me. "I have good references and there are plenty of seniors' homes here, good ones. I think I can get work, no problem. And I might do some study, some painting."

"Have you been thinking about it for a while?" I ask. The way she's looking at me, asking my permission, makes me realize just how cruel I have been.

She nods. "A long while. But I wanted to be sure . . . that it's okay."

"Of course it's okay," I say.

"Yes!" Merriem hoots.

"Of *course* it's okay," I repeat.

Bella reaches for my hand and squeezes it. "I was hoping you would say that. I can let Valentina take my lease; she's already asked if she can. She's fallen in love with Poe."

Bella explains who Poe is to Merriem, and they start talking about cats and how, when their owners move, they often return to their old homes. Bella squeezes my hand one more time and I know that her relocating has nothing at all to do with Valentina or Poe but is about coming home to look after her sister and her papa, to be with her family, as she should be. Only now do I properly recall her the day of the funeral. Getting out of her car to speak to me and I had almost recognized her but refused to.

When I lift my head, both Merriem and Bella are staring at me. Merriem is beaming.

"Were you talking to me?" I say.

"I was just telling Merriem that you might be neighbors."

"Oh . . ."

"Bella was filling me on things I missed yesterday. She said the cabin is yours?" Merriem's eyes are dancing.

"No, well . . . technically, I guess, but . . . They're going to contest the will."

"You don't know that they will," Bella says.

"I'd say it's pretty likely."

Merriem considers. "Surely if it's left to you . . . in a will . . . ?"

I look away, into the forest, thinking of Alex. It's confusing to think of him now, part grief, part anger, so many things I want to know but never will.

Merriem's voice softens. "Hey, you'll work it out. I'm just being selfish. It's been so nice to have you girls here. And your father, your family. I got excited."

"We'll visit, either way. Whatever happens. Right, Frankie?" Bella says.

I nod.

"Good," Merriem says, brightening. "We need some new life in this neighborhood. It's been Huia and Jack and me for too long. We need you Caputos to keep things zesty."

Bella laughs.

Huia calls out. "What's so funny?"

"I'm trying to take Frankie and Bella hostage," Merriem answers.

Huia trots over. "What does that mean?"

"I'm trying to get them to stay."

Huia looks between us. She fixes her gaze on me. "Yes, you need to stay. It's so much funner with you here."

Merriem gives one of her big, deep guffaws. "Much, *much* funner." She looks at her watch. "And now we've got to get you to school, Miss."

Huia starts to protest.

"No, no, we're already late. Your dad will kill me. He asked one favor. I need to keep my promises."

As Merriem starts telling Bella about a friend who has a big, old house on the outskirts of Seattle with lots of rooms that she lets out, I feel a tug on my shirt. I crouch down, and Huia whispers into the cup of my ear, her breath hot.

"You'll stay, won't you, Frankie?"

I don't have the heart to tell her no. Instead I rub her back and look back up to Merriem. "I might come by this afternoon? I have those books to give back to you."

"Oh, no rush now, keep them as long as you like," Merriem says, grinning.

"No, it's okay, I should . . ."

Her grin fades to a smile and she nods. "Okay, honey. I'll be there."

That afternoon, when I arrive at her house with the books, Merriem's expression is more solemn than usual. "Frankie, honey. I'm glad you're here." She lifts the books from my arms. "Let me take those for you."

Behind her, a figure rises from a chair by the dining table. My throat goes dry.

*Summer.*

My hand connects with Merriem's shoulder; she turns her head.

"Don't," I whisper. "I can't . . . Why is she here?"

Merriem twists around to face me properly. "I'm sorry, Frankie. I didn't know that he was the same person. Summer's been waiting for you. She wants to talk."

"There's nothing to say," I say, my voice rising.

Summer steps towards me. I feel hijacked.

"Frankie?"

"Try," Merriem encourages me, with a reassuring smile. "She's really sorry. It might help."

I shake my head. "It won't help."

"Frankie, please?" Summer says, closer now. Her face is worn and her eyes red-rimmed.

Merriem looks at her and then back to me. Her expression is

gentle and sad. I hate her for her sympathy. I feel my own expression harden.

"I'll make tea," Merriem says.

"I have to go."

"No, stay." She wraps her arm around my back, guiding me to the dining table.

Summer and I take seats opposite each other. I hear Merriem filling the kettle in the kitchen. I stare at my hands on the table. When she clears her throat, I speak before she can begin.

"Alex proposed to me here. Did you know that?"

I lift my eyes just enough to see her shake her head.

"Down by the water. He made a picnic." I realize I'm staring at my ring. "He said that we'd been through so much together and we made sense. He said I'd been good to him."

Summer says nothing.

"I thought it was romantic. I thought he was being romantic. I'd been waiting so long. Now when I think about it, I feel like a consolation prize."

Summer is blinking back tears.

"We met in high school. I've never loved anyone else."

Her face is grave. "I'm so sorry. I understand. You had a love story. I ruined that."

I nod. That is true. Partly true.

"I wish you didn't have to know. Don't let me change what you had," she says. "One kiss, a mistake . . . It was nothing."

I can see her pain as she speaks. It wasn't just a kiss. It wasn't nothing. It wasn't nothing to her, and it wasn't nothing to him; that's written all over her face. It was something and it will haunt her. I may never get to be his wife but I was his fiancée. I'm allowed to be sad. I'm left with that and the cabin while Summer has nothing.

The diamond on my ring slides around, and when I make a fist it presses into my skin. Alex has abandoned all of us.

Merriem places a teapot and cups in the center of the table. We are silent. Then Merriem rests her palm against the top of my shoulder and for a moment I don't feel mad. Mainly just weary, like I want to go to bed. I think of Jack's couch, the smell of the blanket, cedar and lavender. Steam streams out of the teapot as Merriem leaves the room.

"Everything's different now," I say.

Summer frowns dolefully. "I really am sorry. Can you believe me?"

I give a small nod.

"It was easier not knowing you," she whispers.

We both stare at the teapot, until she stands and pours the tea, a cup for me and one for herself.

"We can't be friends," I say. My tone is, surprisingly, almost regretful.

"I know," Summer replies.

When I return, Bella is brushing out the tent. She's already packed some of her things. I tell her I'm taking a walk and she studies my face before nodding.

I take the path I took that day Bella arrived. In my mind I have walked it dozens of times. I pick my way through the ferns, looking for things Huia would pluck and eat. I walk past the two identical Douglas firs. I walk past the nurse log with its tiny seedlings reaching up to the sunlight. I walk through the forest, till the trees thin and the ground becomes rocky. I lift my eyes from watching the fall of my feet and take in the ocean, which is suddenly in front of me. I drink in the air and feel the salty breeze tug at my hair.

A narrow path picks its way down the rocky face to the expanse of water. My feet follow the crooked line that many have wandered before me. I walk alone. My steps are quiet. I hear only the gulls and waves breaking against the rocks.

I pause at the place where the path meets the water. Or, I should say, where the water rushes and splashes at the path. How violent the ocean seems after the poise of the forest. How different the sounds, the scents. The nose-prickling, metallic, life-affirming smell of salt.

I take off my shoes and toss them behind me. I dip one foot into the water. The cold rockets through me and I pull it out again. This is always the way, I remind myself. Too cold at first.

I force myself in, still wearing my summer dress, and wade until the water is up to my knees. The chill is a sweet kind of pain. I lower myself in and swim beyond the waves crashing against the rocks to where it's calmer, bobbing like a buoy in the cold, rising and falling with the gentle swell of the ocean. I peer at my hands through the greenish tint of the water. The skin on my fingers is starting to pucker. I stare at my left hand, the diamond glinting like an eye.

*Tesoro mio*, I whisper, though I never called him that other than in my head. *Tesoro mio*, my treasure, my darling.

I imagine him right beside me, like he was all those years ago, that night at the cape, grinning and glowing, lit up from below like a creature from another place. Like an angel.

# Chapter Twenty-three

· · · ·

When I come back, wet, Bella stares at me. The tent is no longer there; a rectangular imprint left on the ground. I know she is ready to leave.

"Are we staying?"

I shake my head. "You're going."

"I'm not leaving you—"

"No, I don't mean it like that. I'll come soon. I just need a little time."

"I don't think you should be alone," she says, frowning.

I know she would stay here as long as I need her to. Would sleep in her car and refuse to leave as she did before. But it's time to go, for now, back to the life I have left.

"I won't be," I say.

She touches my arm. "Ghosts don't count, Frankie."

I smile. "I'll be right behind you. You have a lot to do if you're planning on moving back."

"It can wait."

"You don't need to worry."

She blinks. "It's my job."

"I'll be right behind you."

She makes me promise and I do.

After she leaves, I start to pack my own things, retrieving clothes from the ramshackle closet. My fingers touch something shoved to the back of a shelf, which I pull out and unroll. My black dress. I press it between my fingertips and the material feels foreign. Thick, rustling, and stiff . . . I'm reminded of cucumber sandwiches. The airless room. Seeking freedom.

I pack the dress and slip on a long-sleeved top, stepping out of the cabin with the heavy key in my jeans pocket. The daylight is gone but the sky isn't black yet.

I drive away with my window rolled down. The air is fresh and tingling in my lungs. I stare down driveways, imagining the houses at the end of them. I imagine people all over Washington State, nestled deep in their homes, in living rooms watching television, in kitchens stacking dishwashers.

I remember Alex coming home after a day's work. The way he jangled his keys. The way he huffed as he took off his shoes at the door. Dropped his briefcase by his shoes. Tugged at the knot on his tie. I'd be on the couch. Reading a magazine or watching the news. He'd come over and kiss the top of my head. His breath against my hair.

"Hey, Frankie."

"Hey."

Then into the kitchen to open the fridge door. Searching for a beer, something to eat before dinner.

"How was your day?" I'd call out.

"Same as usual."

That's what he said every day. Same as usual. Until the day there was no answer. And no usual. No sound of shoes coming off, or a briefcase falling to the floor. As far as I know, the briefcase is still where he dropped it that last Friday afternoon.

Reflective mailbox numbers shine at me like cat's eyes. Mine is the only car on the road. Lawns, where there are some, roll down into gutters, where leaves rot, making food for worms and mushrooms. Morels.

Soon there's the mailbox with a sunflower on the side. Yellow and hopeful against the battered metal. I slow down. Then the little green house with the beehives out back.

A sign at the fork in the road points to Edison. I turn in the opposite direction. The highway reaches out ahead, dark and twisting.

Though it's becoming night, the darkness seems to recede as I drive on. There is light on the motorway, then from houses in clusters, traffic lights, floodlights shining on billboards advertising coffee and clothing sales and health insurance.

I drive past children's playgrounds, empty now it's getting late, and gas stations, grocery stores. Neighborhoods that all look the same—garage, fence, mailbox, garage, fence, mailbox.

Finally, a vanilla-colored apartment building strung with little balconies. A kitchen window with a crystal hanging in it. Rooms full of things and ghosts and memories. I park the car and get out, taking only the keys and leaving the rest of my belongings in the backseat. In case I cannot do it. In case I need to escape.

I open the main door and ignore the row of silver mailboxes with dark mouths. I take the door leading to the stairs instead of the elevator and every footfall echoes in the cool, concrete stair-well. My breath quickens and my heart pounds as I climb. When I get to our floor, my key slides easily into the lock though the door is heavy and needs a strong push. It's dark inside. I reach out to flick the light switch.

*Our place.*

I swallow down the fear that rises up into my throat.

There is a briefcase in the hallway. I move slowly into the living room and switch on the light in there too. It is so quiet in here, like a strange cocoon. I see the surfing magazine on the side table, the photograph of us on the shelf. A gray throw blanket folded on the arm of the couch. Everything as it always was. I glance across to the open door of the kitchen, where the espresso machine shines, our two cups sitting on top. I listen and wait for ghosts to come to haunt me. For memories so vivid I could fall into them. Instead there is silence.

I breathe in deeply. There is no scent of soil and leaves and tree resin here. No salt and iron coming from the ocean. It smells as ordinary as any place. I lower myself down on our couch and exhale. There is no birdsong, no guitar being played, no laughter ringing out. It is simply an apartment, still a little warm from the afternoon sun. It is as ordinary as any place and full of ordinary things—just a magazine, just a photograph, just cups. And I start to believe Papa may be right.

Life will be better, *duci.*

# Epilogue

·····

This is where I come to eat lunch most days. The café is generally quiet and cool. It's across the road from the beach, which is rocky and met by the pale green, glittering sea. The café isn't pretty or fancy; the food's simple and traditional. Some days the cook is late and they serve only what the man at the bar can grill or fry—whole fish, the silver scales marked with charred black lines, and home-cut potato fries. On very hot days, I order gelato brioche or granita.

"*Buongiorno*," the waitress sings at me. She's carrying a tray of dirty glasses in one hand. "I'm Carmelina."

I smile and reply in Italian, "You're new."

"First day back," she says. "I was on vacation. Croatia."

"Nice?"

"Very. You been?"

"No. Not yet."

"You have to go. It's so cheap."

"But it's cheap here."

She laughs and shakes her head. "Not like there. Believe me. And the sea . . . It's so clear. But can't be on vacation forever. Back to work, you know?"

I nod, but I haven't worked, not properly, for months now. I've picked fruit on farms, cleaned dishes and floors, even herded goats, all to help pay my board in the places I've stayed. In one place I looked after a pair of four-year-old twins. It had reminded me of Summer, helping out with her nephews.

Now I'm in Sicily I often stay with distant relatives, people whose faces I barely recall but who tell me they remember me when I was "this big," gesturing to a height around their knee-caps. They have noses or eyes or expressions like the aunties and they mother me in the same way, bullying and pampering.

Work the way I think of it—the little desk at the council, my favorite mug, my notice board pinned with lists and old photos and a *Peanuts* cartoon about Mondays—seems a million years and a million miles away. Those things, at least, are a million miles away, and now someone else sits in my chair, her things on the notice board and her mug on the desk.

I inhale the Sicilian air, its heat and salt. "I'm Francesca," I say to Carmelina.

"Hey, Francesca. What can I get you?"

"*Pasta alla Norma.*"

"Good."

She takes the menu from me and I hear her sing out my order to the kitchen as she returns to the bar.

I consider reaching into my backpack for the book I'm currently reading but decide against it. Instead I sip my glass of water, look across the road, and stretch my legs out under the table. They've turned brown in the sun, browner than they've been since I was a kid.

My skin is browner everywhere, as dark as Aunty Rosa's choc- olate *torrone,* and my hair is sun streaked. I got it cut short, just below my ears, before I left Seattle, but it's grown since then, back down to my shoulders. It's ragged and marked with sun- bleached, bronze-colored pieces, tied in a lazy ponytail. Some- times I catch my reflection in the mirror and wonder who it is; I think I look more like Bella than myself, touching my cheeks with my fingertips, noticing new freckles. I wonder if Bella does the same with a mirror in the apartment. Staring at her face, questioning, seeing a new reflection and a different life.

She e-mails me most days after she's finished work, telling me about this patient or another, the art and yoga classes she teaches at the seniors' home. She has her favorites: Magda with the glass eye; Bert with the loud laugh who keeps a parrot in his room; shy Agnes who paints watercolors. She is happy being in the apartment while I travel; after living by herself in Portland she doesn't mind being alone, though the aunties and cousins like to drop by unannounced. She tells me about Daniel here and there too. The gigs he's been playing, a movie they saw. They have become friends and it makes me happy to think of them looking after each other. I'm happy about many more things these days, just as Papa promised. I'm happy to be here and happy she is there where she should be, both of us living our mirror lives.

On the beach, an older couple are coming out of the water. I watch them help each other over the stones, the man steadying himself against the little waves, gripping his wife's hand. She's wearing one of those old-fashioned suits cut low on her legs, a rubber cap, though it doesn't seem as though she's put her head underwater, and pearl earrings. When she almost slips, her husband grips her elbow with his other hand, steadying her, and she turns her face towards him. His expression is stern while she laughs, showing the dark fillings in the back of her mouth.

I trace a finger through the condensation on the side of my glass and watch Carmelina moving between the tables of men smoking and chatting, eating, drinking beer. She's so easy with them, so comfortable in the sway and swish of her body; she reminds me of Merriem.

Merriem refuses to use e-mail so I have to send and then wait for postcards and letters in return. Whoever I'm staying with is always amused by her packages—large, recycled envelopes thickly stuffed with sketches, little boxes of chocolates and sachets of tea, tiny jars of honey wrapped in five or six plastic bags, dried flowers between note pages, pictures and paintings from Huia.

"Here you go," Carmelina says, setting down my meal. It's steaming hot and fogs up my water glass.

"*Grazie*," I reply.

"Pepper? More *ricotta salata*?"

"No, thank you, this is perfect."

Once it has cooled, I pierce a stack of wavy-edged pasta with my fork and eat in silence. The fried eggplant is soft and rich, the *ricotta salata* subtle and salty. Though the aunties make this dish at home, it tastes different here in the place it belongs. Simple flavors, not too many, all working together, accompanied by the heat in the air prickling my skin and sound of water against the stony shore. When I've finished, Carmelina delivers my bill.

"You're not from here," she says. The lunch rush has cleared out and siesta's soon to begin. This afternoon I'll probably go for a swim or write a letter on the beach.

I unzip my bag to retrieve my wallet. "No."

"But you look Italian. And you speak well."

"My family," I explain. "My mother's family are from Calabria and my father's family are from Sicily."

"Ah," she replies, nodding. "So where are you from then?"

I pull my backpack onto my lap, fingers still searching for my wallet. Instead I find something else. I wrap my palm around it out of habit, distracted. The charm I have carried with me on my travels. "Sorry . . . America. I'm from America."

"Oh. Cool," she says.

I watch her face light up and know what she's thinking. She's envisioning California, the sun and surf, the celebrities, fast cars, wide lanes, cheap nail polish. Or perhaps she's seeing her version of New York: the solemn, iconic lady in the harbor, the Empire State Building, lights on Broadway, and horse-and-carriage rides through Central Park. The America of sitcoms and Christmas-holiday movies.

She will not be thinking about the place I'm from. About the skies painted gray and the rain that rolls in, forewarning with that heavy, damp, sweet smell. The huge mugs of coffee. The trees as straight as columns that crowd out the light, the smell of damp earth, and the first, hopeful spring trilliums. Merriem's radiant dandelion bread; Huia, shoeless, joyful, looking for morels; and Jack, his almost-black eyes, the way he laughs, sitting on his couch with him right beside me, almost close enough to touch.

I take a quick breath. I've been speaking Italian for months now, but the words suddenly vanish. Instead my head fills with the memory of his voice, deep and gentle. "Will you be gone long?"

"A while."

"Are you running away?" Laced with worry.

"Not this time."

Such dark eyes. Dark as a crow's wing, dark as espresso. Staring at me like a person looks at a rising sun. I reached out for him.

"There are people I need to come back to." My fingers seeking the warmth of his.

I glance up at Carmelina. "Sorry," I mumble in English.

She shrugs kindly, and waits.

I open my fist, which holds the little matchstick cabin instead of money. Carmelina peers at it.

I place it on the table and return to my bag, pushing the contents around. Towel, book, sweatshirt.

"*Scusassi*," I apologize, my Italian coming back to me. "My wallet's in here somewhere."

Carmelina points at the cabin. "What is that?"

I follow her finger to the log walls made of matchsticks, the miniature windows. The doorknob has fallen off along the way, but other than that it's intact. A perfect, tiny replica of the cabin in the forest. I can almost hear the Steller's jay, imagine its flash of blue, smell the lemony resin of the cedars. See daisies looped flower to stem upon dark hair. Feel a hand with a broad palm and rough fingers linked with mine.

I smile at Carmelina. "That is home."

# Pasta alla Norma

PASTA WITH EGGPLANT,
TOMATO, AND *RICOTTA SALATA*

Pasta alla Norma is one of Sicily's most well-known dishes.
It was supposedly named by Nino Martoglio, a Sicilian writer, poet,
and theater director, who compared the delicious dish to the opera
*Norma* by Vincenzo Bellini. Penne is generally the easiest pasta to
source for this dish, but if you can find *reginette* or *malfadine* (both
are wavy-edged) or *sedanini* (similar to penne but slimmer and slightly
curved), then feel free to substitute.

*Serves 4*

3 eggplants
Sea salt
4 garlic cloves
1 large sprig fresh
    rosemary (chopped
    into one-inch lengths)
5 plum tomatoes
2 tablespoons extra virgin
    olive oil, plus more for
    serving
2 tablespoons *passata* or
    tomato puree

Freshly ground black
    pepper
2 cups vegetable oil
14 ounces dried pasta
    (penne)
1 bunch fresh basil for
    serving (leaves simply
    plucked or torn
    depending on your
    preference)
¾ cup coarsely grated
    *ricotta salata*

## PREPARATION

Cut 2 of the eggplants into 1-inch cubes. Sprinkle them with salt
and set in a colander in the sink to drain for at least 2 hours.

Preheat the oven to 425°F.

To make the sauce: Halve the remaining eggplant lengthwise,
then place the halves, skin down, on a clean work surface. Score
the flesh with diagonal lines one way and then the other to make

a diamond pattern. Thinly slice 2 of the garlic cloves and push the slices into the eggplant halves. Push rosemary pieces into the remaining slots.

Put the eggplant halves back together, wrap in foil, and roast in the oven until soft, 20 to 25 minutes. Unwrap, discard the garlic and rosemary, and scoop out flesh with a spoon. Let the flesh drain in a colander until cool and then finely chop.

Bring a saucepan of water to a boil. Dip the tomatoes into the boiling water for 10 seconds, then remove and rinse under cold water. Peel and discard the tomato skins. Halve and seed each tomato, then halve again.

Finely chop the remaining 2 cloves garlic. In a large saucepan, heat the olive oil over medium heat. Add the garlic and cook very gently until soft and fragrant. Add the chopped eggplant flesh and cook gently to warm through. Add the *passata*, stir, and cook for another minute or so before taking off the heat. Season with salt and pepper, cover, and set aside.

To fry the eggplant: In a deep pan, heat the vegetable oil (the oil should not come higher than one-third of the way up the sides of the pan). To check the oil is hot enough, put in a few breadcrumbs. They should sizzle straight away. Gently squeeze the diced eggplant to get rid of excess liquid, then fry in the oil until golden, one handful at a time. Drain on paper towels and pat dry.

To make the pasta: Bring a saucepan of water to a boil. Salt the water and add the pasta. Cook until al dente (often about 1 minute less than cooking time given on the package). Reserving a little of the cooking water, drain the pasta. Add the pasta and cut-up tomatoes to the eggplant sauce and toss all together. Add the fried eggplant and basil leaves and toss. Toss again with a small amount of the ricotta salata, adding a little of the reserved cooking water to loosen the sauce if necessary. Serve with the rest of the ricotta salata and drizzle with a little olive oil.

i thank you God for most this amazing day: for the leaping greenly spirits of trees and a blue true dream of sky; and for everything which is natural which is infinite which is yes

e. e. cummings

# Acknowledgments

· · · ·

This book was both troublesome and hugely rewarding—in that wonderful way that small children are—and, similarly, required an entire (very kind and generous) village to raise.

In order to create the setting I relied heavily on incredible people who work passionately to ensure beautiful, ancient forests like Frankie's exist, including: Ken Wu and team at the Ancient Forest Alliance, Mitch Friedman at Conservation Northwest, Larry Pynn, Adrienne and Jeff Hegedus, Elaine Graham, Elspeth Bradbury, and the volunteers and teams at UBC Botanic Gardens, Greenheart Canopies, Lynn Canyon Ecology Centre, and Lighthouse Park Centre.

I am truly indebted to the real-life Caputos and the other Italians and Italians-at-heart who tirelessly supported me with translation and the cultural aspects of this book. In particular: Melissa Caputo-Khan, Marcella Caputo, Francie Jordan, Laura Foster and her Sicilian sisters—Marcella and Chiara Gattuso. *Mille grazie.*

Special thanks also to chefs Alfie Spina and Shane Schipper

who ensured food references were authentic and assisted in the creation of delicious recipes.

I feel very blessed to have a phenomenal work family of talented people who coach and encourage me and want the very best for my books. Sincere thanks to Miya Kumangai for her brilliant ideas and efforts and everyone at Touchstone for all their kind support. Big thanks to Alexandra Craig, Emma Rafferty, Nicola O'Shea, Rebecca Thorne, and all the gracious, hardworking team at Pan Macmillan Australia. Love and gratitude to my superb agent, Catherine Drayton, Alexis Hurley, and all the team at Inkwell; and to Whitney Frick who steered me and the manuscript in the right direction. To author plus friend Ria Voros and family plus friend Brianne Collins, who provide endless, professional advice and support seemingly just for the love or torture of it—my sincere thanks and love.

Friendships cannot be underrated in this odd, lonely, wonderful job. I want to acknowledge all those friends (including readers who have become friends) that answer my strange questions and buy, gift, celebrate, and promote my work. Special thanks to dear friends who served as first readers—Lucie Geappen and Elizabeth O'Brien.

To my family—my parents, Glen and Rob Tunnicliffe; my siblings, Kendall Stewart and Greg Tunnicliffe; all my in-laws, the wonderful Ballestys, Stewarts, and Wattses, who continue to raise and nurture both me and my work—I love and thank you very much. Thanks also to Moana Salmon (a part of our family too) who makes life both easier and more fun.

To my husband, Matthew Ballesty, and our girls, Wren and

Noa, you are simply the loveliest, most radiant trio of beings in the entire universe. It's impossible to explain, or express ample gratitude for, the love, kindness, encouragement, pride, and joy you give me. *Arohanui.*

Finally, this book is dedicated to a precious and significant friend—Sian James. The experience of knowing you inspired and moved me and changed my life forever. Thank you.

# About the Author

. . . .

Born in New Zealand, Hannah Tunnicliffe is a self-confessed nomad. She has lived in Canada, Australia, England, Macau, and, while traveling Europe, a camper van named Fred. She currently lives in New Zealand with her husband and two daughters and coauthors the blog "Fork and Fiction," which explores her twin loves—books and food. *Season of Salt and Honey* is her second novel.

# SEASON *of* SALT *and* HONEY

Devastated when her fiancé, Alex Gardner, suddenly dies in a surfing accident, Francesca "Frankie" Caputo abandons her steady job, her comfortable Seattle apartment, and her huge Italian family to retreat to Alex's family's secluded cabin. Surrounded by the Cascade Mountains and a forest brimming with treasures waiting to be found, Frankie attempts to grieve and heal herself from the devastation of losing the love of her life—but it isn't long before the outside world comes to find her. Jack, the Gardner family caretaker, is sent to oust Frankie when the family claims she is trespassing on their land; Bella, Frankie's estranged sister, arrives seeking sanctuary and solace from her own problems; and Frankie's father, aunties, and cousins come bearing gifts, concerns, and baskets of delicious, soul-nurturing Italian food. As Frankie attempts to move forward with her life and form relationships with her new neighbors and friends, she learns secrets about both her family and her former fiancé that make her question everything she thinks she knows about love, loss, and forgiveness.

*For Discussion*

. . . .

1.  When faced with difficult situations, both Frankie and Bella resort to running away from their problems. Why do the sisters rely on escape as a solution to their issues? In what ways does running away help Frankie and Bella, and in what ways does it hurt them? Have you ever found it beneficial to run from the things that are troubling you?

2.  "Perhaps Italians know that hunger feels too much like sadness" (page 45). Describe the role that food plays in Frankie's grieving and healing processes. How is hunger similar to sadness and grieving? Why is everyone in Frankie's life, from her aunties to Merriem, so intent on feeding her? What was your favorite passage about food in the novel, and how did the addition of recipes at the end of the chapters enhance your understanding of the role of food in Frankie's journey?

3.  The forest is a mystical place in the novel, home to Merriem's lush vegetable gardens and hidden treasures that Huia finds on her foraging expeditions. Why is the forest the perfect setting for Frankie's escape? What does it offer her that the

city cannot? How does the forest change Frankie's identity over the course of the novel?

4.  "The thought made me shiver a little: how limited the control we have over the things that matter is. My generation expects the world to yield to our command, to do as we bid it. How naive we are" (page 69). Explain what Frankie means when she makes this statement. How does Alex's death impact her view of the world, and her role in it? What does Frankie's realization about her lack of control mean for her life going forward, and how does her awareness of this fact change her?

5.  What does being Italian mean to Frankie and how does it define her identity? How does Alex's refusal to travel to Italy on their honeymoon impact her? How did the inclusion of Italian words and phrases affect your reading of the novel and your understanding of Frankie and her upbringing?

6.  Compare and contrast the Gardner family and the Caputo family. How are Frankie and Alex able to make their relationship work despite the differences between their families? Do you think the Gardner family would have changed their opinions of Frankie when she was officially a member of their family?

7.  Throughout the novel, Frankie recalls scenes from her relationship with Alex as if she were watching a romantic comedy where everyone ends up living happily ever

after. In grieving, however, she comes to realize a number of truths about their relationship that she was previously blind to. How did your feelings toward Alex shift throughout the novel? Do you think he loved Frankie, or was *in love* with her? How does their love change as they evolve from high school sweethearts to an engaged couple leading busy lives? Do you think it is inevitable for love to change over time?

8. Since they were little girls, Frankie and Bella have been categorized and put into boxes by their family members: the good girl versus the bad girl. How do the sisters each play into the expectations of their family? How does being cast into a certain role impact their decision-making and their relationships with each other? Would things have been different if Frankie had been deemed the bad girl by her family?

9. Both Frankie and Huia have grown up without a mother. Describe what we know about each of their mothers, and how each character remembers her mother. Who do Frankie and Huia each look to as mother figures, and why? How do Giuseppe and Jack both attempt to provide their daughters with mother figures?

10. Why are the Gardners so adamant that Frankie leave their cabin? Why don't they respect her grieving process or feel that she is close enough to family to allow her to stay? Did your feelings toward Mrs. Gardner change when you

learned about the secret of her marriage and the true reasons she has for disliking Frankie?

11. Do you think Frankie is right to hold a grudge against Bella for what she thinks she saw at a party? What prevents Frankie from confronting Bella, and how might their relationship have been different if she had confronted her sooner? How did you react when you discovered that Bella had been falsely accused?

12. Forgiveness is a major theme of the novel. How and why does Frankie come to forgive Bella, Summer, and even Alex? Do you think she is right to forgive each of them? Share stories with your book club about circumstances when you have forgiven someone.

13. On grieving his wife, Giuseppe tells Frankie, "Life becomes better. Things become better. But it remains. It always remains. I never had this closure" (page 280). By the end of the novel, do you think Frankie has attained any degree of closure about Alex's death? Do you think that it is necessary to find a sense of closure after a loss, or do you agree with Giuseppe that it is not possible?

14. How did you feel about where Frankie ends up at the end of the novel, both physically and emotionally? Were you surprised by her decision? Where do you imagine she will be in five years?

A Conversation with
Hannah Tunnicliffe

· · · ·

**Your previous novel, *The Color of Tea*, was set in Macau. What made you decide to move across the ocean to set *Season of Salt and Honey* in the Pacific Northwest? Were you surprised by any similarities you found in writing about these two locations?**

To put it simply—*I* moved across the ocean! I lived in Macau for three years, where I wrote *The Color of Tea*, and then relocated to the Pacific Northwest and was immediately awed by the marked contrasts between the two environments. The beauty and impact of the ocean, the majestic ancient forests, the ever-present tones of green and gray and blue. The two settings of my novels—Macau and Washington State—are very different, but what struck me as I wrote this story was how similar people are, no matter where they are. Love and family are the most meaningful elements of our lives; food is used to soothe and celebrate, and grief sears, no matter where we go to escape it.

**Did any person or situation provide inspiration for Frankie's story?**

I was very curious about the account of Julia Butterfly Hill, an activist who lived in a California Redwood tree for 738 days in order to save it from felling. Butterfly Hill's documentation of sacrificing years of her youth to live in a tree led me to explore the idea of a similarly young woman escaping to the forest for protection, privacy, purpose, and comfort. Various Pacific Northwest writers and poets such as artist Emily Carr, who describes the forests in this region so poignantly, and the environmental activists who diligently strive to preserve them also provided rich inspiration for the writing that became *Season of Salt and Honey*.

**Frankie and Alex's love story is obviously the focus of the novel, but I loved Frankie and Bella's sister story. Did you always envision the sister story as being so central to the narrative, or did that emerge through the writing process?**

I always envisioned a central sister story for Frankie, but the dynamics of the relationship and its significance evolved over the course of the writing. I really enjoy writing about female relationships, and sisters are no exception. Sister relationships can be so complicated and yet, at the core, so simple. It seems to me that a sister relationship is not the same as a friendship, differs from a parental relationship, and is dissimilar from a competitor or foe; yet it contains the elements of all of those kinds of relationships in varying and unequal measures. This makes sister relationships very satisfying to write about.

**Which character in the story do you empathize with the most? Which would you most like to have a cup of tea with? Merriem in particular was such a vibrant character—she really came to life on the pages!**

That's a great question—can I have a tea party with all of them, plus a steaming hot loaf of Merriem's dandelion bread? I probably empathize most with Frankie, whom I got to know best, but sympathize with both Bella and Summer, adore Papa, Merriem, and Huia, am charmed by the aunties, and have a crush on Jack. I would love the opportunity to return to Washington State and Edison in particular, to explore the region and its food, including the small bakery that inspired the one in the book named Breadfarm. I'd constantly be on the lookout for the characters from the story and wishing for that tea and bread with butter and honeycomb.

**It would be great to have Sunday dinner with the Caputo family! What are gatherings with your family like? Are there special foods you always have on the table when you're together?**

My family gatherings were all-or-nothing affairs—simply meat and three vegetables or soup or huge feasts with friends, family, flowers, and themed table settings. My mother steers away from repetition, so every big gathering, even Christmas lunch, is different. I am from New Zealand, where Christmas is in our summer, which makes some of the more wintry traditions a bit misplaced. One year for Christmas lunch we hung pink and yellow streamers and paper lanterns and ate at a long table outside, finishing the meal with the pièce de résistance: a beautiful spherical mascarpone and berry frozen dessert my mother had spent a long time making. Unfortunately, it was so frozen solid we couldn't slice it no matter the various ways we tried! So we left a huge knife in it, laughed till we cried, and waited until it melted a couple of hours later. I admire my mother's enthusiasm for gatherings, bravery in trying new recipes, and good humor when they don't go according to plan. No party with my family is ever the same, but the compulsory elements are: teasing each other, pretty paper napkins (a weird family obsession), everyone helping, laughter, and wine.

**Your descriptions of food are positively mouthwatering. What research did you do to learn about Italian food and cooking? Did you have help developing the recipes, or did you come up with them on your own?**

As soon as I decided on Frankie's ethnicity, I began my research into southern Italian food and cooking. For me, food is a crucial aspect in understanding a culture; it can explain so much about geography, influences, wealth, values, and relationships. Personally cooking, testing, and adapting the recipes taught me a lot about Sicilian culture that I would not have appreciated otherwise. The recipes in the book are a mixture of those I created from scratch and traditional recipes I minimally adapted. The traditional recipes (e.g. *nzuddi*, mother in law's Tongues, Pasta alla Norma) are as close to the original, uncomplicated versions as possible, because I hope readers will discover more about Sicilian culture through making them, just as I did. Other recipes (e.g. banana bread, spring risotto) I invented or took more liberties with to adapt to my personal taste. I also consulted Sicilian-Australian chef Alfie Spina regarding the recipes I had chosen, and he gave me hints and tips, some of which have been passed down from generation to generation within his family.

**It seems sweet that Jack likes Frankie so much, but she clearly isn't ready for a relationship yet. Some authors might have pushed for a romance here. Did you ever consider a scenario in which Jack and Frankie end up together?**

Absolutely—I'm a romantic at heart; I couldn't help but foist my matchmaking upon them! I did explore other endings in which Frankie and Jack more obviously wound up together, but given Frankie's grief and Jack's diplomacy, these endings didn't ring true to the characters. I'm pleased with the final outcome, which I think is more delicate and authentic to their natures.

**The overarching message of the value of forgiveness in the novel will really stick with the reader. Have you ever been torn over whether or not to forgive someone in your life?**

That is a fascinating question because generally I forgive very easily. I like to believe in the good in people. I'm not great at self-forgiveness, though, and guilt sometimes stalks me. In the book Summer is the character I worry about the most because, other than grief and guilt, she is left with so little compared to the others. I think she struggles with self-forgiveness. I wonder if readers will forgive Summer for her actions or not?

**You are a self-described nomad who has lived in Canada, Australia, England, and Macau. Where was your favorite**

**place to live and why? Where would you most like to travel that you haven't been yet?**

That's a tough choice to make because every place I have lived has been so different and offered so much. I joke that I am always missing someone and somewhere no matter where I am. The beauty of living abroad is that you leave pieces of yourself, of your heart, all over the world. The pain of it is exactly that, too! For now I will say that New Zealand is my favorite place to live. It is where I was raised and where I am raising my own children—there is a lovely, familiar, cyclic feeling to that. Plus, my family is here, the air is good, and the baking is great. As for where I'd most like to travel to—what I have found is that the more I see of the world the more there is to see! So my wish list is very, very long. Currently at the top of the list are: Turkey, Burma, Portland, New Orleans, Sweden, Beijing, and back again to Japan, Bali, New York, California, and France. I might have to win the lottery.

**What are you working on next? Will we ever see Frankie and Bella, or Jack and Huia, again?**

I am very excited about my next project—another novel filled with food and love and set in an evocative location. I feel very blessed that writing is my job and I get to explore all these imagined characters, settings, and stories and then share them with you! As for Frankie and Bella, Huia and Jack, Merriem and Papa, and the rest of the *Season of Salt and Honey* characters, I think of them often. I would love to drop in on them again and see what they are getting up to.

## Enhance Your Book Club

· · · ·

1. Using the recipes provided throughout the novel, cook an Italian feast!

2. Research foraging opportunities in your area and go on an expedition with your book club.

3. Write about your most memorable meal or dining experience and share it with your book club.